Beyond This Bitter Air

by Kristin Sherrard

Fernweh Press

to Garry and Victoria

Co-conspirators extraordinaire

I pray you

you (if any open this writing)

Make in your mouths the words that were our names

–Archibald MacLeish, Epistle to Be Left in the Earth

Prologue (by skywave, 5985 kHz)

As we drift along this green and empty shore, I cast my thoughts back across wide waters to the days of my youth. Then, the world was but a single land, called Nuatha. And our youth stretched long as shadows on a summer's day — which in Nuatha is very long indeed. Yet we have learned to our sorrow that winter can be longer still.

So it was, and so I shall tell you, that in those days everything moved in gracious circles. The sun wheeled its summer course round the sky, the stars and the moon's broad lamp in winter. And the waters of the Circling Sea flowed widdershins, opposite the heavens. Now that the circles have been broken, and the very heavens pulled askew, we know that life was never so simple, nor so safe.

Erkanni would say there are better things than safety.

We send our story out into infinite ether in the hopes that it will make its way back to poor, beleaguered Nuatha. Perhaps it may also find its way to other people, living in lands as yet unknown to us.

Listener to this tale, whoever you be, doubt not that you have heard of my country, though likely by another name, as the merest whisper in the corner of your ear. The Nuatha that is for me the heart of all and my holdfast, for you hovers uncertainly at the edge of your maps, caught between actuality and potentiality, prophecy and exhortation; haunting, impossible, and yet real. Be not ashamed of your ignorance. Like you, we believed we were the only ones with thoughts and stories, cities and books, reverence and wisdom; that the world we knew would last for ever, but it was never so.

I will begin our transmission with the traditional widecast call: Hear ye, here we, we seek you, we seek you; this is Rowan Askve Yngling calling faraway and wide . . .

Chapter 1. The Finding

Remember how your father would send a stone skimming far out over the water with a flick of the wrist? How the broad arc touched down on the lake's silvery skin, only to skip up again, twice, thrice, so many times you lost count. That was how Rowan would eventually come to the little casket. In the centuries following the Exodus it had been repeatedly found, hidden, forgotten, and rediscovered. Suspended for an indefinite stretch of time between clear blue sky and murky depths, it carried a message that could change the world. Although Rowan as yet knew nothing of all this, tonight the dirt-encrusted object tucked between mattress and headboard was driving away all hope of sleep.

Rowan threw the bedcovers aside in sudden decision. Grandmother might still be up, even at this hour; and there could be no better time to tell her what they'd found.

Summer's late and slanting light streamed up the narrow staircase, setting Rowan's hair ablaze in an incongruous halo. At the end of a dim passageway, Rowan eased open the door to Grandmother's chambers. Rugs rich in hues of amber and garnet graced floorboards burnished by long years of use.

A haze of dust motes hung in the air, swirling like galaxies in a faint breeze. Otherwise, all was still. Perhaps Grandmother was already asleep after all.

"Rowan, is that you standing there? Goodness, I'd have expected you to like your bed well enough, after your weeks in the mountains."

Grandmother was beckoning from the open window. Just outside, a crow peered at them suspiciously, then ruffled his wing feathers.

"Hey now, sa-sa-sa; there's no harm in my Rowan." Grandmother offered the crow a bit of oatcake from crumbs scattered about the sill. The crow made a couple of sideways hops toward them, one bright eye on the intruder. It wasn't the one who sometimes threw rocks, but the tree-climber who lacked the sense to stay down on the ground where long-leggers belonged. He snatched the largest crumb and flew off into the gloom, croaking disdainfully.

"Don't tell me that's another friend of yours!" said Rowan with a laugh.

"Oh, crows are terrible nuisances at harvest-time, but they really are such interesting creatures. Mind, don't tell your mar I was feeding him." Grandmother dusted off her hands outside the window, and latched it shut; the gloaming was apt to get chilly so late in the season. "Let's see your arm."

Rowan held out a sturdy, well-tanned arm, and Grandmother placed her leathery one beside it, an end-of-summer ritual for the two of them. Rowan groused, "Oh, you're always darker! But I bet Orry beats you."

"How do the sheep fare, by the way?"

"The sheep are grand; wool right up to your elbow, and fat as butterbeans from the mountain grass. —But Grandmother," said Rowan in a changed voice, "I wanted to tell you about something we found, up in the mountains."

Grandmother gave her middle grandchild a sharp glance, then went over to the teapot that sat beneath the solar multiplier. She poured two mugs of apple blossom tea, and beckoned jhm over to a pair of worn armchairs flanking the empty fireplace.

This was where Grandmother used to tell them stories beside the leaping firelight, back when they were too young to go to town for the winter: tall, serious Dialfi staring into the fire with dark eyes; restless Rowan who was always asking what happened next; and little curly haired Orry struggling to stay awake with the others. She'd told of gnomads wandering the Waste under the endlessly circling stars of winter; of Syowyans raiding the coast in the teeth of a winter storm, the skua-man in the prow beating his night-black wings to keep time for the oarsmen; of fisherfolk from the far northern isles finding strange objects washed up on storm-wracked beaches, gifts from the sea that launched them on marvelous or disastrous adventures far from their snug stone cottages.

Grandmother sipped at her mug, then took up her knitting from the broad arm of the chair. "Now, tell me all about it." She settled back, fingers busy but eyes on her grandchild, in the fading hours of dusk while the rest of the house lay dreaming.

"We never would have found it, if not for the game of flag-tag," began Rowan. That was the childish sort of thing they all reverted to up in the mountain pastures, after the older ones arrived to join the youngsters who'd been up there since midsummer. Dialfi hadn't wanted to play, of course — jhe'd been keeping them busy from one suncircle to the next, practically, finding dye-plants for Mar, cutting hay to send downslope on the autotram, and making sure the sheep didn't wander into any trouble.

But in truth the sheep now took little looking after. From their weeks of feeding on the lush mountain grass, the lambs had grown too large to fall prey to foxes or skuas. They'd lost the urge to explore, content to graze in the endless daze of sunlight.

Rowan tried to convey all this to Grandmother: how the clean, pungent scent of pine, dry grass, and sage made every breath a delight; how the sun beat insistently on your closed eyelids, but the shade was always cool, the oven-dry air holding no heat of its own but transmitting it with utter clarity. Towards the Northwest, the smoking peak of Mt. Terebus rose out of a sea that shone like beaten silver. Looking southwards, the hills with their tawny grasses waving in the wind slept like immense and benevolent creatures, and gave way to range after bluer range of mountains and at last to the great shield that guarded the realm of the gnomads.

Grandmother said with a hint of impatience, "My dear, I too have watched sheep in mountain pastures in my day, you know."

"I'm just setting the scene," Rowan replied innocently, using one of Grandmother's stock phrases; for Grandmother had always been rather prone to digressions in her own storytelling. “In the mornings, if you can call it morning, when the sun never goes down but only circles round and round in the sky, while the others are all dead to the world, I’d go down to one of the tarns. When you dive in, it’s like diving into a cool twilit sky.”

“Do you ever see any otters?” Grandmother asked, drawn in despite herself.

“Yes, going like shooting stars one behind the other, with streams of bubbles trailing from their pelts.”

Grandmother’s eyes were closed, as she smiled at her own memories. “And shafts of sunlight making underwater nets of light. Oh yes, I have seen such mornings in the mountains.” Then her eyes snapped open. “But what was it you were going to tell me about a game of tag?”

Rowan nodded, and explained how Orry and rest of the small fry had been angling to play flag-tag all week. They’d finally worn down Dialfi, and indolent Dana too, who would have preferred to laze about smoking (a recently acquired pretension) and philosophizing.

Dana had half-listened as Orry excitedly outlined the rules, and had finally interrupted: “So the gist is that two teams hurl lots of overripe bush plums at each other to defer discovery of a scrap of fabric hidden somewhere on the grounds. I think I get it.”

“Great. And Dana, if you and Dialfi want be on the same team, no problem. I’ll take my chances with Rowan.” Rowan punched jhr younger sib in obvious concurrence, which led to a bout of wrestling. Rowan was overconfident, and Orry managed to pin jhm momentarily. Dialfi laughed, "Watch out Rowan, your days of careless domination may soon be over!"

The rest of the small fry divided themselves according to whether they thought age with its presumably attendant wisdom, or youthful vigor, the greater advantage; and the game began.

It was the sort of afternoon that felt everlasting: the sun hot on their shoulders, the blood singing in their ears, the very dust from a scuffle that hung in the air humming in praise, Rowan's team having just fended off the enemy with a particularly fierce barrage, that had been aided at a crucial juncture by a fortuitous incursion by wasps. Orry and the others had gone off scouting, leaving Rowan on guard duty. The only sound to be heard was the far-off creaking call of a raven. No one was anywhere nearby. A long time passed, and still no one came to relieve jhm of this boring and currently pointless business of guarding a flag against a nonexistent threat. At last Rowan, fed up with all the waiting, took off to search for their opponents' flag. Jhe made jhr way towards an exposed slope, exactly the sort of devious place Dialfi and Dana would choose, using the tumbled boulders of an old avalanche as cover.

There it was! The merest hint of blue peeking out from a rotting stump. No one seemed to be watching it, either. Rowan hesitated, then dashed out of cover at full speed.

A plum shot past, but jhe dodged and kept going. Dana leaped down from a tree and smacked jhm, hard, with a gnarled plum-branch. That was typical. You'd never catch Dana breaking rules, only bending them out of all recognition. But Rowan only laughed: though short, jhe was strong and quick, and more than a match for gangly, bookish Dana. Circling warily just out of reach, jhe feinted towards the stump, dodging Dana's attempts to strike again.

Dana called, "Dialfi, a vile knave intrudes; remember your swashing blow." Rowan looked up to see Dialfi on the ridge above them with a shirt-load of ammunition. The next moment, something soft and warm gushed into jhr ear. Dialfi, unlike Dana, could aim properly.

Rowan darted for the flag, but jhr toe caught on a sharp-edged stone, and the ground rose up with a crash. Laying there with the wind knocked out of jhm, Rowan saw small, golden heads of mountain sunflower tossing against the azure sky. Interspersed with these were snow-white flowers sticking out their long frog-tongues, and as extravagant a growth of copper nettles as Rowan had ever seen. *Rowan, Rowan*! came faintly through the dizziness and pounding of blood. But these plants, now: all of a sudden, Rowan grinned up at the sky. This would show Dialfi, who thought long hours of toil were such a great virtue. For Rowan knew deep in jhr bones that life was full of unexpected gifts, as well.

Dialfi came running over. "Oh, Rowan, you're filthy. You look like you've made a blood-pact with Gaea Herself!" The hint of impiety made Dana scowl.

Rowan sat up and took inventory. On top of the grime, a trickle of blood was welling down jhr arm, and one ear was gritty with dirt where jhe had scratched at it. "It's nothing. But look at this false kingsfoil, and all the rest!"

Dialfi took in the flora into which Rowan had tumbled, and whistled appreciatively.

"When you Ynglings are done marveling at a bunch of plants, I'll conduct Rowan to the jail. Jhe is my prisoner, you realize," said Dana. But no one bothered to answer. Dialfi and Rowan were already eagerly pulling out plants and sorting them into piles.

"Hey, what's this?" Rowan had just managed to extract a tough clump of sunflower, along with a huge clod of dirt and stones, and had glimpsed a blueish-green object where the roots had been. Rowan enlarged the hole, using a stout stick to pry the rocks out of the hard-packed earth. At length jhe was able to extract a flat object of tarnished blue-green metal, not very large, encrusted with dirt and clay.

Dialfi came over to see. "Hmm, that might account for all those copper-loving plants growing here. Might be worth something, too."

"If it is," said Dana, "we should all have a share in it."

Rowan glared. Dana's family was one of the richest in the district, and had no need of such gleanings. They didn't even keep sheep, but had sent Dana up there for a vacation, of all things.

Using the already filthy edge of jhr shirt, Rowan rubbed at the object. Patterns began to emerge from the grime. "Back off; I can't see what I'm doing," jhe grunted, as the others crowded round. It looked like some sort of a miniature casket, about two hands wide and half as thick. It was sealed shut, but whether by age or design was impossible to tell.

One side was plain, while the other was marked with irregularly spaced lines swirling outwards, from a lumpish spiraling shape in the center. All along the side, tiny raised figures followed one another in an endless round: stick-figures of people and animals, deer with branching antlers, and small boats of odd design, and other shapes unrecognizable, possibly letters, though in no alphabet Rowan knew. Whichever way jhe turned it, Rowan could find no crack, keyhole, or hinges.

"Why don't you open it?" urged Orry. "Here, I'll do it."

Rowan frowned but handed it over, knowing from long experience that Orry would give jhm no peace otherwise. Rowan hovered protectively as Orry got out a pocketknife and pried at the edges. "Be careful, you'll scratch it!" Orry put the knife away, then held it up to an ear and shook it. Hearing nothing, jhe shook it harder. "That's enough!" protested Rowan. Jhe tried to grab it but Orry danced out of reach. "Dialfi, could you. . . ." Dialfi reached out a long arm, and Orry surrendered it.

Then, to Rowan's unreasonable dismay, Dana softly slipped the casket from Dialfi's hand. Jhe examined it carefully, looking at each side in turn, while puffing thoughtfully at a pipe.

"What a strange motif," jhe commented, tapping the shape under the spiral with the pipe stem. "Of course, we'll need to consult an expert on antiquities when we get to town."

"No, one's asked your advice, Dana," Rowan told jhm.

Dana smirked. "Still, I offer it freely to those so obviously in need." Pursing jhr lips to thoughtfully blow out a thin stream of bitter-smelling smoke, Dana declared, "This is a historical artifact, not some sort of knick-knack to adorn the corner shelf of a farmstead in the hinterlands."

Rowan waved the smoke to one side, and reached for the box. "It's no business of yours what we do with things we find on our own land."

Dana shielded it smoothly with jhr body, and told Dialfi, "Maybe you'd better explain to your sib, in simple words jhe's sure to understand, that such a discovery falls within the provenance of Akademe."

Rowan had always detested Dana for no particular reason beyond the instinctive hatred of the guileless dog for the artful cat. Jhe hurled a pebble at a tree trunk a good ten meters off, where it hit with a satisfying thwack. "Why can't you mind your own business for once?"

"Rowan," said Dialfi, relieving Dana of the casket before anyone came to blows, "Dana may be right, you know, that we need to show it to someone."

Rowan replied, "Great, so I'll take it to the museum myself, when we go to Adare this fall."

Coolly, settling jhr glasses higher on jhr nose, Dana said, "As representatives, however junior, of Akademe, I believe Dialfi and I would be the most appropriate ones to present our discovery."

"You had nothing to do with this discovery, Dana," Rowan said furiously.

"No? Who recognized the significance of the find, and who just wanted to sell it?"

"I never said a word about selling it! And as you're just trying to hog some kind of scholarly glory, there's no need to act so pure and virtuous!"

"Scholarly glory, forsooth!" scoffed Dana. "You shouldn't hinder the increase of knowledge, just because you're not Akademy material."

"As if I'd want to join that herd of nether-clipped bell-wethers!" This insult had the desired effect. Dana stalked off, and the air was the fresher for it.

Rowan glanced several times at Dialfi, but jhe was deep in thought. At last Rowan said, "We can't just sell it, Dialfi."

"No, of course not; not if it's of scholarly interest. But either way, Rowan, you shouldn't count on being able to keep it." Nonetheless, Dialfi handed the casket back to Rowan, and walked after Dana.

They all visited the tarn below camp to rinse away accumulated layers of squashed plum, dirt, and campfire soot. The otters made themselves scarce as these clumsy giants splashed about with great bellows and walloping belly flops. After a hastily thrown-together supper, the small fry dropped off to sleep, rolled in their wool blankets on the springy heather. They looked like a row of tousled raccoons, in their dark eye patches that kept off the sun's glare. Dialfi and Dana as usual sat talking by the dying embers of the campfire. Rowan wandered over to a huge boulder, where jhe sat fingering the raised designs on the casket.

The sun wheeled low and lower in the southern sky. Rowan squinted at its shimmering oval, fire-bright and defiant as it traversed the jagged knife-edge of the Shield Mountains that formed the border between Nuatha and the Waste. Would it manage to complete another circuit whole and unharmed?

As Rowan watched, unconsciously holding jhr breath, a dark peak reached up to stab its naked belly. It raked across the barest fringe of golden disc, before the sun sprang up again, whole and seemingly unscathed. Yet this brief eclipse meant summer's long day was drawing to a close. Tomorrow the sun would sink lower yet, and before long there would be real twilight, and then times of darkness.

It would soon be time to head home for the harvest-work, and then, to town. Rowan heaved a deep sigh. True, winter in town did bring interesting changes: all the people arriving for the season, the bells and tower lights that marked the darkling hours, the boisterous games that would range all through the streets before the rain and darkness drove everyone indoors. But mostly, winter meant school, and work indoors, and all the things Rowan did badly at.

Sitting there as the low and changing light played over the landscape, holding the mysterious casket in jhr arms, Rowan felt a fierce protectiveness well up for this relic rescued from its long interment, and knew what jhe must do.

As the sun climbed back up into the sky over the Helluland peaks, Rowan crept back to camp, quietly gathered a few things with a wary eye on the sleepers, and then set off, following the stream bed. There were dozens of ways out of the mountains and jhe knew most of them, having spent many a fine, long suncircle wandering their slopes to find berries, or dye plants for Mar, or tracking deer or cooncats. It was impossible to get lost once you had learned the streams and their tributaries, which sooner or later always brought you down to familiar places. The way jhe meant to go was too steep for the sheep, and much shorter.

Rowan went swiftly over narrow deer paths, as marmots piped warning to each other of jhr coming before diving into their burrows. The sun ran the gauntlet of the inland peaks and climbed higher, warming Rowan's back with golden light. Jhe slept a few hours in a sheltered hollow, then went on, through alpine meadows filled with the year's last wildflowers, and through stands of fir, spruce, birch, aspen and, lower down, cool, spongy groves of vine maple, alder, and devil's club. Not long after sighting the red-roofed farmhouse, Rowan caught a tantalizing whiff of frying onions and baking bread, and ran the rest of the way down.

Jhr parents were a bit surprised at jhr arriving alone. They hugged jhm warmly, and Far joked that Rowan must have grown tired of roughing it, and had come home for a bath and some home cooking. Of their three children, this was least likely to be true of Rowan.

Rowan explained that they'd thought it best to give some notice of the sheep's immanent return, with the mountain grass withering earlier than usual. Dialfi had said something of the sort, a few days back.

"Just wait 'til you see the load of dye plants we sent yesterday!" Rowan told Mar. "I found them — copper nettles, sunflower, false kingsfoil — you can't believe how much!"

"Wonderful!" exclaimed Mar. "I've been wanting more ocean shades."

Rowan drained jhr tea in one gulp, then told Grandmother, "But I wanted you to know the rest of what had happened."

"And a long story you made of it, too," said Grandmother with a twinkle.

"No more than you always did!"

Now Rowan drew out the casket, and Grandmother examined it carefully. Then she shook her head. "I can't see how to open it either, not without damaging it." She poured them some more tea, adding two lumps of white sugar this time, with a wink. Rowan's eyes widened at the sugar.

Grandmother sipped thoughtfully at her tea. She'd long suspected that Rowan's path would be as precarious as her own daughter Askve's. To be sure, there was a streak of wildness running through the family. Dialfi didn't have it (took after steady Sol, thank goodness Askve had found him in the end); whereas Orry's mischief was of a simpler kind. At last she said, "So, the treasure has finally been found."

"What do you mean?" Rowan asked in great excitement.

"My own Grandmother used to tell us that some kind of treasure had been hidden here, somewhere in the hills of Yngencloven, long ages ago when this land was nothing but rock and dust. None of the other farms could boast of such a legend. We dug so many holes looking for it, you could have broken your leg a hundred times over stepping into them!" Grandmother shook her head and smiled at the memory. "And it's to you that it's come at last, Rowan; only think of that."

"Dana thinks we should take it to the scholars."

"Maybe so, maybe so," answered Grandmother. "But long as it's been waiting, there's no need to rush into such decisions, is there?"

"That's what I thought, too," said Rowan. "At least we should see what's inside, first."

Chapter 2. Harvest

Efts: How can I possibly describe them? Girls without the giggles and shrieks; boys without the swagger. I'm talking about the sort of boy who has no interest in besting his fellows or in running with the raucous pack, but who follows his own lights. Or they're like those rebellious girls with long, tangly hair and nut-brown shoulders, the ones who are always climbing trees and running wild and beating everyone at chin-up contests. Freer than any boy, they wear a skirt when they feel like it, and balk at nothing. Your grudging esteem is mingled with pity; for you know how soon she will be thrust into an alien world, all the rules changed, her power stolen away in the night.

These efts — as tall as adults, and as knowing (save in one regard), with the unthinking arrogance of adolescents, but none of the hormonal mayhem — they are monarchs secure in their birthright. Not for many years to come will they be deposed and banished by their bodies' revolt. New creatures for a new world, they are inventing themselves before our eyes.

— Kassandra Morgan-Ávvu

The morning after the others had brought the sheep home, Rowan and Orry got up early. They climbed out the bedroom window, slid down the bamboo drainpipe to the porch roof, thence to one of the great oak's broad highway branches, which was smooth from untold years of such use. Down in the yard, Orry got the pump going with a few practiced strokes. Jhe bent over to plunge jhr head under the cascade, then straightened up and shook shining drops all over Rowan.

"Hey!" Rowan jumped back.

"That's what you get for running off and leaving us to bring all the sheep home. Where'd you put it, anyhow?"

"Somewhere safe." Rowan slid open the barn door and grabbed two baskets off a hook just inside.

"Boy, was Dana mad when we woke up to find you gone." Orry's voice rose in pitch, imitating Dana's pompous manner: "'Notwithstanding questions of provenance or surterranean property rights, such a discovery may be of incalculable intellectual worth, that is to say, in its potential to confer upon me the opportunity to write my name in gold letters upon the Philosopher's Wall beside those of the great sages. . .'" Orry dissolved into laughter.

"And what did Dialfi say?"

"Oh, jhe just let Dana talk on until jhe ran out of breath."

With baskets slung over their arms, they crawled around the nooks and crannies of the barn and then out in the yard, finding all the eggs they could. It was almost as fun as hunting mushrooms in the woods, though the chickens' hiding places were smellier. The ducks for their part hid their eggs outside in the tall grasses, as did the geese, who defended their would-be progeny with hissing, outstretched necks.

They brought the treasure trove to their mother, who was slicing the season's last peaches in the open air of the summer kitchen. This was a lovely place framed with apple boughs and a wisteria vine, visited by small green frogs and whirring dragonflies.

Mar lifted her hands in mock amazement at the number of eggs they'd found. She set about scrambling a number of them. Seeing Rowan's surprise, for ordinarily she did not consider herself the household's cook, she smiled and said, "I thought we should have a breakfast feast, to welcome everyone home."

It was a dewy morning with the first hint of autumn in the lucid air, and the outdoor breakfast table soon took on the trappings of a banquet. Dialfi contributed a broad, turquoise bowl filled with dew-drenched raspberries, that held the faded red-gold hues of autumn sunshine. Rowan was adding a few strawberries when Grandmother came out with a jar from her precious store of honey and a plate of oatcakes. Far appeared, fingers ringed with mugs, cradling a carafe that exuded the luxurious aroma of *coffee*. A feast indeed.

Rowan made sandwiches of egg and oatcakes, and wolfed them down with gusto. Jhe leaned back and let out an appreciative, rolling belch. Orry tried to do one of jhr own, but it fell flat. "Heis, Orry, you've really got to practice that," Rowan told jhm, and started giving pointers. Orry enthusiastically gulped milk while trying to take in breaths at the same time, which predictably ended in a coughing fit.

"Grow up, you two," said Mar, with a glint of amusement in her eyes.

Far began regaling them with tales of his egg-hunting tribulations while they'd been away. He contorted his tall, lanky form through imaginary crannies with many a grimace. "The long and the short of it is, we've hatched out a lot more birds than I'd intended this year. We may have to spend the winter eating little but roast chicken and goose."

"That will be a lot of plucking for you, Sol," Mar told him, only partly in jest.

"Feather beds, mounds of feather beds!" yelled Orry, arms stretched wide, pretending to fall backwards into a soft pile.

"And quill pens," added Dialfi. "I need some new ones, in fact, before the start of school."

"That won't be for a bit longer," said Mar, growing serious. "We've got a great deal to do before you leave for the winter."

"When is Anno getting here?" asked Dialfi. Anno was an older cousin who always came to help with the harvest.

"Anno's gone on ordeal." Mar got up and began to clear the table. Dialfi and Rowan looked at each other, taken aback. Already? Anno wasn't all that much older than Dialfi.

"And, and, and?" asked Orry, with irreverent curiosity.

"Do you think your cousin is a kitten whose tail you can peek under?" answered Grandmother, and Rowan just managed to stifle a giggle.

Orry said, "Come on, that's all anyone wants to know about a new imago!"

"Anno should be with us by Midwinter," Mar said with dignity. "The monks said she needs more time to adjust."

She. Rowan tried to picture Anno as a woman. Their adventurous cousin had worked jhr way up through the ranks on various merchant ships, and had been well on the way to earning command of jhr own vessel. Now that would have to be put on hold. Imagoes generally kept to the more circumscribed world of home and family, at least until they'd raised children.

Orry was muttering, "Time to adjust, time to adjust. . . *I* for one aim to stay an eft forever." As the youngest, Orry was the only one who got away with talking to Mar this way, but the others quietly enjoyed the show.

Mar answered, "It's not anything you'll have a choice about. Although I should warn you that sailors aren't exactly known for lingering in efthood." Orry, whose ambition was to sail, grinned and helped jhmself to more oatcakes.

Dialfi asked, "And what news of Kiril?" Kiril was Anno's constant companion, who had become practically a member of the family.

Mar said harshly, "Kiril has proven false, as boon friends often do."

Far explained, "Anno stayed when the change came upon Kiril, unwilling to be parted even if it meant changing before jhr time. But then Kiril forgot what lay between them, as if it had never been. To some, the change does that."

Dialfi said, "But Anno did not forget Kiril?"

Far looked grave. "Take my advice, Dialfi and Rowan — and you too, Orry — don't go seeking a boon friend. Our family isn't cut out for them. I think we must be too faithful, and it's best to save that for imagohood."

On that sobering note, they all helped with the rest of the dishes, knowing how Mar despised the unending drudgery of household work that dominated the summer season. For Askve was first and foremost a weaver, famous for her tapestries throughout the Victoria highlands and all the way out to Adelie. Yet she would admit to no more than an unusual obsession with color. Most weavers focussed on texture or on such clear contrasts of dark and light as could be managed by winter's lamplight. At most farm-holdings they could not spare the electricity for brighter lights, and Yngencloven was no exception. This meant subtle variegations of color were both difficult and highly prized. Yet Mar would claim to be far braver with colors for being unable to see them outright. Each year at Sunreturn, she would act surprised at how well the patterns showed in the daylight, though Rowan had lately begun to suspect the surprise was at least in part feigned.

Mar's hands were agile and heavily knuckled, and her arms roped with muscle from the heavy dye work. This time of year, they were generally stained to the elbow in muddy hues. Her hair was always plaited into a long, grayish braid. The effortless dance of her fingers each morning as she waited for the kettle to boil had captivated Rowan since early childhood.

Rowan loved to wander through Mar's spacious workroom, with its dark floor of polished oak. It had shelves and bins lining all the interior walls, a treasury of rich colors: the teal of a drake's wing, the scarlet of a poppy, the shadowy green of pines, browns like newly plowed furrows, dusty cornflower blue, rich purple of twilight sky on the season's shoulder, and all the yellows: egg yolk, dandelion, rich amber of honey and mellowness of beeswax, pine's new-sawn brightness, oat-straw's lustrous sheen, the vivid glow of alder and birch leaves in October rain. To Rowan, it seemed the entire world lay there, contained in those colors, waiting to be assembled into new and wonderful patterns.

Arching overhead were the beams Far had carved for his wife long ago when they'd begun their married life: fish, vines, birds, snakes, foxes, funny grimacing faces — all sorts of fanciful creations. The roof-beam was an entire trunk, bowed and curved. Its natural form had inspired Far to shape it into a woman arched with her back to the floor, hands and feet braced against the opposite walls as if holding them together and apart. She was at once strong and graceful, and her head was turned so that she looked over her shoulder. You could see a hint of a smile on her face, as if she was amused by her own predicament, up there among the rafters. Far called her "the Supine Caryatid" and was very proud of her. Once, gazing up at her admiringly, he'd commented, "She's another one that had the wit to fall upon her back, wouldn't you say?" and Mar had shushed him while laughing, and Dialfi had gone to consult a well-worn book, and upon finding a certain passage had laughed too, but had refused to explain it to Rowan and Orry.

The next few weeks were full of urgent work, before the rapidly encroaching winter darkness eclipsed the daylight hours. Still, in whatever quiet moments jhe could find, Rowan would slip upstairs to take out the casket and study it, and rub jhr fingertips across the embossed decorations. Orry had finally given up asking where it was, and Dialfi did not raise the subject at all, for which forbearance Rowan was grateful. If they handed it over to the experts, they'd probably never lay eyes on it again.

At first, jhe'd only wanted to keep Dana from unfairly taking credit for the discovery, but jhe'd grown more and more curious about what the casket could be, and above all what was inside it. Yet jhe could discover no non-destructive way to open it. Dialfi might have been some help, or Far, but Rowan was afraid that involving them would lead to the casket's passing out of jhr hands.

Mostly, though, Rowan had little time to puzzle over the casket. For starters, there was the twice-daily milking, and the last of the year's cheese- and butter-making; the aforementioned egg-collecting; and the feeding and watering of the stock. Breakfast was a hasty, catch-as-catch-can affair, and then they'd tackle the end-of-summer garden harvest. They dug onions, carrots, potatoes, parsnips, and beets, and put them carefully in the cool cellar, in storage bins lined with sand. From withering vines, they cut squash in many shapes, dappled yellow on dark green, or warmly glowing orange, and lay them gently in hammock-nets strung about the storeroom. Cabbages went on shelves above, and long vines of beans hung to dry in the barn, to be threshed at their leisure.

One whole day was spent apple-picking. With large baskets strapped over their shoulders, they swarmed through the old orchard and filled the wagon, while the ponies ranged free to graze on windfall. They stored the best apples in the cellar with the vegetables, and set aside the damaged ones to be made into cider.

While Rowan and Orry saw to the cider-making, Dialfi hitched a couple of ponies to the wagon and brought back load after load of mown hay from the autotram depot, stacking it in the loft of the big barn with Far's help. Mar and Grandmother busied themselves blanching green vegetables for freezing, and canning tomatoes and other fruit, which fortunately, as the afternoons remained hot, could be done in the breezy outdoor kitchen.

In any spare moments, Rowan and Orry hauled loads of fallen branches and logs that Far had cut and left lying, and stacked them against the lee wall of the house, or else (Orry's preferred method) sent them hurtling with a great clatter down the long chute from the upper woodlot into the woodshed.

Rowan was in the woodshed tossing logs up into the crib, when jhe heard a voice just on the other side of the thin-planked wall.

"How now, my fellow scholar? Is your swashbuckling pen poised for its winter labors?"

It was Dana. No one else talked like that.

"Hey, Dana," Dialfi grunted, tossing down jhr load with a thump. "How goes the harvest?"

"Not bad, not bad." There was a rustling sound near Rowan that must be Dana leaning up against the wall outside. Rowan pictured Dana lounging just a few centims away, smooth, clean hands resting in jhr pockets. Dana did not do much farm work, and was for some reason proud of this. "But I didn't come to talk about the harvest."

"No?" Dialfi was slapping jhr hands together to stay warm. Rowan could tell jhe was impatient to get back to work.

"Where's Rowan?" Dana asked abruptly.

"Oh, around somewhere. Probably off in the kitchen sneaking a donut and a sit-down." Rowan scowled; jhe kept a jar of donuts handy in the barn, precisely so jhe could grab them on the run.

"See, Dialfi, I've been thinking some more about that casket we found in the highlands."

"Well, you're right that it's Rowan you need to talk to." Good old Dialfi. Rowan would share some donuts with jhm as soon as Dana cleared out.

"It may be of great significance," Dana was saying. "Who knows, it could even make our careers. What good is it to Rowan?"

Dialfi murmured something inaudible. Rowan put jhr ear to the wall. Dialfi was saying, "I may never get to the Akademy, with money as tight as it is now."

"Oh, you'll win a scholarship, no fear of that. But look, Dialfi, you've really got to convince Rowan that jhe can't keep illegally harboring an antiquity – if word got around the Akademy, such a thing might even do you harm."

Dialfi said, "Well, that's hardly likely, unless you went bearing tales."

"I didn't mean to imply—"

Rowan burst out of the side door, and was briefly gratified at the startled look on Dana's face. From an insolent slouch, Dana quickly straightened. "Were you *spying* on us?"

"Why, are you ashamed of what you were saying?" Rowan stepped closer, and Dana hastily pulled jhr hands from jhr pockets, as if expecting Rowan to strike jhm. It was tempting, but instead Rowan attacked as a scholar would, with words. "How dare you talk to Dialfi like that, you — you Junior Cleric of the Cowbird's Plume, or however it is you style yourself these days!"

Dana said stiffly, "I had the honor of being made Ancillary Scrivener last spring."

"Oh ho, now that *is* a fine thing!" hooted Rowan. "It *sounds* much fancier than Assistant Scribbler, at any rate."

"You know nothing of such matters," Dana replied, "any more than you understand the significance of the artifact you tripped over while playing childish games among the sheep, which you now cling to with grubby hands rather than passing it on to those who could unfold its meaning."

"Stuck-up prig, you were looking after the sheep and playing flag-tag with the rest of us!"

"I was only there to keep Dialfi from moldering for lack of intellectual discourse. These months of hard manual labor take their toll, even on jhr fine mind."

Heavy footsteps approached. "Mornin', Dana," said Far. "You'll forgive me for not stopping to join your chat, as we're over busy just now. Dialfi and Rowan, I need your help."

"Just a moment, Mr. Yngling," said Dana, stepping into his path. "Are you aware that we brought back a potentially valuable artifact from the mountains last week? Valuable in the intellectual sense, I mean."

"I've heard nothing of that," said Far, glancing at Dialfi.

Dialfi explained, "That bale of dye plants that Rowan found, they were growing all around an old copper box buried in the ground."

Dana went on talking to Far, as if Rowan were not there, "I'm concerned to see this artifact turned over to the proper authorities, but Rowan's acquired the unaccountable notion that it belongs to jhm."

Rowan shot back, "Whereas *you*'ve acquired the unfathomable notion that it concerns you at all, Dana!"

Far's look of amusement would not have been evident to any but a close member of the family. "Dana, I appreciate your bringing the matter to my attention. Never fear, we'll make sure this article ends up where it belongs." Far strode off.

Rowan jogged after him, and when they were out of earshot, said, "Please, Far. You have to promise you won't let Dana get hold of it."

Far shook his head. "How could I, when I don't know where it is, or for that matter what it even looks like? —No, I don't want to hear any more about it right now. Time enough when things have calmed down around here."

Chapter 3. Gnomads

Great rumbling herds of mehemoths will one day wander through the broad grasslands of the uttermost south, realm of the night's night, where stories pour onto the sleeping earth through a hole in the heavens.

— Kassandra Morgan-Ávvu

They'd just sat down to supper when they heard a dull rumble in the distance. Everyone rushed out to the porch. From away down the road came a series of trumpeting calls that echoed about the hills.

Rowan wrapped an arm around a column and leaned way out, shading jhr eyes, and was rewarded with the first sight of great shaggy beasts coming around the bend. "It's the gnomads, all right!"

"They're early, this year," Dialfi said, going to radio the neighbors.

Mar muttered, "Oh, marvelous, so now I have to feed gypsies, on top of everything else." But she put on her apron and began to set out refreshments, while Far cleared away the supper dishes.

Orry ran to pull aside the heavy fence to the outer corral, which held the largest trough. The dogs were barking like mad, running in circles at the gate. In the distance, the lead animal slowed to a shuffling halt. "Get those ill-mannered curs out of the yard," ordered Far angrily, for gnomads were not over-fond of dogs. Eager not to miss anything, Orry and Rowan hurriedly tied up the dogs behind the house.

By the time they'd finished, half a dozen well-laden mehemoths were pouring into the dusty yard, swinging their tusked heads in time with their steps. They varied in hue from pale ivory to red-brown to smoky grey. A small figure perched high behind each broad skull.

Grandmother walked over to the lead animal and bowed, her arms spread wide in welcome. The rider dipped his head, while the beast too appeared to return the courtesy by lowering itself to its knees with measured dignity, whereupon the rider slid smoothly down to land on the ground with a flourish. He was in full regalia, boots upcurled at the tips and trimmed above the knee with white wolf fur, rich embroidery glowing along his cuffs and shoulders, and bells tinkling along the edges of the dark blue scarf that covered his face, showing only his bright grey eyes. Gnomads always seemed to be swathed in layer upon layer of clothing. However, Rowan caught sight of someone at the end of the line hurriedly yanking on jhr boots, and suspected that this youngster, at least, had been riding barefoot in the mild evening.

The appropriate greetings made, some of the riders began to deftly untie colorful mounds of trade goods and pile them beside the porch. Others took beasts laden with their own gear to the far side of the pasture, where they would make camp.

Once unburdened, the thirsty beasts made their way over to the trough, where Rowan and Orry were pumping water. They drank in the oddest fashion, by reaching their long, flexible snouts though the fence (for they were not permitted into the corral, lest they upset the stock) and filling them with liter upon liter, then bending the snouts around to discharge the load into their upturned mouths. In this manner they emptied the trough faster than Rowan and Orry could replenish it. Then they stood back expectantly, eyes glistening with pleasure, to watch spurts of cool water gushing from the pump's spout.

When the beasts' great thirst was at last assuaged, Rowan edged closer to one of the dangling snouts. Jhe was curious to touch the leathery, wrinkled appendage that was snuffling around in the dust of the yard. Jhe held out a hand, palm up, as if this were a pony and not a five-meter tall, shaggy, tusked, giant-headed monster. The tip of the snout lifted and moved towards jhm. Rowan felt a strange thrilling in the air, vibrating through the soles of jhr feet.

A shout rang out. Next moment a gnomad came hurtling over the fence and shoved Rowan back. He spoke some low words to the mehemoth, who with immense dignity slowly backed away, then turned and ambled back to the others. The gnomad ordered Rowan with vehement gestures to stay away from the beasts henceforward.

Rowan noticed the formerly barefoot eft sitting on the fence, watching. The eft smiled, revealing strangely ornamented upper canines, with capped tips that curled upwards in minute mimicry of mehemoth tusks. Rowan shyly smiled back.

The gnomad eft hopped down nimbly, and gave a slight bow. "*Tehru*," jhe said in a voice hoarse from the dust of the open road.

"I'm Rowan."

They sat down side by side. Rowan expertly extracted a long shoot of grass and offered it to the gnomad before pulling another for jhmself. They chewed on their tender ends companionably. Rowan took strange scents into jhr nostrils, the sour sweat of another body, hints of unfamiliar spices, the musky stench of mehemoth. What would jhe smell like to the gnomad? Probably like the potatoes jhe'd been digging all afternoon.

The gnomad touched jhr own shock of pale hair, while pointing a pinkie towards Rowan and raising jhr brows questioningly.

Puzzled, Rowan touched jhr hair, which was tied back in a short ponytail. Efts often grew their hair long, to mark the transition out of childhood, but Rowan's had never had more than a glancing acquaintance with the comb. Besides, jhe had little wish to draw attention to jhr hair. Most Nuathans were dark, but this time of year Rowan's was a sun-bleached brown, shot through with bright gold and copper streaks. Jhe'd been teased often enough over the years, for that and for the dizzying explosion of freckles that summer always bestowed from forehead to shoulders.

Rowan longed to ask what it was like to ride the great beasts, and travel the open road through the shortening days of autumn. But it proved impossible to convey such questions by gesture alone, and they were reduced to shrugs and smiles. Seeing Mar advancing in the distance, Rowan jumped up. "I've got to go. See you later?"

The youth smiled, so jhr little tusks disconcertingly poked out.

Rowan, Dialfi, and Orry hurried through the evening chores. By the time they'd finished, groups from neighboring farms were calling out greetings as they drove their wagons into the yard.

The gnomads had laid out a collection of goods attractively on felted mats near the porch. In addition to a large array of practical items, there were carved ivory drinking horns and leather canteens, decorated hats and cloaks like the ones the gnomads were wearing, though of lesser quality to Mar's practiced eye (as she had told Rowan in years past, when Rowan had begged for such clothing), and precious stones of all colors, some made into jewelry. Far would never waste money on such trinkets, Rowan knew. In good years, he might be interested in such items as lanterns made of intricately carved bone or hardwood, or cutting tools with razor-sharp blades of obsidian and handles of wood and leather. This year, Rowan noticed Far bargaining over a pile of some type of ore.

As usual, Mar examined minutely the collection of dried plants peculiar to the lands of the interior, and lovingly fingered the incomparably lofty skeins of long-haired wool from their beasts. She always selected a few to add to her weaving in small amounts. Grandmother for her part would contrive to purchase a few coveted items for her grandchildren, having first quietly observed their inclinations. This year, Orry was entranced by the wooden bird whistles and little carved animals, while sober Dialfi, rather to Rowan's amusement, was browsing through the hair ornaments.

In return, the gnomads were content to take such mundanities as bags of salt, bundles of dried fish, sewing needles, cooking pots, and antibiotics; farmers in the area made sure to lay in a good supply of this sort of thing from town. Sometimes the gnomads would also bargain for bags of green coffee beans, and smaller ones of sugar. This time, though, they wanted bullets and gunpowder. Their extravagant gestures indicating explosive weapons entertained Orry greatly. Jhe imitated them with great glee for weeks afterwards, long after the others had tired of the show.

After the trading was finished to everyone's satisfaction, and the neighbors had gone home, the gnomads and the Ynglings settled down on the porch to drink small glasses of akkavita. As the dusk deepened, one by one the gnomads unwound their scarves and bared their heads to the evening air with sighs of appreciation. Their cheeks were pale, with wide slabs of cheekbones, small-bridged, upturned noses, and the tanned skin around their deep set eyes was densely traced with fine wrinkles.

One gnomad sitting near Rowan wore a broad silver ornament on her chest. Something about it caught Rowan's eye, and jhe looked closer. It had the same stylized figures marching around the edge, as were on the casket! These were etched more sharply and Rowan realized it was a train of caribou pulling sleds, with people and mehemoths striding along amongst them. Did the casket have something to do with gnomads, then?

Rowan jumped up to fetch the pillow-case-wrapped casket from its nest between mattress and headboard, to ask them if they knew how to open it. But as jhe clattered back down the stairs, jhr footsteps slowed. What if the gnomads did recognize the casket, only to claim it as their own? Or what if they offered to trade for it? With money as tight as it was, Far might be tempted.

Back out on the porch, Rowan noticed Tehru watching jhm curiously. Jhe sat down on the lowest porch step, and carefully, making sure Mar didn't see, gestured around towards the back of the house. After a moment, Rowan slipped away into the shadows of the yard.

Jhe found Tehru settled comfortably against a rise in the ground, as if it were a fine couch. The chatter from the front porch reached them only faintly; cool darkness cloaked them and a half moon hung low in the sky. Not far away, a mehemoth, eyes half-closed, leaned on three legs, with one tree-trunk foot delicately tipped diagonal to the ground.

Rowan unwrapped the casket and showed it to Tehru. Moonlight shone on the burnished surface.

Tehru ran a finger slowly along the line of marching figures. Rowan turned it to show the top, with its irregular swirling shape. Seeing it, the young trader gripped jhr wrist. "*Emru*," jhe breathed, amazed and clearly frightened.

"I don't understand," whispered Rowan.

"*Emru*!" Tehru fluttered a hand above their heads, then made it descend in slow circles to chest level. To Rowan, it looked like a carrion bird scanning the ground for a meal. Tehru met Rowan's eyes intently.

Suddenly Rowan felt jhmself hauled bodily to jhr feet. "Go check on our stock," said Mar stiffly, not looking at Tehru, nor noticing the casket clutched under Rowan's arm. "That monster—" she gestured at the drowsing mehemoth, "is making them nervous."

"We were just talking—" Rowan protested.

"Talking!" scoffed Mar. "You don't even speak the same language. I mean it; off with you, now!"

Late that evening, Rowan once again slipped through the silent house to visit Grandmother's rooms, and tell her about how Tehru had reacted to the pattern on the casket. "It meant something to jhm, Grandmother."

"Did it, now? Well, come to think of it, it may have been Granny Rilla herself who hid it in the first place."

"Granny Rilla?" asked Rowan. "Wasn't she your own grandmother?"

"Yes indeed; Rilla with hair of golden flame, and a temper to match, so they said. Oh, surely you've heard the story: how my great-grandfather lost his heart to her after seeing her at the midsummer Fair. They danced the valse, so floatingly . . ." Grandmother closed her eyes and waved a hand back and forth in time to imaginary music.

"But did she have something to do with gnomads?" interrupted Rowan.

"I should say so! Rilla was a gnomad princess."

"A princess?" Rowan asked skeptically. "Do gnomads have that sort of thing?"

"Well, something like that," Grandmother waved a hand carelessly. "Anyway, she was one of the wandering folk, and settled here at Yngencloven. That used to happen now and then in the older days, but not now, not now."

"So you're saying we're part gnomad?"

Grandmother nodded. "Not that anyone likes to speak of it."

Rowan suddenly understood something. "Wait, is *that* why my hair is so light? You used to get so angry at Orry for teasing me, and I never knew why."

"You've got more than a drop of that blood running through your veins, or so I would guess."

Rowan felt strangely excited at this revelation. "Is it because of Rilla that the traders always stop at our farm?"

Grandmother shook her head. "Do you know the old stones, out beyond the north pasture?" Rowan nodded. A ring of jagged stones stood, half-buried in moss, beside the spot where the gnomads were camped. Grandmother continued, "Those stones go back much farther than Rilla's time, and mean something to them, though I don't know what, exactly. In any case, our family has always welcomed the wandering folk."

"Mar doesn't," said Rowan. "I was talking with one of their efts, and she just dragged me away."

Grandmother said, "There's a gulf between their people and ours. I've never really understood it. Maybe it's nothing but the scorn of a settled people for wanderers."

Rowan thought of the word Tehru had kept repeating, upon seeing the casket. "Grandmother, do you know any of their language?"

"Only some old songs; I used to sing them to you, when you were little." She sang a few haunting lines, faintly familiar to Rowan.

"Oh, what does it mean?"

"Something like this: *The long night is coming, is coming; the wind is blowing the stars to us. The windnoses are running to meet them, meet them, their treehorns tossing apace.*"

"What are windnoses?"

"That's another word for caribou; for they like to run straight into the wind, or that's what Granny Rilla said. Treehorns are their antlers."

Rowan put jhr hands behind jhr head and gazed up at the shadowy ceiling. "You know, I used to imagine running away to join the gnomads, when I was little. I'd forgotten all about that! It seemed like such a perfect life, to wander the wilds of the Inner Waste, never tied down to anything, going where you please."

"I too have dreamed of that, Rowan. It must be that gnomad blood in our veins, don't you think?"

The next morning, Rowan got up while the light was still dim, and hearing no sounds from the yard, was certain that for once jhe'd gotten up early enough to see the gnomads break camp and set off. But when jhe ran downstairs to look, both yard and campsite were empty, the dust of their passing long settled.

Chapter 4. Cold Snap

A raven on tilted wings, veering outward from the center, is how I see the map of this land. A circling raven spells warning, and doom.

— Kassandra Morgan-Ávvu

As the weather cooled and dimmed, tempers began to fray. Mar spoke more sharply; Far grew quieter. Orry began to balk in little ways. Rowan found jhm chopping wood in bare feet, and sent jhm in for boots. Rowan finished the job and put the axe back on the porch, where jhe found Orry fiddling half-heartedly with the laces. "When you've managed to tie your boots, come help me set the haystack to rights," jhe told jhm sharply. "If you think to get out of the job by doing it sloppily, you'll soon see you're mistaken."

"Next year I'll be off to sea with Uncle Narv," Orry retorted, "where no one'll care about splitting kindling or laying haystacks just so."

"And a good riddance, too!" muttered Rowan, though jhe didn't like the idea of Orry riding the storm-tossed seas.

Rowan spent what time jhe could find on jhr own investigations of the casket: trying to get it open (there had to be a hidden mechanism somewhere) and making rubbings and drawings of its raised decorations, and molds with some clay jhe dug up from a stream-bed. Sometimes, struck by a new idea, Rowan would become lost in thought, causing Mar to say sharply, "Rowan, what's gotten into you? Stop daydreaming, and get back to work!"

Far intervened. "Now, Askve, Rowan's always been one to pitch in with a good will, you know that."

Mar answered quietly, but not so quietly that Rowan did not hear, "At least jhe could save the laziness for winter-school like jhe usually does, hard-pressed as we are this year."

Far murmured something, and Rowan slipped away, resolving to stay out of Mar's way until her mood improved, which was looking like it might take until Midwinterfest, if not longer.

One afternoon when Far was fetching potatoes from a distant field, and Mar and Grandmother were hard at work canning, the three sibs climbed over the fence rails to feed apples to the ponies. Yngencloven had half a dozen ponies of various temperaments. They were an ancient breed whose colors ranged from dun to copper-bright, all sporting a dark dorsal stripe that ran from their tails along their backs and up through the midline of their cream-colored manes, which bristled up like shocks of oats. They were sure-footed and nimble, strong enough to plough and haul on the sloped fields and hardy enough to spend the winter outdoors. Far had lately acquired a pair of fine-boned horses, but Rowan much preferred the ponies.

As they lingered there in the lowering sun, Orry suggested some pony races, just one or two, to liven things up a little. They persuaded Dialfi to join them, pointing out how in past years there had been time for play, even during the harvest.

Rowan coaxed Berta over to the fence rails and slipped onto her back. She was a spirited mare who had a mind of her own, but didn't spook at every falling leaf. Orry, with not a little tugging on her mane, managed to clamber onto patient little Mari, while long-limbed Dialfi swung jhmself onto Mattias, the tallest of the lot. They dashed bareback round and round the horse pasture, egging the ponies on with their heels, yelling with abandon at unexpected turns and near accidents.

One thing led to another; Rowan went and got bridles from the barn, and they ended up spending a good part of the afternoon messing around, making a course with jumps and other obstacles. Rowan whooped as jhe and Berta shot past Mari and over the pile of oat sheaves to grab the prize willow ring from under Dialfi's hand yet again. Of course they were too old for such antics, but Rowan would forever after treasure the memory of the wind in jhr hair and the cold, bright sun on jhr back, and the exhilarating recklessness of galloping around the rough pasture with jhr sibs, through that full and glorious autumn afternoon.

Over a hastily thrown-together supper of leftovers from the canning, they learned that their antics had not escaped

Mar's notice. "So, you three find time for riding ponies, while the rest of us are run off our feet."

"Now, Askve," said Grandmother, "we've all been working hard these past weeks."

Far gently tucked a loose strand of Mar's hair back into her braid, adding, "Soon enough, my love, you'll be back to your weaving."

The real trouble began with the shearing of the sheep. Being longhaired shermunrardos for Mar's fine weaving, they were normally sheared both Sundip and Sunreturn. This year, Far was inclined to leave them their summer coats, as the coming winter looked to be a hard one.

Mar disagreed. She said that if not clipped, they'd grow little more wool that winter; and moreover, if shearing was delayed until Sunreturn, the fleeces would become matted, dirty and difficult to work. Far nodded thoughtfully, tuned in to the weather reports on the skywave, and went out to the yard to squint at the different quarters of the sky. At last he agreed to go ahead with the shearing.

On a beautifully sunny morning they drove the sheep into the lake, splashing in after them and whooping from the cold. They chased the sheep all around in waist-deep water, and rubbed and beat their coats (and did the same to each other when they saw a chance). At last they drove them back up onto the grassy shore and into a straw-filled pen, where they could dry. That was the fun part.

Then Far showed Dialfi how to manage the electric clippers, which had always been Anno's job. Only Far was strong enough to wrestle each reluctant sheep into position, rolling it this way and that for clipping. The others ran the stationary bike to charge the spare batteries, since no one had remembered to cycle them through the solarator when the sun was still high enough. They also picked the fleeces clean of twigs and burrs, and laid them out along the sawbuck fences to dry. It was hot, dusty, and tedious work, and the smell of lanolin so permeated everything that their appetites were blunted. Supper hardly seemed worth the bother, when they finally finished.

The next morning dawned grey and misty. When Orry and Rowan scrambled down the tree to hunt for eggs the eaves were dripping, the firs were weeping, and the grass was soaked. Rowan shivered, but didn't bother to dig out a musty sweater from the back of the cupboard, figuring the fog would burn off soon.

It didn't. During breakfast the wind came up strongly, and rain began to beat against the windowpanes. Mar took one look, then hurried out of the room. Grandmother said, "Quick, Rowan, go shut all the windows, and don't forget the upstairs ones! Dialfi, you see to the sheep; Orry, you bring in the hens!" Then she dashed out to do some other urgent task. From an upstairs window Rowan saw Far bringing the mare and her new colt into the barn. The ponies and cattle could stay in the pasture. They were already growing their shaggy winter coats, and there was a thick copse of firs at one end where they could shelter.

Everyone came back shivering to the living room to find Mar had lit a precious charcoal fire, almost unheard of so early in the autumn. They finished breakfast huddled around the heater, and neither Mar nor Grandmother complained of the drips on the carpet. On the skywave the radio announcer spoke of freezing temperatures throughout Victoria, right down to the lowlands around Adare. "Folks, we could be in for a tougher season than the record-breaker of three years ago, so you'd best fill in every chink, batten up the storm windows, and see to any repairs to wall or roof that you've been neglecting. And if you find you're in good shape, please check on your neighbors!"

All that day they blundered through their tasks, as if the chilling fog had penetrated to their very bones. Nothing went smoothly. The pump broke while Dialfi was watering the stock, and it took Far all morning to fix it. He swore under his breath with uncharacteristic ill-humor as he hammered a new pin. Trying to be helpful, Rowan began to knock the ice off the still-damp fleeces. But Mar stopped jhm angrily, saying it would wreck the fibers. She brought them inside to dry by the living room stove, fussing over them and turning them this way and that. Soon the nauseating smell of wet wool filled the house.

Rowan, wandering aimlessly in the yard, heard a chorus of skirling cries. Jhe looked all around, and at last overheard. Black shapes of geese were flying by in straggling lines, their long necks stretched out. Flock after flock went over the farm. Rowan wondered where they could possibly be headed. Did they spend the winter on warm seas faraway?

Far came out and put an end to Rowan's musings. He set the three of them to filling the woodshed, a job more tiresome than usual as the slippery wood kept crushing their numb fingers. Every so often one of them would duck into the house to warm their freezing hands. On one such occasion, Rowan was upstairs fingering the casket when jhe felt a slight discontinuity along one edge. Tarnished metal or else grime made it impossible to see whether this might be a tiny crack. Picking at it with a fingernail was no good.

Rowan ran out to the tool barn with it. The tool barn was a drafty outbuilding across the yard from the main barn, used for spillover storage and odd jobs. At one end was a little stove for heating pots of glue and the like. Beside the stove, a rough shelf was crammed with boxes of bolts and other bits of hardware, its edge rimmed with clamps and screwdrivers stuck through drilled holes. A variety of hammers hung jauntily from pegs on the wall below. Of course Rowan wouldn't think of doing anything that could damage the casket.

Jhe got down a bottle of alcohol and daubed at the edge where jhe'd felt the tiny crack with a dampened rag, trying to clean out the caked grime. It was finicky work, and Rowan wasn't sure it was making any difference, but jhe was unwilling to give up just yet. Suddenly, something blocked the light streaming through the doorway.

"What are you up to, Rowan?" Mar asked sharply.

"Just fixing something." Rowan hastily shoved the casket behind some canisters.

Mar raised her eyebrows, and glanced around for the remnants of a snack; if it had been Dialfi, she'd have looked for a book. Seeing nothing, she spun on her heel, saying, "Repairs can wait for winter." Mar set jhm to gathering cow pats and filling the chinks in the barn walls, a deeply ignominious punishment. As Dialfi and Orry virtuously hauled the sledge back and forth to the farther woodlot, they'd call out things like "Honey, what is that new fragrance you're wearing?" and "I hear that manure softens the hands!" Rowan didn't take any notice of them. The sting lay in being ordered about by Mar, as if jhe were only a youngster.

As the afternoon wore on, Orry began fussing and fumbling and dropping things on purpose, and generally being maddeningly underfoot, in a transparent bid to get sent inside. Rowan grew wild with irritation, which was Orry's other aim, should the primary one prove unobtainable. At last Orry managed to gash a knee open, and ran off crying for Mar. By that time, even Dialfi and Rowan were bickering, and they finished their work in grim silence. As jhe drifted off to sleep, shivering under heavy layers of covers, Rowan thought, *Thank the Sages today is over and done with.*

But the next morning was even colder. Though the freezing rain had stopped, the air held a strange dankness, chilly as a lake in early spring. When Orry and Rowan looked out the window, their breath made puffs of smoke. They tried to blow smoke rings, like Uncle Narv, but couldn't get the trick of it.

Downstairs, Mar and Far were deep in conversation. Heading out to the barn, Rowan skidded on a puddle and bent down to look, astonished. Ice, so early in autumn? Jhe'd never heard of such a thing. Jhe looked around, and saw that a sheath of ice coated the bushes and trees in dreadful beauty.

Dialfi and Rowan talked while they milked. "No, that year it was All Howls at least before the cold hit," Dialfi said, huffing out a great cloud for emphasis. Rowan's cow heaved a sigh, in an even better demonstration of the difference between inner warmth and outer chill.

Rowan suggested, "Maybe it's just that it's come on so suddenly. It might not mean such a bad winter ahead."

Dialfi said slowly, "I don't know. It's worrying, though."

The worst of it was how they'd only just done the shearing. The sheep huddled their close-cropped, pink-skinned bodies together miserably in their indoor pen, refusing to go out to graze on the still-green grass. Far came in and watched them for a while, then shut their door to keep out the wind.

At lunch, Far told them he'd decided to get a fire going in the tool barn, and move the sheep and the colt in there temporarily. As crazy as it seemed to light a stove for stock, he'd seen it done by relatives who lived among the southern mountains of Helluland, with whom he'd spent time in his youth. "It's a different sort of farming they do; their land is much stonier, and the winters are like nothing we ever see here. The winds go howling about the house like enraged ghosts, and the snow piles up until the door freezes shut, so you can't go out for days. You've never seen such snow! Not many live there, for it's a harsh and unforgiving land."

"I don't see how anyone could manage it," Dialfi said.

"They build the walls of their houses and barns as thick as they can, with packed earth and straw between layers of wood, and connect them with tunnels so there's no need to go out when icy winds are whipping around. Big families share a compound, which is good since you get hardly a visit from a neighbor from one moon to the next, in winter. It gets so stuffy, with the windows shut tight, and the smell of tallow candles and charcoal. Oh, that smell, how well I remember it!

"Right about this time of year, when the harvest is in, the children all trek to a forest cave to make charcoal, then haul it back home by sledge." He shook his head, eyes resting on Orry. "Children making charcoal, just imagine. But they think it's great fun. Anyhow, what I meant to say was, no matter how bad things may get this winter, we'll be able to manage. Though maybe it's time we threw up a covered walkway to the woodshed . . . " He gazed up at the ceiling thoughtfully.

Though Far had meant this speech to be reassuring, it made Rowan wonder just how bad he thought the winter would get.

Dialfi objected, "But Far, we don't have time to build walkways. It's nearly Allthanks, and we have to get to Adare right after that, at the very latest."

"I hadn't forgotten that," said Far. He looked around at the three pairs of anxious eyes, and said, "At the moment, I'm only planning to run the stove for those poor new-shorn sheep. Why don't you all come out and help me."

They worked with Far to set up a barrier at one end where there was room for the sheep and knocked together a stall for the tiny colt. They spread fresh straw all around, and brought in hay. The tubs had to be filled by hand, a laborious process that splashed them with freezing cold water when they impatiently carried too-full buckets.

Orry began topping off the wood-bin, but Far stopped jhm. He brought in a wooden container, took out a small number of black rocks, and placed them in the stove. Dialfi picked up a piece, puzzled. "What is this? It's too heavy to be charcoal."

"Coal," said Far quietly.

Orry dropped the piece jhe'd picked up. Shocked, Rowan said, "We can't burn coal!"

Far said quietly, "The stove isn't big enough to heat this drafty place without someone adding little logs to it continuously, not to mention using more wood than we can spare."

"But coal is undead," cried Orry; "it's supposed to stay under the earth!"

Far said, "I've only thought to use it ever so often, when wood wouldn't do the job. . . You three don't know what it's been like up here lately. When you were little and we used to get excited about the occasional deep snowfall, that was one thing. Last year, we ran out of wood a few weeks before Sunreturn."

"You never told us," said Dialfi, shocked.

"We didn't want to worry you."

"We'll cut more wood," Dialfi said. "There's no need to start burning coal, Far."

Far sighed, and gathered the lumps of coal back into the box. "You're right, of course."

Far split kindling and got the stove to a good, steady glow. Orry and Rowan began to bring in the miserable, shivering huddle of shorn sheep, while Dialfi brought in more loads of hay and straw, piling them against the wall furthest from the stove. By the time they'd finished, the sheep were contentedly munching hay, and the colt, a delicate, long-legged creature who had at first been distraught at being separated from his mother, now lay calmly in the warm straw.

Far surveyed the scene with satisfaction. "Now, my fine and pious offspring: keeping this drafty place warm with such a little stove will be a touchy job. The three of you will have to take turns watching around the clock. It should only be for a few days, just until the cold spell breaks."

Being in the heated space was a respite from the cold, at any rate. They took to sleeping there, burrowed into a huge pile of hay carried in for that purpose. It was certainly more comfortable than the frigid house, where no more fires would be lit for some time. They were spending so much time there that Rowan smuggled in the casket, hiding it on a roof beam, to look at it in quiet moments.

One evening, Rowan and Dialfi stayed up talking long after Orry had gone to sleep. They lay head to head in the scratchy, sweet-smelling hay, and every so often one of them got up to add a log to the stove.

Dialfi said, "It was strange to see Far almost burning that coal. I wonder how many others are already using it."

"Not Dana's family, anyhow," said Rowan. The Ettencotts were renowned for their strict interpretation of the Commandments, and rather looked down on the Ynglings for being so immoderate as to raise three offspring.

Dialfi ignored the fling at Dana. "If all it takes to make people start breaking the Commandments is a little spell of cold . . ."

“It was you Far listened to, about not burning it, not Orry or me. Why does he treat you so differently?”

Dialfi shrugged. “I'm eldest.”

“Not by all that much," objected Rowan. “Maybe it's because you're going to be a scholar.”

Rowan felt Dialfi shake jhr head. “That isn't it.”

“What, then?”

“Oh, I don't know; maybe if you were more serious about something.”

“I'm serious about all sorts of things!” Rowan got up to stir the stove, then burrowed back into jhr warm spot in the hay. Sleepily, jhe asked, “Where did Far get that coal, anyway?”

“Bought if off the traders. But they've never been miners. Maybe they got it from some folks in Vinson, or cash-strapped farmers in the Shield.”

“Hmm,” mumbled Rowan, only half-listening.

Dialfi sat up and leaned against the wall. “I need to do some thinking. I'll take the first watch and wake you up later, all right?”

“Wake up Orry; it's jhr turn.” Rowan rolled over, and fell asleep like a stone dropping into deep water.

Chapter 5. Fire

In this frozen land, we remember with disbelief how we used to curse the heat: blazing summers and baking autumns, winters that never came and springs comprising only a few muddy days. Now, we long for the ice to melt utterly, the sooner the better. We gaze in shameless ecstasy at the widening cracks in the ice fields and gaping sapphire-blue millraces, where the meltwaters dive down into unknowable depths, as if someone had yanked out the stopper of the world. We cheer on the creeping exposure of new rock, month by month, and waves of tundra spreading ever further south.

— Kassandra Morgan-Ávvu

As each frigid morning dawned later and darker, Rowan found it increasingly hard to stagger up out of bed and start the day's work. Jhe felt out of sorts, and jhr hands were stupid and weak at the morning milking. Orry was unusually silent in the evenings, fingering new blisters and calluses on jhr small hands, and Dialfi went about each task with grim determination. Far looked so worn out that they didn't complain of their own weariness.

The radio reported that the colder weather would likely go on for some time yet. Far thought they'd best keep the stove going at night while the cold spell continued, but leave off during the daytime, so as to gradually harden the sheep and the colt. Thankfully, it was looking like they'd manage to finish the work of harvest in time for school.

Then one night disaster struck. When Rowan came on watch in the tool barn, jhe found Orry had let the fire nearly die out, and it had become quite chilly. Jhe had to keep adding wood to the little stove, and then, since Orry had also neglected to fill the wood bin, jhe had to make a bunch of trips back and forth to the woodshed, too.

Coming back with one last armload, Rowan saw that the moon had risen above the trees. It was the glorious globular moon of winter, unseen these many months. Bone-tired as jhe was, Rowan couldn't resist the enchantment, and sat in the doorway watching the silvery light. The fanciful thought came to jhm that the casket might reveal its secrets by moonlight. Rowan made sure the others were sound asleep, then shimmied up the post and felt around the dusty surface of the roof beam to find it.

Jhe held the box to the otherworldly light pouring through the doorway, turning it this way and that. The tiny figures marching around the edge flickered and seemed to move under jhr hands, walking, walking endlessly into the unknown waste. . . Rowan shook jhmself awake. Jhe climbed up to put the casket back on the beam, and added more wood to the stove. The fire roared up, and at last the little barn began to feel comfortable.

Lulled by the warmth, Rowan closed jhr eyes, still seeing the figures on the casket. Gradually jhe drifted into a sort of half-dream, where, as if from a vantage high above, jhe watched a long column of figures stretching ahead and fading into the dim twilight of early winter. Mountainous mehemoths laden with poles and bundles walked beside caribou mares, who drew sleds filled with round, boisterous children. Older children darted in and out of the column on geldings, while imagoes on foot smacked at the offending hindquarters of child and beast alike. Through it all rang the ceaseless tinkle and din of bells of many shapes and sizes. Their combined notes verged tantalizingly on song, like waves striking a pebbly shore. At the very front of the column walked an unladen and riderless mehemoth, followed by a bent figure leaning on a tall staff.

In the way of dreams, Rowan now found jhmself within the scene, riding double behind an eft on the broad neck of an oak-brown mehemoth. Its swaying gait had a wider, slower arc than that of a pony. At first the motion felt precarious, but it became gradually more comfortable. In time with the loping strides, the eft was chanting softly. The words were mostly beyond Rowan's understanding, but a few phrases stuck out like boulders from a swift, dark river: *ice out of time, the ends of the earth, drowned undersea, death into birth.* From somewhere ahead in the column came a faint throb of skin drums, and a lower, deeper rumbling, felt more than heard. The looming sense that something important was about to happen grew upon Rowan, making jhm faint with expectation. Any moment now it would reveal itself. The drumming and throbbing came from all sides. Bells shrilled.

Rowan awoke to a loud roar from the stove. The dogleg section of pipe that ran under the beam was pulsing orange. Desperately jhe clamped shut the dampers to suffocate the fire, but the sound grew to a wavering roar as the pipe glowed yellow, then white. Jhe could see the bright fire inside, through many small but widening cracks in the pipe. The roaring increased; Dialfi and Orry came stumbling out of sleep; and they all ran for water, though Rowan feared no amount of water could stop the fire now. While the others refilled their buckets, Rowan stood frozen in horror as the glowing section of pipe began to dissolve and rain down drops of molten steel, sowing a vigorous crop of flames.

Now the tool barn was filling with smoke and with the crackle of rapidly spreading fire. The panicked colt screamed; outside, its mother neighed frantically in reply, her hooves pounding up and down the paddock as she desperately sought her offspring. It was like a nightmare, confusing and relentless and outside of time. Mar and Far rushed in, shouting for them to help get the stock out. Dialfi saw to the rearing colt, while Rowan and Far tried to herd the panicked sheep past the spreading flames and out the door. Mar asked, "Where is Orry?" in a voice terrible to hear. But just then Orry came racing in to hurl more buckets of water at the fire, dodging the colt's flying hooves. "No use!" Far yelled, then began to cough and cough. The stupid sheep kept going the wrong way, back into the far corner, where soon they would be cut off from escape. Already the beam over the pipe was smoking. But then one old ewe lunged for the open doorway, and the others followed in a great bleating stampede.

All at once Rowan remembered the casket. Ignoring Mar's frantic shouts, jhe ducked back inside to scramble up the dreadfully warm post, reached up to the beam — then snatched back jhr hand with a cry. The casket was burning hot.

Gripping the post tightly with jhr legs, Rowan yanked off jhr sweater and wrapped it around one arm. Choking and eyes streaming, Rowan felt around on top of the beam with the clumsy sweater-mit, terrified lest jhe knock the casket into the inferno below. Not far away, the beam was in flames. How hot could copper get before it melted? Jhe felt something, and hitched jhmself higher up the post to slide the awkward burden into the crook of jhr arm. Then, leaping down over the flames, jhe burst out the doorway into the frosty night.

The family stood numbly watching as the roof of the tool barn collapsed into the hungry flames. Fortunately, there was no wind that night to spread the fire to any of the other buildings. There would have been very little they could have done.

Far was saying something about how the sheep were going to have to manage in the main barn now. The throbbing pain in Rowan's arm was growing worse; but it was no more than jhe deserved. "Far," Rowan choked out, "I'm. . . I'm sorry."

Far looked at jhm with surprise. "Rowan, you're not thinking the fire was your fault?"

Rowan hung jhr head. "It was my watch."

"No, it was that damned doglegged pipe that was at fault. Some fool of an Yngling (I'm sorry, Askve, but it's true) must have got lazy and put in a flat stretch to reach the chimney hole, and worse still used cheap simple steel to do it. It didn't matter for warming glue pots and branding irons — who would have thought we'd ever use it for heating the place?"

"What's so bad about a flat stretch of pipe?" Orry wanted to know.

"They collect too much residue from the smoke. After all these years, that pipe must have been full of creosote."

"But I still stoked the fire too high," said Rowan.

"You were only doing as I asked, trying to keep the place warm. Truly, Rowan, this fire was not your fault."

Up on the porch, Mar lit the large overhead lantern, for no one felt able to go back to bed yet. Grandmother brought them mugs of tea and tucked quilts about their shoulders, then set about dressing Rowan's burn. Rowan had been cradling the casket in jhr shirt all this time. At last jhe dared to take it out and see if it was unharmed.

Far said, "I suppose that would be the 'artifact' Dana was asking after?"

Rowan nodded. Though smudged with ash, the casket seemed to be intact.

Mar asked, "Is that why you went back in there, Rowan? When you disappeared into the smoke, I thought. . ." Orry was snuggled up to her on one side, and she'd put her other arm around Dialfi's shoulders; but her eyes were on Rowan, and they were bright with unshed tears.

"I had to save it from the fire."

"Wherever did you get it? And why does everyone but me seem to know about this?"

"They found it up in the mountains, Askve," Grandmother explained. "It's Granny Rilla's lost treasure, I'm sure of it!"

"Oh, Mother," sighed Mar, "wasn't that just a story you told to get us searching far and wide, and out of your hair?"

"It most certainly was not!" Grandmother said indignantly.

"But we don't know what it is," Rowan said. "I can't figure out how to open it."

Far turned the casket over and over in his large hands, peering at it closely under the lamplight.

"Hey, it wasn't like that before!" Rowan pointed to the edge, where gaps had opened up, separated by beads of solder that had been melted by the fire's heat.

Far strode into the house and came back carrying a fine-tipped awl. Carefully, using a pair of tongs, he held it in the still-hot coals where the tool barn had stood. Rowan hurried to bring a light. He delicately placed the red hot tip of the awl here and there against the soldered edges of the casket, shaking the melted drops off as soon as they formed, and pausing every so often to let it cool. "Don't want to incinerate whatever may be inside," he called to his rapt audience. All at once the heavy lid parted from the lower half, and he carried it in triumph back to the porch.

They all clustered around the opened casket. Inside was a soft wrapping that crackled like finely spun sugar (glass wool, said Far, to insulate the contents). So perhaps they had opened it in the intended way.

Rowan gently eased the glass wool aside. Within lay a metal and plastic object no bigger than the end of your thumb, but flatter, with a crack radiating and ramifying out from one corner. "Is that some kind of a device?" jhe asked.

Dialfi shrugged. "Not like any I've ever seen."

Underneath was a small book in a cracked yellow binding. The cover had an odd drawing of teardrops falling diagonally within a square. In flowing script across the top was written "Rite in the Rain" and lower down, in square, blocky letters, "ALL-WEATHER **UNIVERSAL FIELD BOOK** No 374". The pages were stiff and shiny, much thicker than pages of a typical book. They were filled with closely written text that was utterly incomprehensible.

They all stared at the squiggly lines. "I wonder if that could be gnomad writing," said Rowan.

"What makes you say that?" asked Dialfi.

"I saw one of the traders wearing a brooch that had figures a lot like the ones marching around the box's edge. And if it was Granny Rilla's originally — well, she *was* a gnomad, even if no one ever likes to bring that up." Rowan gave Grandmother a slight smile.

"What would gnomads be doing with *writing*?" asked Orry.

"They are people of the book, even as we are," Grandmother reminded jhm.

"Even so," said Dialfi; "it's hard to believe they would still have the Humanual after all this time, living the way they do."

"Why do people always act like gnomads are no better than Outlanders, anyway?" demanded Rowan. Outlanders were barbarians who lived on the far side of Terraus, who had no efts but were like beasts in being male or female from birth. Appallingly, they were said to be indistinguishable from imagoes.

Far said, "A long time ago, Rowan, the gnomads abandoned the path that the Founders laid out for us. They turned their back on learning and chose to live as primitive hunter-gatherers. They refuse even to farm the land, and shun metallurgy and all but the simplest of crafts – though you may have noticed that they are happy enough to buy our medicines. They make no settled abode, but wander ceaselessly, following their half-wild herds."

"That doesn't sound so bad to me!"

"Of course it doesn't," said Orry. "You practically live like that already, outside of the school year."

"Oh, and sailing a boat is so very civilized."

"It requires mastering the venerable arts of navigation, weather-casting, and aerodynamics, among others," Orry loftily replied.

Grandmother had been carefully rewrapping the book to return it to the casket. Rowan protested, "We only just got it open; aren't we going to look at more?"

"Not tonight," Mar said firmly. "It's time we were all abed."

"Quite so," agreed Grandmother. She patted the casket, adding, "I believe I'd best hold onto this for the time being."

Rowan began to protest. Grandmother sniffed at the smoldering remains of the tool barn. "Never fear, I'll take good care of it." She added to Rowan by way of consolation, "You'll have fresher eyes tomorrow, anyhow."

Far had been watching all these disputations with much amusement. "A buried treasure come to light, a box without hinges or key unsprung by a fire, an alphabet no one knows; why, it's enough to make my head spin! What say you, Askve?"

Mar shook her head wearily, and hugged the quilt about her shoulders as though it were the only thing holding her together. "I say there's been quite enough excitement for one night. There will be plenty to do and decide by daylight."

Mar reached up to turn out the lantern.

Next morning, as they sleepily applied themselves to breakfast, Far came in looking grim. "Where has all the hay got to?" he demanded of Dialfi.

"What do you mean, sir?" Dialfi replied, startled into formality.

"The loft is barely half-full, though you told me you'd finished bringing it in from the fields."

Rowan and Dialfi looked at each other, aghast. Dialfi explained dully, "It was in the tool barn. We figured, if the sheep and horses were to be there a long time . . . . "

Far roared out, "You figured! You figured you'd rather toss hay in a warm barn than do work that needed doing. You figured you would make yourselves cozy beds! —But of course, you didn't expect a fire—" his tirade faded as quickly as it had begun; like many farmers, Far did not find that anger answered, in most circumstances.

Mar had been drawn by the shouting. "How bad is it, Sol?" she asked him quietly.

"Bad enough," he answered. "We'll have to make some hard choices." They talked awhile of selling the new horses, most of the ponies, and some of the sheep. Far went off to the radio and came back discouraged. "No one was interested; they're worried about feeding the livestock they already have." He and Mar looked at each other.

"Give it a few more days," Mar said at last.

In the end, he managed to sell the two horses; there are always people who cannot resist the beauty of a good horse, however impractical. He arranged for the colt to remain with its mother through the winter until it was weaned. All but three of the ponies were dispersed among neighbors as well. But this was not as much help as one might think: except in the worst of winter, ponies can pretty much forage for themselves.

It was the sheep that were the problem. No matter how he calculated, Far couldn't find a way to make the hay last, even had he been expecting a mild winter. It was far too late to cut more; the rains had spoiled whatever remained in the fields. No one was willing to sell their hay. And even as a gift, no one wanted to take on the sheep right at the start of winter. Nor, from respect for Mar's weaving, would anyone think of buying them for mutton.

It came down to the hard choice Far had feared. He told Mar that with the horses gone, he figured they could feed twenty of the flock, providing they did not delay. Then he left Mar to do the choosing. They all stayed away from the barn while she separated the sheep into two pens. One pen had the best ram, many young ewes, and a few older ones who were especially good mothers. Mar came in after many hours, straw in her hair and streaks of dirt on her face, and went upstairs to her work room, not looking at her family or stopping to wash. Far looked after her, then headed out the back door with set shoulders, taking Dialfi with him for the task they both dreaded.

The surprisingly early cold was a curse, that yet held some meager blessings. It would preserve meat slaughtered so early in the winter. And Far told his children that he would send some of the cured sheepskins with them to town. "Your mar will never touch them," he said, "and who knows but that you may need them this winter. Nothing should go to waste . . . isn't that in the Commandments too?" he tried to smile at them. But Mar did not smile for days, and they gave up trying to cheer her, as it only seemed to make her more upset.

Chapter 6. A Charge

You, my reader — whoever you are, and however far away — reading my words, you are a traveler in time.

— Kassandra Morgan-Ávvu

Some days later, Dana rode into the yard on a gleaming bay mare, head held high as though jhr very presence bestowed honor on their humble household. "Still haven't made it to Adare?" jhe asked Dialfi carelessly.

Dialfi and Rowan were breaking out chunks of ice from the sheep's trough preparatory to refilling it. Dialfi answered, "We thought we might as well stay for Allthanks this year, to save the older folks the trip to town." Rowan suspected that this delicate reference to tight finances went right over Dana's head.

"Yes, I've just come back for Allthanks, myself, though I'd much rather have stayed in town. But as my parents say, next year I'll be on the Isle of Getz," Dana shrugged casually, "at the Akademy, you know."

"Yes, of course," Dialfi answered neutrally. Rowan began to pump vigorous jets of water into the trough, even though there was still some ice in the way.

Dana backed away from the resulting splashes. "Rowan, about that casket we found."

Rowan scowled. "What do you mean, we? As I recall, *you* were off having a smoke when *I* found it."

"I really must insist that it be given into the proper hands without further delay, so that its provenance and significance can be established."

Rowan answered, "I already told you I'd bring it to the museum. But it happens I've learned some things about it already."

"Is that so?" Dana rolled jhr eyes at Dialfi. But Dialfi watched Rowan with interest.

In the best scholarly fashion jhe could muster, Rowan explained, "The decorations on the casket were in the same style as an ornament one of the traders was wearing. Remember the odd little figures going around the rim? They're a line of migrating caribou and gnomads, with their sleds and everything! It's easy to see them, once you know what you're looking at." Jhe rubbed at the itching skin where jhr forearm was healing from the burn; but catching Dialfi's eye, stopped short of mentioning that they'd managed to open the casket, as well.

"So you style yourself an archaeologist, now?" Dana said, laughing and shaking jhr head. "In truth is it said that the arrogance of the ignorant is boundless."

"It's nothing to the arrogance of the learned!" Rowan said, stung by Dana's scorn. "You'll see, your precious experts will say it's from the gnomads when they get a look at it. Besides, it's more than likely that it originally came from our many-times-great grandmother Rilla, who was a gnomad herself!"

"Ah yes, your unconventional great-grandmother. She seems to have bequeathed her fabled temper to you, at any rate."

Rowan ground jhr teeth; Dana was the most infuriating person jhe'd had the misfortune ever to meet.

"But as for what the experts will say," continued Dana, climbing back onto jhr fine-boned horse, "if it really did turn out to be of gnomad origin, like yourself, then it's worth a lot less than I'd hoped. Scholars care very little about the trinkets of gnomads." Jhe rode off with a jaunty wave of jhr cap.

Rowan yelled after jhm furiously, "In that case, I guess I won't bother about taking it to the museum!"

Dana's parting retort ate away at Rowan all day, so that jhe became ferociously determined to prove Dana and all the scholars in Nuatha wrong. Rowan was convinced the little book had something important to tell them, if only they could figure out how to decipher the strange writing.

That evening after supper, it being more seasonally mild than of late, they sat out on the porch to see the evening sky. With the harvest winding down, there was time for such things. By now, it was quite dim after supper. Rowan looked and looked around the darkening horizon, but as yet not a star, nor even a planet, were to be seen.

"Hold still," Grandmother ordered. She was changing Rowan's bandage. The burn was healing well, though there would be a scar. The spiraling shape that had so disturbed the young trader was seared into the flesh of Rowan's forearm near the elbow. "Well, you've been marked by the treasure, and no mistake. There's no telling where that may lead."

There'd been talk of whether they ought to seal up the casket again, the way it had been. Rowan argued against it, wanting a chance to look at the book some more. Dialfi thought they should make a scan of it, but there were no devices for scanning at Yngencloven, nor at the Ettencotts' either; in fact none closer than Adare. In the meantime, Grandmother promised to keep the book and casket safe. "Maybe I'll start my own museum," she winked at Rowan.

"Tell us about the treasure again," Orry begged. There was time again for stories now, too.

Grandmother sat back, and wrapped her shawl more tightly about her shoulders. "Every Midwinter's Eve, Granny Rilla would speak of the treasure that lay somewhere up in the high hills of Yngencloven." She slipped into a singsong cadence. "So it was, and so I shall tell you, it is a treasure not of gold, nor of jewels, nor of any such worth, but of wisdom from the past, that will shine its light in a time of great need . . . ."

Orry interrupted, "Does that mean the treasure could decide when to be found?"

"Of course not," said Dialfi. "Such a thing would be impossible."

"How could you know that?" Orry argued.

"Hush, you two," said Rowan; "I want to hear what Grandmother was saying."

Grandmother was patient with their bickering. "O my children of a reasonable age, when you are as old as I, you will have come to know that Logos moves in mysterious ways, and gives you glimpses of a greater pattern . . . ." Her voice was soft and intent, the way it had been when she would tell them great legends and marvels by the flickering firelight. "The treasure will set in motion things that have long been still. It will bring you and those around you into trouble, and danger, and grief. And yet — take heed, my dear ones — it would be far more dangerous to remain in ignorance. It will lead you into the distant past, and shape for all of us the future . . ." she trailed off, nodding to herself.

Low on the northern horizon, Rowan saw the first glint of a winter star.

That night, Rowan once again tiptoed into Grandmother's room. "Can I look at the book tonight?"

"Again? Are you becoming a scholar too?" Grandmother's eyes twinkled.

Rowan snorted. "Hardly."

"Do be careful with it. It seems quite sturdy, whatever it's made of, but still—"

"Of course I will," answered Rowan.

Grandmother went to bed, leaving jhm at the small table bathed in warm lamplight. Slowly Rowan turned the pages, and studied the spidery writing that looked like no alphabet jhe'd ever seen. Jhe began to copy out the letters onto a bit of scrap paper, just to get a sense for this strange alphabet. It was no help: every so often a letter would repeat, but for the most part they were dizzyingly distinct, and fitted together in intricate ways.

Was this gnomad writing, or might it be something else entirely? Maybe it was something out of the ancient world that had been forgotten long since. Writing that no one could read was tantalizing, and maddening.

At last, in frustration, Rowan began flipping ahead in the book, seeing page after page of the indecipherable squiggles. Some parts were written neatly, but as it went on, it became more variable, and others were scrawled rather carelessly, even running downhill from the ruled lines. Long, unbroken passages gave way to shorter and more fragmentary bits. Then there were a couple more long sections, followed by a blank page. Was that the end?

Rowan turned the leaf over. No! Rowan sat up straight, stifling an exclamation. Here were letters in Anglic!

Unfortunately, they were arranged into words that by and large made no sense. A few pages on, though, recognizable words and even phrases began to pop out. The final passage, before the pages went blank for good, was readable, if rather quaint and peculiar.

> I cry to thee, O most distant Dream of my grandchildren's children, through a long-linked Chain of Voices . . .

It was nearly dawn by the time Rowan put the book carefully back in its encasing casket and slipped into bed, stupid with exhaustion. When Orry shook jhm awake to go collect eggs, jhe at first burrowed into an unassailable fortress of covers; but a bit later, waking up enough to remember what jhe'd found out, jhe jumped out of bed and ran downstairs. Dialfi was just coming in from the milking.

"Show me," said Dialfi, following Rowan to Grandmother's rooms with eyes alight. Orry, sensing something afoot, soon joined them.

Rowan opened the book and found the place where the cryptic squiggles gave way to recognizable Anglic letters. "See? It's not all gnomad writing. But it's still impossible to understand."

Jhe began thumbing jhr way through the book. *Wait, wait*, they cried, but Rowan kept slowly turning the pages until jhe got to the last passage. They stared at it, taking in the words.

"My goodness, what's all this?" said Grandmother, coming out still in her nightgown, to see the three of them huddled around her living room table, their heads like three petals of a flower.

So Rowan read the passage aloud.

I cry to thee, O most distant Dream of my grandchildren's children, through a long-linked Chain of Voices.

After terrible Troubles, we have found a Place of Refuge. Yet I fear a Grievous Peril will one day menace our Realm. Once more, the pitiless Finks will emerge to pose the Conundrum that every wise, tool-wielding Species, dwell they on any Sphere in the Multiverse, must surely answer, or else be rendered again to Stardust.

Yet I would not make the error of the Dolphin Oracle, and by my cryptic Utterance chase thee into a Doom ye would otherwise not have found. How are ye to know whether or not ye have been born into that Time of Testing? In answer to that I offer my Tale Entire, written in the timeless Runes of the wandering Folk.

Ye need not be someone rich in Knowledge, nor yet schooled in the ways of Power, but rather one like unto an Hero of Old: pure of Heart, clear of Soul, strong of Spirit, open of Mind. If our Human Species cannot produce even one such an Hero, it may be that after all we are not meant to persist as part of Creation, but rather to perish.

But be consoled, o distant Reader: the time of the Crisis may not yet be come. Then ye must only add thy Link to the Chain of Anglic herein.

Afterwards I ask that ye once again consign this Book to the Earth, that in due Time it may again be rediscovered.

"What a bunch of gobbledegook," said Orry.

"No, it isn't!" cried Rowan, eyes shining. "Don't you see, it's talking about some sort of quest."

"I guess you're thinking you must be the hero," said Orry, "since you found the casket."

Rowan blushed, for of course jhe'd been picturing whether or not jhe might qualify for the role.

Orry added, "Plus, you qualify in being none too rich in knowledge or schooling."

"Very funny."

"And your mind is certainly open enough; at any rate, nothing ever stays in it for long!" Orry crowed, delighted at jhr own cleverness.

At this, Rowan moved threateningly towards jhm. Orry ducked out of jhr reach, crying, "Spare me, Sir Rowan the Empty-Headed, for I foresee a grievous peril!"

Putting jhm in a headlock, Rowan growled, "Oh, I'll show you a grievous peril!"

Dialfi ignored these antics with practiced dignity. "We need to find a way to decipher the rest of it."

"I've looked back through the earlier Anglic parts, too," Rowan told them, giving Orry's scalp one last scrub before releasing jhm. "As far as I can tell, it's the same thing, in older and older versions, as if people had copied it over and over again. Those must be the links of the chain, see? This book is like a stone skipping through time. Every so often someone must have found it, and rewrote the Anglic in the current form, so the next person who found it was able to read it."

"The scholars might be interested in this, you know," said Dialfi.

"Oh, I don't think so," Rowan said hastily, glancing at Grandmother for support. "They must have tons of examples of that sort of thing already. The important thing will be to figure out what the other part says — what it calls 'the Timeless Runes of the Wandering Folk.' That *has* to mean the gnomads! And we already know from your dear friend Dana how the scholars don't care about *them*."

"Still, Rowan, don't you think . . ." Dialfi began.

"Look, this came to *us*, Dialfi! If we hand it over to Dana or jhr precious experts, it will just end up in some dusty cabinet. Oh, they'll be happy enough to take it and lock it up somewhere, with a little tag on it that says 'Gnomad knick-knack from the vicinity of Yngencloven.' But as for taking it seriously, and figuring out how to read the runes, if that's going to happen at all, it will be up to us."

"You're probably right," sighed Dialfi, though not looking entirely convinced. "Well, how would you go about it, then?"

"Find a gnomad, of course! It's too bad the traders have already been and gone this year, but maybe there will be someone in town."

Orry suggested half-jokingly, "You could always ask the Drummer-Man." This was a shambling, drunken figure of a gnomad who haunted alleyways near the harbor.

"Maybe I will!" said Rowan.

"But do you think it's a good idea to bring the book to town?" asked Grandmother worriedly.

"We'll have to, anyway, if we're going to scan it," pointed out Dialfi.

"And afterwards we'll bury it again, like it says to," added Rowan. "But I don't know if I like the idea of having it in town. . . I wouldn't put it past Dana to put the scholars on the scent of it, just to mess with me."

"I could try copying the runes by hand for you," offered Grandmother. "Then the book can stay here, safe and sound."

"Would you really, Grandmother?" Rowan knew firsthand how difficult this would be.

"I'll do my best. 'The timeless runes of the wandering folk': that sounds like something worth knowing about."

Dialfi looked concerned at the rapid settling of the book's fate. "You know, Rowan, the book may turn out to be something really important and of interest to the scholars, after all."

"I hope it does!"

"But, see, they won't be satisfied with just a copy, or even a scan. They'll need to have the actual book to authenticate it properly."

Stubbornly, Rowan said, "I've got to do as the person who wrote this book says, at least until I know more about it.

It's a message for the future, and not necessarily for our time at all."

"And if it is for our time?" persisted Dialfi.

"We'll burn that bridge when we come to it," said Rowan, then over Orry's laughter, added, "or cross it; you know what I meant. But the first thing to do, is to write out this passage in modern Anglic, like it asks."

"I don't know, Rowan," said Dialfi; "do you really think we should be writing in the book?"

"It says we're to add our link to the chain of voices," Rowan insisted, "like this Ravn did."

Startled, Grandmother asked, "Did you just say Ravn?"

"Right here," Rowan pointed to the name at the bottom of the passage.

Dialfi added a bit apologetically, "It's written pretty small, so maybe you can't see it."

"My eyes are very well, thank you. Ravn, my goodness . . ." She looked around at their blank faces. "Ravn was my great-grandfather's name."

Rowan exclaimed, "The one who danced the valse, and —"

"Who married the gnomad princess," confirmed Grandmother.

"Wow," said Orry. "So it really *is* her treasure."

"I knew it!" exclaimed Rowan.

"We shouldn't jump to conclusions," said Dialfi. "It's just as likely that Ravn dug it up like we did, and then met Rilla because he was looking for a gnomad who could read it."

They all looked at Grandmother, and she spread her hands in puzzlement. "I never heard anything about that. I didn't even know the treasure was a book."

"Then she wasn't able to read it," Rowan said, fearing jhe'd have no luck in this regard either. "It all came to nothing in the end!"

"It hardly came to nothing," Grandmother reprimanded jhm. "Their blood runs in your veins. They are bound up in your story, whatever it turns out to be."

Rowan unexpectedly found jhmself in charge of writing out the Anglic passage in modern language. Dialfi had plenty of advice to offer, though. For example, jhe took exception to the word "multiverse." Jhe called it a pretentious piece of outdated astrophilosophy, and Rowan wasn't about to argue with that. But when Dialfi said the phrase "again be rediscovered" was redundant, Rowan insisted that was exactly the point, for it underscored just how many times the book must have been found and then reburied.

Orry's numerous suggestions were of more doubtful value. However, they agreed when jhe said that the word Finks was ridiculous. Dialfi thought it was most likely a corruption of "Sphinx," which he explained was a mythological creature that waited on a mountain pass asking travelers impossible questions, and killing them when they couldn't answer.

"That's mean. Didn't anyone ever get the right answer?" Orry wanted to know.

"One man did, but then he went on to commit a terrible crime, through no fault of his own. You really don't want to know the rest, Orry, believe me."

"I do so!" Orry insisted.

Meanwhile, Rowan was hunting down some clue by comparing earlier passages. Jhe saw dozens of names, increasingly strange the farther back in the book they were. It made Rowan wonder if others had found the casket by noticing the copper-loving plants, as they had. Of all these people who'd found the book and copied out the passage over however many centuries, had any of them actually managed to read the runes? "Oh, I get it!" Rowan exclaimed. "It's meant to be Delphic, not Dolphin. Wasn't there a Delphic Oracle?"

Dialfi nodded. "It's yet another legend of the Hellenes — they had a lot of legends for people who systematized rational thinking, didn't they? The Delphic Oracle would inhale volcanic gases, and then utter brief pronouncements about the state of affairs or about the future. That man I was talking about before, who'd committed the crime—"

"Which was what, by the way?" interjected Orry.

"—the Delphic Oracle had predicted it all when he was born, that he'd grow up to do this terrible thing—"

"What thing?" demanded Orry.

"—and so of course his parents did everything they could to prevent it, and he did too; but everything anyone did to stop it, only worked to make the prophecy come true."

"Why won't you tell us what he did?" Orry asked, exasperated.

"Because it's far more entertaining not to. Not to mention, it might persuade you to pay more attention in school."

"*Anyhow*," said Rowan, who'd been busily paging through the book, "someone writing in here a few links back changed Delphic to Dolphin."

"I wonder what else may have been lost, along the way," said Dialfi.

With a sinking feeling, Rowan asked, "Then how in the deep blue could the runes still be readable, if this is what happened to the Anglic only a little ways back?"

"The runes weren't written over and over," pointed out Dialfi. "Lots of errors creep in during copying."

"But we can't read the oldest Anglic passage at all!"

"That's true," admitted Dialfi. "Maybe the runes are only a ghost of a message, lost for all time."

At last their version was as clear as they possibly could make it.

"Let me see," said Grandmother. She read it through carefully, mouthing the words. "Well done, you three! You didn't fiddle with it too much, nor use fancy words where a simple one would do better. No doubt it will sound quaint and old-fashioned to whoever digs it up next, all the same."

Rowan carefully penned their entry into the book. The others sat around the table watching quietly. A hushed calm was beginning to settle on the household after the frantic work of harvest, in peaceful if somewhat melancholy accord with the darkness steadily closing in on the shrinking light of day.

They each signed their names at the bottom, and Grandmother said, "Now you too are part of the grand chain stretching back and back into the past."

I cry to you, most distant dream of my great-grandchildren, through a long-linked chain of voices.

We have lived through terrible times, and have found a refuge here. Yet one day, a danger will come. The merciless Sphinx will pose her Riddle once again, as she does to every intelligent, tool-wielding species, living on any planet in the cosmos. We must finally answer, or else be utterly destroyed.

Yet I do not wish to fall into the error of the oracle at Delphi, and point you toward your doom with too simple a warning. How are you to know if you were born into the time of Testing? In answer I offer you my whole story, written in the timeless runes of the wandering people.

You need not be very learned, nor one who knows the ways of power, but rather like a hero of old: pure of heart, clear of soul, strong of spirit, open of mind. If our human species cannot produce even one such hero, perhaps after all we are not meant to persist in creation, but rather to perish.

But be comforted, future reader: that time of crisis may not yet be here. All that will be asked of you, then, is to add your link to our chain of Anglic words, and commit this book to the earth, that in due time it may again be rediscovered.

— Rowan, Dialfi, and Orry Yngling

Chapter 7. Allthanks

Ah, this grand, heroic endeavor of composing the Humanual. What, of all we have learned, shall we pass on? Perhaps it's just as well there's neither room enough nor time to include everything. Knowing too much is the curse of our age.

Ironically, the oldest media remain the most durable: undisturbed cave paintings, cuneiform writing inscribed on fired clay, thousand-year old velum manuscripts. Even rag paper can last for centuries. But 99% of what we know was learned in the past hundred years, and our electronic media evolve and go extinct with blinding speed. They are also far more vulnerable to civilization's collapse.

Our fervent hope is to save something from the ashes. The scientists think of their science, and the Kymrans of their legends and history. They contend that knowledge of the material world can be rediscovered, whereas a story once lost is lost forever. But the scientists fear that superstition will once again take hold, and are concerned above all to pass on the hard-won treasure of reasoning from evidence.

It seems to me both paths are wise, and not wholly divergent. Yet so much cries out to be saved; and we have besides to find our food, and shelter, and love. We are poor limited creatures after all, reach as we must for the heavens.

— Kassandra Morgan-Ávvu

It was a subdued Allthanks they had that year, what with having to sacrifice half the sheep, and worries about the coming winter. Mar flat out refused to slaughter a single goose or duck for the dinner; not even a chicken would she allow; and no one wished to cross her. It was true that to feast as abundantly as they usually did for the holiday would feel frivolous. It might also be unwise to cut deeply into their winter stores so soon. On the other hand, not to honor Gaea's bounty at harvest time seemed an ill omen. Not that Nuathans believed in omens, priding themselves on being a rational people.

The family sat around an oval table of polished oak, down the middle of which ran a long piece of Mar's weaving in blues and greens. Tall red candles burned serenely in pewter candlesticks. At the table's center stood a small statue Far had carved from rosy, fine-grained mountain juniper, its natural swirls and protuberances suggesting a woman's graceful shape. She looked both strong and kind, and held her hands outspread. Although it represented Gaea, the personification of the living planet, it was neither altar nor idol. Nuathans were not generally prone to wishful thinking about gods, and the Ynglings had always been strict rationalists. The statue was placed there at Allthanks to remind them that the planet was, in a quite literal sense, their mother, to whom they owed thanks for the continuing gift of life.

They sang the hymn of thanks, Grandmother beginning it in her dry alto, and each joining in turn, from oldest to youngest, until Orry's clear voice rang out completing the fugue. The familiar sound made Rowan feel that perhaps this Allthanks was not so different from other years, even if the food awaiting them in steaming dishes was not the usual fare.

They dug into the meal with unfeigned eagerness, just as if it had been the traditional roast goose with gravy. A platter of lake trout caught by Dialfi and Orry that morning was in the place of honor, surrounded by bowls heaped with kale and turnip greens that Grandmother had gleaned from the now-ragged garden, and a tureen of leek soup with wild mushrooms, the latter courtesy of Rowan's foraging up the creekbed.

When they had all had their fill, and were lingering over Grandmother's inevitable and formidable squash pies and gingerbread, and sipping large mugs of mulled cider, and eking out small cups of coffee, Far got down the tome of the Humanual from its place of honor on the mantlepiece. He located the Great Book's traditional passage for Allthanks. It concerned the beginnings of the cosmos, perhaps because at this time of year people turned their thoughts from the fruitful earth to the skies above, which were filling with stars not glimpsed since the previous spring.

In the beginning, we know not why, 1.375 x 10^{10} years ago, everything exploded out of nothing with tremendous heat: cause and effect,

space and time, energy and matter, and, finally, darkness and light. At first only a pinprick, everything grew; and as it grew it cooled; and as it cooled it unfolded like an immense and wondrous flower. Thus did the cosmos give birth to itself.

Rowan leaned back and listened to the majestic, rolling words. Far's voice was always very deep when he read from Genesis, and a lilt came into it, echoing his own father, a bard who'd traveled the sunwise reaches out beyond Adelie. The beauty of the words also held a strange sadness for Rowan, perhaps because they'd become linked with the immanent departure for winter schooling.

Far went on with the litany of bizarre features of the early cosmos.

First gravity separated itself from the rest, then the strong nuclear force and afterwards the weak leaving electromagnetism, all in the first 10-36 seconds (see Timeline in Appendix 1A; note that 1 second = 9,192,631,770 vibrations of Cesium-133 and 1 standardized sidereal year = 31,558,118.4 seconds). Light already did exist in those earliest seconds, but could not yet escape the dense tangle of forces and parti-

cles. All was enfolded in a fog of blankness.

In the first 10^{-10} seconds, the fundamental particles that would give rise to energy and matter began to appear, and sometimes to annihilate one another. Nuclei, the hearts of atoms which in turn form all matter, began to form at 3 minutes; they ceased forming as it became too cool 17 minutes later.

It took a further 377,000 years for the first atoms to stably form, as nuclei captured electrons, whose orbital interactions drive chemistry and indeed the very processes of life. At first all matter took the elemental form of explosive hydrogen, but gradually some fused into the more quiescent helium, with the barest fraction merging further to form metallic lithium and beryllium. As matter thus began to mature to its current form, after some one million years, it no longer trapped the light, but allowed it to escape. The cosmos became transparent, and light shone through and around and about it, and so it has been ever since.

Rowan shook jhmself wide awake; the next bit was worth listening to.

From that earliest instant to this very day, and onward into the farthest future we can imagine, came into being Logos: laws of physical existence, omnipresent and inviolable, to which all objects and creatures are subject. We assume that the implacable action of Logos orders all things from one moment to the next, without interference or exception. To understand its laws is to begin to be able to read wisdom from the world itself.

Far handed the book across to Mar, who sat lost in thought. She rubbed at her forehead, then began to read in a soft but intent voice.

So it was that by studying the orderly movements of the heavenly bodies we gradually discovered, to our great astonishment, how the cosmos is ordered and how it began; and indeed that it had a beginning before which we as yet can discover nothing, though it is likely some form of Logos exists beyond time itself.

We have been gradually uncovering such truths over a great many lifetimes of seeking to understand the nature of things, from our earli-

est beginnings as animals full of wonder and curiosity, love and poetry, with keenly thinking minds. With telescopes we have looked outward to planets, stars, and galaxies, even to the edge of creation; while with microscopes we have peered inward to our cells and their marvelous molecular machinery. We have decoded the intricate dance of the hereditary message that unwinds itself to instruct the cell how it is to live and grow, even as it links the remotest past to the most distant future, and all life forms to one another, in a wide-branched tree of earthly being.

Where telescope and microscope could take us no further, we travelled by imagination, using mathematics and digital approximation and theorizing. In this manner, we edged back to the time when space and time began, and worked our way even to the heart of the atom, whose spinning and orbiting parts recapitulate the motion of solar systems and galaxies.

Here, then, are enumerated the discoveries we have made and the knowledge we have so far amassed, and the means by which we have done so.

Rowan's mind began wandering again. The Ynglings never stinted on the traditional readings. From Allthanks at Starreturn, to the nadir of Midwinter, to the spring-new hopes of Sunreturn, not excepting the minor litanies for the cross-quarter days between, you could be sure of hearing the proper sections of the Humanual read out in full. But the Allthanks reading was by far the longest. Now they'd gotten to the part about how the stars had forged the elements.

At the heart of the first stars, the dust of hydrogen and helium began to be fused into new kinds of matter, including with great abundance life-weaving carbon and nitrogen, the trickster oxygen, and all the others up to hard iron (see the Periodic Table in Appendix II).

The second generation of stars were more massive and longer-lived. Within their mighty furnaces, more elements were crushed into being from the lighter ones already in existence, copper and silver and the other precious metals, the heavier minerals, the rare earth elements, and radioactive exotica. Thus do the stars themselves forge the matter that forms the water, the air, the solid ground of rocky planets, and the elements essential for life. We know this to be true because spectro-

graphs show that later-born stars contain more heavy elements than earlier ones, and because the composition of matter in stardust extracted from fallen meteorites matches the predictions of the detailed theory of nucleosynthesis (see Appendix 1B).

Orry piped up, "Why does it always have to break in with all that 'see Appendix 1' stuff?"

Far said firmly, "In this family we stick to the classical version of the Humanual, even if some parts are dense and complicated. The modern versions leave out too much."

Dialfi added, "See, Orry, the details are there so we may test the truth for ourselves, to understand how the Sages learned these facts in the first place, and not just take them on faith."

Orry wasn't satisfied. "But what is an appendix? We never read them." *Oh no,* thought Rowan, *that's all we need!* At this rate, they'd be sitting there all night.

Far answered, "They are part of the Esoterica; only very advanced scholars study them. Many are full of terms whose meanings have become obscure, but if nothing else, they serve to remind us how much we have lost since the time of the Sages."

Rowan said, "Or it's just a bunch of mumbo-jumbo the Sages put in there to convince everyone how smart they were."

"It isn't," said Dialfi. "One of them has instructions for making a microscope. With one of those, you can see things like the hairs on a fly up close."

Orry said, “Why in Gaea’s name would you want to do that?”

“You wouldn’t say that, if you knew what they really looked like. They have an especially high-powered microscope at the Akademy, that can make a speck of dust look like a whole world, with mountains and valleys and all.”

Far took up the Book again.

> **The death throes of those massive, second-generation stars can still be seen at the distant reaches of space, using a powerful telescope, because to look out into the cosmos is to look back into time. Light itself, the fastest thing we know of at 299,792.428 kilometers/second, takes many thousands of millions of years to traverse the vast reaches of space. Yet note that the universe extends much further than the edge that marks the oldest and most distant light we can see, which is estimated (at the time of this writing) to be 46 billion light-years away.**

“Wait,” said Rowan, never before having noticed this odd claim. “Shouldn’t the oldest light be 13 billion light-years away?”

“Lots of people make that mistake,” said Dialfi. “You’re forgetting about the cosmic expansion; it’s all explained in the Appendix.”

Orry groaned, “You looked at *that* Appendix, too?”

“Sure.”

“And Sadoctor Yngling will now tell us all about it,” Orry intoned, with a flourish as though introducing a famous lecturer to the podium.

Ignoring this, Dialfi continued. “Since the entire fabric of space is always stretching in every direction, very distant things are actually moving away from us *faster* than the speed of light.”

“Stop messing with us, Dialfi. Everyone knows nothing can move faster than light.”

“Right you are, Orry-dyu — but space itself is always stretching out bigger, so if two things are already very far apart —”

“Oh, I think I get it!”

“What?” said Rowan.

“Uh, you tell jhm, Dialfi.”

Dialfi continued, “The oldest light, the light that’s been traveling through space towards us ever since it first escaped from the rest of creation, 13-odd billion years ago; well, that light has had space stretching under it, as it were, all this time.”

Rowan asked, “You mean a light year now is a longer distance that a light-year was billions of years ago?”

“Just so; it’s creepy, isn’t it? That’s why you can see a red shift in distant objects, their wavelengths have literally been pulled out longer in the time the light’s been traveling. It’s precisely how the sage Hubble long ago figured out that everything must be expanding. He ran it backwards in his mind, and saw how it must have started with the Big Bang."

Orry shook jhr head. "Do you really *believe* all this stuff from the Humanual, Dialfi?"

"Of course I do. So many of its assertions are demonstrably true, I see no reason to disbelieve the ones we no longer have the means to test."

"Come on," said Rowan, "Let's hear the rest of it; there's only a little more."

Far handed the Humanual to Dialfi, an unexpected honor. In a solemn voice, jhe read,

> **We are uncertain of the ultimate fate of the cosmos, for it depends on its fundamental nature, of which we still have much to learn. One chilling possibility, based on what we have so far been able to measure, calculate, and discover, is that it may continue to expand ever faster, and to cool, until no more stars can form after some 10^{14} years, and all will sink back into darkness. Another possibility, considered unlikely at the time of writing, is that the cosmos will cease expanding and instead begin to contract. If so, it would reach an infinitely condensed pinprick after another 10^{11} years, out of which it might again expand, in an immensely slow heartbeat. Or there may be oth-**

er ends concerning which we as yet know nothing.

Rowan loved that last sentence. Some years back it had occurred to jhm that this word, "ends," didn't necessarily just mean something was over and done with, but could also signify "purposes."

Orry commented, "The Sages sure say an awful lot about how much they don't know."

"There will always be limits to knowledge," said Far. "Still, the Sages discovered much that we cannot hope to equal, in these lesser days."

Dialfi bristled at this. "Why do you say 'lesser days'?"

Far paused to formulate an answer, and Orry chimed in, "I think it's just the cold, shrinking people in." Jhe mimed a person hunched over with chill. They all laughed heartily at the weak joke.

Far said, "No, no, Orry; we've been having a bit of a cold patch, but that's just the lot of a farmer. Too dry, too wet, too hot, too cold . . . it's always something." He reached for another piece of pie.

"Speaking of farming," announced Orry, "next summer, I'm going to sail on the *Nioren*." This was a trading vessel captained by their Uncle Narv, which plied the inland sea each summer from Adare to the large isle of Getz, and on down through the northern Archipelago.

"That might work out," Far allowed, "if Anno is back with us by then."

"And if I take to it, I might find winter work on a herring fisher," Orry added. Far didn't dignify that with an answer.

"When I was young," said Grandmother, who'd been following her own thoughts, "we used to eat outdoors at Allthanks, the better to see the returning stars. We had swimming races in the millpond, too." She chuckled. "I hadn't thought of that in years!"

Mar said, "Oh, Mother, past summers always seem more golden."

Rowan commented, "The millpond's iced over. The ducks have been walking around on top of it all week, looking puzzled."

"Never mind about the weather!" Dialfi said, fed up with all the rambling talk. "I want to know why Far thinks we live in lesser days."

Far sighed. "I suppose I was thinking how much more careful we are in all our endeavors."

"If the Ancients did everything without thought for the consequences, it makes *them*, not us, the lesser people." Rowan had rarely seen jhr sober sib so visibly upset. Something must really be eating jhm. Dialfi continued, "They used up all the surface metals, and most of the liquid hydrocarbons. Just think of all the useful plastics we could have made with that, instead of having to laboriously purify algae."

Far shook his head in somber agreement. "Well, they were punished for it, in the end."

"Hey, are you talking about the Ages of Bronze, Iron, and Carbon?" asked Orry. "I know about that! My teacher said they mined so much that they dug the mountains flat, and started earthquakes . . . copper and iron and titanium and cobalt and tar, and I forget what else—"

"Coal," Rowan reminded jhm, casting an anxious glance at Far. "To burn in their machines."

Orry stared. "To *burn*? But didn't they know that was wrong?"

"If they knew, they didn't care," said Rowan.

Dialfi said, "Yet their great discoveries and their destructiveness went hand in hand. Maybe there was no other way to have learned so much."

Far said quietly, "At least we can keep alive the knowledge gained in those times, by reading from the Humanual."

"Right," Dialfi said bitterly, "so we can get our noses rubbed in their glory over and over. It's humiliating, to hear about ancient experiments and not be able to replicate them properly ourselves. They've been working on that radio telescope array in Randestad for over a century now. Whereas the Ancients had heavier-than-air flight and sent people to the moon, and probes to other planets, just to see what they could see. Once they even launched a spacecraft on an endless voyage far beyond our solar system, carrying a message on a golden disc."

"What was the point of that?" asked Orry.

"I think they wondered if intelligent life might be living elsewhere in the galaxy, and wished they could hear word of them, so they decided to send word of themselves. That craft will keep traveling on and on, outwards across the galaxy, for a billion years and more. It's probably the most incredible thing our species has ever done. But as for us," Dialfi sighed, "we'll never do anything remotely like it: to fire off rockets you need to use mined hydrocarbons, and that's forbidden by the Commandments."

"For good reason," admonished Mar.

"Really?" asked Dialfi. "I tell you, the more I think about these Commandments, the less I understand them. Some are just unnecessary, while others are downright obstructive."

Rowan was shaken that jhr revered older sib would think to question the wisdom of the Commandments. And on Allthanks, no less! "Is this the sort of thing you and Dana talk about?"

Dialfi shook jhr head. "Dana would not approve of such talk."

Far said, "The Commandments were written in a very different time from the one we are now living in. If they seem unnecessary, that's a mark of just how far we've come."

"Yet is it really cause for pride, to have constricted our endeavors to such an extent that we'll never accomplish anything of note?" Dialfi took up the Humanual and turned to the frontispiece. "*1. You shall know your place as a part of creation.* What does that mean, really? Why should we, and what happens if we don't? *2. You shall take only your share to live, and no more.* A bit better, though subject to broad interpretation, of course. And where does it leave a scholar who needs a fine telescope? *3. You shall not overpopulate the land.* Well, that's hardly likely, given the difficulty of maintaining a decent demographic curve."

"We'd be better off if more couples had three children," agreed Far, "with so many people who never get around to having any. But it's not everyone who can pull it off as handily as your Mar and me."

Dialfi said, "Moving on, number four: *You shall not burn the heat of a thousand summers in a single winter, nor take more than the fruit of the season, lest the core of the world-tree become rotten.* That is, no burning of coal nor hydrocarbons, the undead carbons that were long ago taken out of circulation. The longest and most flowery of the Commandments, and by far the most specific, yet again no reason is given other than that poetic nonsense about the World Tree. Not very scientific, is it?"

"But Dialfi," said Mar, "we don't need a reason; burning coal or oil is disgusting and unnatural, as Orry said earlier. It would be like — like eating dung."

"There are simple hygienic reasons not to do that. I see no reason for the prohibition on coal."

Grandmother said, "I've always thought it's a matter of not mingling the living and the unliving. Coal isn't merely *dead*, like a downed tree made into charcoal. It's passed outside of the living world altogether, and it's not our place to change that."

Dialfi frowned, "Then the fourth commandment is nothing more than a taboo. And it's a taboo that keeps us from using efficient closed combustion engines for anything but special cases like the sky-train. They say making more biofuel would use too much cropland. If we could simply mine coal and hydrocarbons, there'd be no end to what we could do:

build ships that could easily travel upwind and up current; do experiments that use more electricity per day than all of Adare uses in a year. We could even make flying vehicles again."

Orry pointed out, "You're the one who told Far not to burn coal to heat the tool barn."

"Yes, well, maybe I was wrong about that! If we'd used coal, that chimney fire might never . . ."

Mar's face stiffened, and Dialfi said hurriedly, "But let's finish the list. *5. You shall seek the truth, and shun falsehood,* and *6. You shall honor and make good use of your mind.* Those are my favorites, of course. And here's one for you, Rowan: *7. You shall take delight in living.* I won't argue with *8. You shall help those in need,* but it's vague, vague: where in the deep blue north do the obligations end? —All right, all right, I'm almost finished; just humor me a little longer. Good old *9. You shall carry forward the light of civilization.* That's what we're here for, we Nuathans, but surely it goes without saying. *10. You shall faithfully teach your children all these things.* That one's nice for its recursiveness. Then there's the disputed Eleventh—"

"Is that the one that says we are never to cross the Circling Sea?" Orry asked, thinking about sailing, as usual.

"No," said Dialfi, "the Eleventh is *You shall not suffer an Outlander to live.*"

Far said, "Our promise to stay within the bounds of the sea that encircles us, Orry, is the last and most essential of our commandments. We have chosen to leave the rest of the planet for the other creatures, that they too might thrive without hindrance."

"Isn't there nothing but deep blue sea out there, anyhow?" asked Orry.

"Some say all those lands drowned in the Catastrophe," answered Far, "but no one knows for certain. Nor is there any need to know." Far balanced a pewter plate on his finger, and set it spinning. "It's funny, come to think of it: the Ancients used to think their world was flat, surrounded by endless seas; and for all practical purposes that's the world we live in now."

"A lesser world for a lesser people," said Dialfi with bitterness.

Far leaned back in his chair with his arms over a full belly, surveying the scattered remains of the Allthanks feast. "No, Dialfi, we are not a lesser people. We have learned to live within our means in a way the Ancients never did. And according to the Humanual we have at least 100,000,000,000 years more in front of us — plenty of time to make new discoveries, even without the forbidden fruit of the earth called coal."

Chapter 8. To Adare

I've been dreaming of the future: of little harbors scattered along the coast, bristling with masts; of rocky mountaintops that have shaken off their snowy mantles, and clothed themselves in forests of birch and fir; of red farmhouses dotting the hillsides, windmill blades flashing in the sun.

— Kassandra Morgan-Ávvu

At last they were ready to leave for Adare, where they would go to school at the Collegium under the watchful care of Mar's sister Matti and their Uncle Narv. Whether at school or work, the efts overwintering in town always generated a whirlwind of activity, from masquerade balls to wild street games to beach bonfires and expeditions to uninhabited islands down the bay. And there was Olioli—a kind of hide-and-seek that ranged widely through the streets and backyards and roofs of town, deplored by imagoes for its practitioners' disdain of private property and risking of head and limb — and for these same reasons beloved by efts. Adare was always lively, though (as Rowan remembered with a pang) Anno and Kiril would not be around this year.

They sat out on the front porch amid their bulging packs, passing early morning yawns back and forth and waiting for last-minute details to be sorted out. Far was tapping out a message on the skywave to Uncle Narv to expect them that afternoon. Mar came out with thick sandwiches and flasks of cider for the trip.

Looking at Orry, Mar suddenly exclaimed, "Oh goodness, I forgot to cut your hair for the winter!" She was about to go in for the scissors, when Orry shook jhr head.

"I've decided to grow it out, Mar. A sailor needs a proper braid, after all."

Mar gazed at her youngest a moment, then nodded. After giving each of them a tight hug, she went back inside. They could hear her footsteps going up to her workroom.

Grandmother came out and handed Rowan a packet of paper neatly bound up with twine. "Here you are: this is as much as I've been able to do so far. Copying an alphabet that you don't know is surprisingly difficult, especially one that has hundreds of different letters."

"You've done so much! How did you ever find the time?" Rowan danced her around the porch, nearly lifting her off her feet; Grandmother laughing and patting jhm on the shoulder, eventually gasped, "Enough, enough, you mad creature; I'm not so young as you anymore. —I'll soon finish the rest, with the unfortunate peace and quiet that's about to descend on us Yngencloven homebodies."

Dialfi went off to help Far harness the shaggy ponies to the wagon, in lieu of the fine horses that had been sold. While they worked, Far said to Dialfi, "Rowan seems so excited about that book. I've never seen jhm taking an interest in any indoor thing."

"Well, jhe did find it on a mountainside."

"True enough," laughed Far.

Far drove them to the depot, the wagon looming preposterously high over the ponies' sturdy backs. The three sibs joined the small crowd of students and families waiting for the midmorning run to Adare. "Wait!" Far grabbed one more bundle from underneath the seat, and passed it down. Dialfi took it with lowered eyes. It was some of the cured sheepskins. "See if your Aunt Matti will help you make them into coats," said Far.

Rowan watched Far driving slowly back towards the quiet house, and hoped Mar would not be brooding at the window as she had been of late. Far turned back to wave; his beard had gone grey, but Rowan hadn't noticed until now. But after all, they had celebrated his 89th birthday in July. What was it like for them to mind the farm in winter, with their children all grown and gone to town? wondered Rowan. It could be a long time before the house was lively with little ones again. But maybe Anno would bring a spouse home soon, if she could forget Kiril. Maybe all the ewes would have twins next spring, or even triplets. Maybe next summer's harvest would be a bumper crop, and they could see about buying back the horses . . .

A mournful whistle sounded in the distance. "Here it comes!" shouted a young child.

On the ride down, Orry and Dialfi played one card game after another, leaning out into the aisle and bantering with people trying to walk past. There was constant chatter up and down the train car. But Rowan curled up by the window and watched the countryside rolling by hypnotically, as the soothing rumble of the wheels vibrated jhr forehead against the glass pane.

Sometimes they would pass a rider on horseback, or a wagon piled high with produce, making its way along the road beside the track, which was the lifeline connecting the mountain farmsteads to the port of Adare. Every so often, there would be a sudden sensation of wind pushing at them, and an uphill train would pass so quickly that the faces in its windows were nothing but a blur.

Down and down they went, past trickling streams that would in the spring become rushing cataracts fed by snowmelt, to drive turbines that now hung motionless; past dark, impenetrable forests of fir and spruce, relieved by the occasional farmstead wherever the ground leveled out. First would appear arrays of windmills with majestically cartwheeling arms, or geothermal chimneys pouring out white clouds of steam. Or there might be straggling lines of wind turbines, following the sloping contours where the katabatic winds were strongest. Next there'd be cleared fields and fenced-in pastures, silos, outbuildings, and barns, most painted a dark red to stand out against the landscape's dominant greens and grays. Finally the farmhouse itself would come into view, a comfortable sprawl of roofs and porches that had grown to its current form over the course of many generations.

Over the years Rowan had become familiar with the succession of farm-holdings along the way, and always watched for favorites. There was the Hurry-house, where jhe'd once seen someone running full-speed toward a cow-barn, mouth open in a silent shout, on what desperate errand Rowan would never know. And the Tater-pot place, where there'd been a group of children tending a huge kettle hung over a bonfire, probably full of pig-potatoes, for they'd been cradling half-eaten potatoes in their chubby hands.

This year, the landscape looked bleaker than usual, and there was no work of harvest being done, even as they approached the lowlands. The grasses were bleached to dullness, and the stubble in the brown fields looked weary and discouraged. Even the normally emerald-bright evergreens were somehow leached of color. Probably, Rowan told jhmself, everything looked so dreary only because they were headed to town later than usual. An early and cloudy darkness had set in, with the faint lights of farmhouses appearing without warning and quickly receding behind the branches of the encroaching forest, before they at last came into town.

Uncle Narv was at the station to meet them, his cheerful grin, rolling gait, and shaggy sun-bleached hair marking him out as a sailor. "You've cut it close this year! The Opening Ceremonies are tomorrow," he told them, jerking a thumb at the hill above town where the Ceremonies were always held. He swept up most of their bags "No, no, I can manage these just fine, need them to balance the others — you farmers are a soft lot anyhow, compared to us sailors." Rowan and Dialfi trailed behind, chatting, as he led the way through winding, well-lit cobbled streets. But Orry, lugging the unwieldy bundle of sheepskins, jogged along trying to match their uncle's pace.

The streets were filled with the marvelous commotion of Starreturn, when the overwintering folk came to town. Some were merely passing through the port on their way to the bigger cities on Getz. These swelled the hotels near the wharf while awaiting passage on the last ships to set sail before the winter storms. But many families, when not tied to farms, simply preferred the bustle and activity of town life during the season of darkness. Children and younger efts came for school or apprenticeships, and older efts for amusement and work, while young imagoes were there looking for partners. Winter was the time for study and socializing, for parties and dances and theatre; it was the time for living off the hard-won fruits of summer.

"Goodness, there you are at last!" Aunt Matti cried from the porch. She gave them warm hugs, adding, "Come in, come in, you must be worn to the bone! I've got a little supper ready for you."

Uncle Narv's and Aunt Matti's house was spacious and well kept, but not overly fussy. The downstairs was generously provided with lamps to cheer the winter months. Mar's richly colored hangings and carpets made it feel like an extension of Yngencloven.

While Uncle Narv ferried their bags upstairs to the large communal bedroom, Aunt Matti welcomed them to a table piled with baked delicacies and luscious fruits brought back from her husband's recent voyages. Unlike Mar, Aunt Matti seemed to positively enjoy feeding hordes of hungry youngsters.

Next day at the Collegium's Opening Ceremonies, somber clouds hung in the northern sky, but the sun pierced through underneath. The broad hilltop was decorated with laurels and ivy, and bursts of flame-colored marigolds, the last brave blooms of the dying year.

The townsfolk were gathered to witness the induction of that year's batch of students: younger children beside themselves with excitement at their first winter in town, world-weary efts who preferred school to the more focused work of apprenticeships (or whose families sought the honor of a diploma), and the earnest ones hoping for a place at the Akademy someday. Seated in rows on the grass, people listened attentively to speeches by various dignitaries. For the most part everyone in the audience knew everyone else, at least by reputation. It was a small enough town for that.

Two efts sitting together towards the back, though, were clearly newcomers. One was tall, dressed in the exotically patterned textiles of a northern islander, blue eyes startlingly bright in a dusky, tanned face. Islanders saw more sun down there in the North, where even in deepest winter the sun peeped up briefly every noontime. In contrast to the long, dignified plaits that most efts wore, the Islander had a bushy loft of hair, with tiny braids sprouting out of it here and there decorated with beads and small shells that rustled and clinked.

The other newcomer had a very pale complexion, with reddish hair poking out under a cap of odd design. Jhe was smaller than jhr companion, and wiry under loose-fitting clothing, with shoulders carried high and tight as though warding off a blow. The small one whispered something, and the

Islander nodded while answering. Their words were drowned out by the vigorous clapping accorded to the final speaker. Everyone stood up and made their way downfield to the gates.

The time had come for the entering students, beginning with the youngest, to pass through four ceremonial gates. The gates, different every year, were planned and constructed in great secrecy by professas of the Collegium. Each had an inscription posted high on its arch. This year they read: "Knowledge is Power," "Abandon pride who enter here," "Whosoever would taste of the fruit of the Tree of Knowledge," and "To Know is Not Enough." The older students debated the meaning of the inscriptions both seriously and facetiously, and guessed what passing through them would entail, amid hoots and jeers and a certain undisguised apprehension. Some years, the gates could be rather an ordeal.

"Maybe Knowledge is Power gives you an electric jolt," suggested someone.

"With a voltage proportional to your erudition!" another speculated.

"Well, then, Nokti, you at least have got nothing to worry about!" the first replied with a laugh.

The two strangers hung back from the crowd, watching as the younger students pressed forward impatiently. After making it through the gates, most of them hurried on to the refreshments tent, but one lively youngster came running back to inform some of those still waiting, "Guess what – it really *was* an electric shock!"

A serious-looking eft reprimanded jhm, "Better let us find out for ourselves." The youngster darted back to the tent.

"Well, Yrssu, I'd better take my turn," said the tall, lanky newcomer, and joined the line of older students.

On the other side, where folk were milling about sampling food and drink, Narv called out, "Erkanni, me lad! Come meet my nevvies, who've just arrived in town." To a trio of efts, he explained, "Erkanni's here for some mainland schoolin' – joined up at Faraday and sailed with us the rest of the summer."

"So you're the nevvies I've been hearing about!" Shaking hands with each of them in turn, Erkanni said, "Let's see, Dialfi the scholar, Orry the sailor, and Rowan the, um . . ."

"It's all right," said Rowan; "I'm nothing in particular."

"Rowan of the infinite possibilities, then," the Islander said grandly, and Rowan laughed despite jhmself.

A short while later, Erkanni found Yrssu hanging about at the far edge of the field. "The gates were kind of cool, I guess; at least, we never had anything so elaborate back home. —Hey, and I met those nevvies of the Captain, that he told us about. Remember? They were just like he described: the eldest was very serious and scholarly, the youngest was a merry prankster, and the middle one, well . . . the middle one is different. Jhe's barely any taller than you—" Erkanni rubbed the top of Yrssu's head affectionately.

"Hey!" Yrssu ducked around to the other side.

"Do you want to meet them? They're right over there."

"Neh, I must go now." Yrssu took the long way back to town, following the stone wall along the edge of the forest, and looking as singular as a hawk against an empty sky. Erkanni watched a moment, then turned back towards the happily chattering crowd.

With school set to begin the next day, Rowan regretted their late arrival to town that year. Usually, they had a week or two of settling in. In the first excitement of seeing winter friends again, everyone would be tearing around in a frenzy, getting no more sleep than in summertime. The country folks would unpack their city clothes, strange finery that would in time grow familiar again. There'd be the shopping for candles and lamp oil, for luminous ink and neat new brushes for school, and black seaweed-paper — all the things not needed or thought of in months. Everyone would rush around making the most of the fast-vanishing daylight. Before long, the trees would have lost their leaves in a great rush, and the street lamps have come on for winter, not to be turned off until the following spring.

During Starreturn, each day flashed back and forth between light and darkness, as if summer and winter were two kittens fighting over a piece of string. On cloudless nights, the stars would blaze out, and you would want to stay up and watch them wheel in that calm velvety blackness after their long absence, but then you would yawn gaping yawns, and your eyelids would keep closing. Imagoes would laugh as they tucked in their leaden-limbed, sun-browned children for a real sleep in the deep and restful darkness . . . and then they, too, must have fallen asleep in sweet release. At Starreturn, people would drink sleep like water, inhale it like air, devour it like meat; lovely, swimming sleep. The house cats would curl up next to people, purring. The dust would settle on the windowsills. The birds would be still, and the streets quiet.

Then, the bells in Adare's age-old granite towers would be awakened to their winter duty. Adare was an old city, said by some to be the oldest settlement on the mainland; and its bells had been tolling the winter hours for a great many centuries. All the big towns had winter bells, but none so fine as the bronze bells of Adare, the deep ones tall as a tall man, the highest ones clear and bright as a thrush's song. In winter, it was the regular succession of the bells and the light of the lamp-clocks that told people of the passage of time, in the otherwise changeless darkness.

The first bells would sing the Dawn Trill, its ripple of birdlike notes clear in the dark streets. Three hours later, the Midmorning Call would ring out, a robust and reasoned melody that evoked the work of the mind. At the Noon Peal, a long, tumbling crescendo piled notes one upon the other like fireworks springing ever higher. The Afternoon Cheer was similar in character, but shorter and more subdued. The Dinner Gong would sound its stately march, followed by the sedate tones of the Evening Waltz; and still later the Midnight Tolling echoed through placid streets. Last of all came the three faint notes of the Black-night Sigh, meant to be heard only if you were already awake.

Each period of the day was likewise marked by colored light that shone out from the bell towers, street lanterns, and indoor lamps, evoking the changing colors of the summer sea. Early morning, though dark as a cellar, was lit with a pale yellow glow, later moving to turquoise; the grass-green afternoons gradually shifted to a rich golden honey color, thence to red-orange and magenta as the evening wore on; while the nights were indicated by a deep violet-blue (the lamps at that hour giving little useful light, but rather serving as a reminder that it was time to sleep). The transition from today to tomorrow was marked by a brief spell of faint pink light, like the inside of a clamshell.

As the bells began to toll the familiar calls of winter, and the many-hued lamps shone out, people one by one would stretch and yawn and look about them with new eyes, feeling a different sort of energy from that of the summer, a wondering, questioning sort of energy. Children and efts, wide awake again, would pour out of the houses to run up and down the twisted streets of Adare, and drink hot cocoa in the squares. People would put on heavy sweaters, more for the novelty of their rich patterns than against any real chill. It never grew bitingly cold so close to the sea. In those days, the warm wind always blew in from over the waters, breath of the absent sun. Usually the fog would roll in and cover the briefly glimpsed stars of autumn. Soon the rains would come, the gentle misting rains of the coast that meant winter had arrived in earnest.

Chapter 9. Town Schooling

It's unlike any other place I've seen. People go everywhere on foot, using pull-carts for transport. Still there are plenty of electrical appliances, and the absolute necessities of light and heat are abundantly provided by wind, waves, and geothermal. It's a strange mix of the most modern technology and the most old-fashioned.

— Kassandra Morgan-Ávvu

Rowan woke to the clatter of milk carts over cobblestones and the blare of infuriatingly cheerful foghorns echoing through the narrow streets. Town was nothing if not noisy. When it wasn't milk carts and foghorns, it was crows screaming over garbage, or drunken revelers singing and shouting along the sidewalks, or the trash-squad whose hearty chants were apt to disturb the sleep of those not on duty that month.

Jhe sat up in bed, blinking stupidly in the dim lamplight, and scratching at the mess of hair jhe'd neglected to comb out and braid the night before. How could it possibly be morning already?

Then Dialfi, bless jhm, brought a cup of first-day coffee to share, there on the rumpled bed. Dialfi's pleasure to be starting school at last carried Rowan like a rising tide through mismatched socks, a hurried breakfast, broken pens, and misplaced books ("It's much easier if you keep your things shipshape," Orry pointed out, buckling up a meticulously organized knapsack); carried jhm down the steep and winding streets to the imposing façade of the Collegium. At the top of the steps, Rowan paused. Jhe always wondered whether the ornate hinges spreading over the doors were meant to be branches, or roots.

"Come on, we're late enough already!" urged Orry, as a bevy of efts clattered up the stairs behind them. So they opened the heavy doors, and went in.

Rowan's first classroom was abuzz with chatter, the professa not having arrived yet. As Rowan rummaged through jhr pack looking for a brush with a decent tip, a tall form folded into the empty seat across the aisle with a friendly grin: the Islander they'd met the day before, who'd sailed with Uncle Narv.

The professa entered. Conversations were instantly suspended, except for a few unfortunates who found themselves speaking too loudly in the sudden stillness. The professa introduced himself as Sa Torin. He wrote "Foundations of Philosophy" in impressively large letters on the dark-board, then, without further preamble, launched into a monologue concerning the philosophical foundations of the knowable. After following the first few sentences with faint but fading interest,

Rowan sighed, and slumped down in jhr seat glumly contemplating the weary months ahead.

Sa Torin was droning on: " . . . from the premises articulated by Svarrhanius, we are unable to avoid the conclusion that the potentially knowable is not merely more vast, but crucially, unknowably more vast, than the potentially unknowable, which in turn leads to—"

The newcomer sitting across from Rowan raised a hand and, without waiting to be acknowledged, asked, "Excuse me, but who was Svarrhanius?"

Sa Torin stopped short to stare at this marvel of presumption who'd dared to interrupt him mid-flow. The Islander smiled winningly and added, "Apologies, Sadoctor, sir, but my old school wasn't very strong in Philosophy."

Glancing at – Erkanni, that was the name – Rowan caught a flash of laughing eyes, edged with the fine lines sailors and fishermen tend to get from squinting at bright water.

The Sa answered stiffly, "I have not the honor of a doctorship; I should be addressed simply as Sa Torin." Gazing speculatively around the room, his eye fell on a notoriously studious eft. "Aron-dyu, would you be so kind as to summarize concisely the relevant discoveries of Svarrhanius."

Aron, looking suitably modest, reeled off, "Svarrhanius was a follower of the philogician Gerstein, and extended her Theorem of Unprovability to show that, at any given time, in an actively developing field of study, the limits of truly undoubtable knowledge will always be contained within the bounds of that which had formerly been considered to be certain. This he recognized as forming a discouragingly regressive series, out of which no one has yet been able to discover any egress."

"Oh, yeah, *that* guy," murmured Erkanni.

"Thank you, Aron-dyu. To continue, then, and hopefully without further interruption, this unknowably vast potentially knowable, which we will call p_{kn} for brevity's sake . . . " Sa Torin droned on. To nearly everyone's delight, however, Erkanni did keep asking questions, both on and off the topic, with a genuine curiosity that seemed impermeable to any barb of sarcasm. Sometimes Rowan was sure jhe caught a twinkle of amusement in Erkanni's eye. At last, the Sa lost his composure entirely. "If you would be so gracious as to curb your interest to a manageable level, sirrah, you will find all your questions answered in due time, and the lecture might then proceed in a more orderly fashion." The class shook with smothered laughter.

The next subject, Choir, was one that Rowan generally enjoyed. For one thing, Sa Hesperides was notorious for his tempestuous and entertaining tirades. Hardly a week went by that he didn't throw the baton at someone or some section (for which the students had a long-running betting pool). Rowan never much minded being berated by Sa Hesperides; everyone was sooner or later, whether justly or unjustly, and it signified no more than being caught in a rainstorm.

Sa Hesperides was also famous for a musical commentary during rehearsals that ranged from the bizarre to the opaque. Rowan had a habit of scribbling these asides in the margins of the music score whenever they particularly struck jhm. *Diction is the eye-contact of singing. It really is all about intonation, ever since the dawn of time and the Renaissance . . . well, mainly since the Renaissance. I hope you can all feel the hemiola coming on here, just like when you're coming down with a cold.*

Orry and Dialfi were also in Choir. Since they all sang different voice parts, though, they had little chance to chat. Orry stood with the sopranos, perhaps for the last year as jhe was growing so fast; while Dialfi had worked jhr way into the honored depths of the second tenors, by dint of months of larynx-stretching exercises. Rowan's own voice was the most ordinary of altos. But jhe liked hearing how the music fit together from the relative inconsequence of the middle part.

Before the longed-for lunch break came gymnasium, and afterwards an hour of Geometry with the exceedingly rigorous Sa Osten. She was not impressed with Rowan's casual and intuitive approach to problem-solving. "It avails nothing if you arrive at the correct answer with no notion of how you might do so again," she told Rowan sharply on seeing jhr hastily scrawled answers. "A donkey can do as much, on a good day." With Sa Osten, it always came back to donkeys.

Still, Sa Osten did have some good points. She was prone to flights of fancy inspired by the unlikeliest subjects, her explanation of the number pi serving as a fair example. She began class that day by sweeping her arm in a grand gesture to draw a circle on the board, then marking a dot in the center with an emphatic smack.

She labelled its radius r, and then drew a square outside it so the curve of the circle just touched its sides. She drew another square inside, rotated like a diamond, so its corners met in the same place.

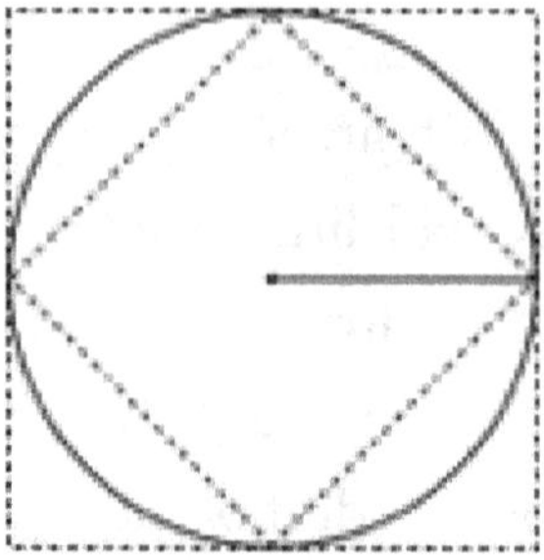

"Now, any child can tell you the area of a square. The larger one is obviously $4r^2$, and those of you who have forgotten your trigonometry can take my word for it that the smaller square's area is precisely half of that. But what is the area of the circle?" Eager hands cropped up thick as masts in the summer harbor, but she shook her head.

"I want to reason it out, people; I am not interested in your donkey-memorizing. Evidently it must be r^2 multiplied by some intermediate value between these two squares, that is, between 2 and 4. The ancient Gypsans, who liked their math simple, thought it was 3, but they were dead wrong. In fact, they utterly missed the clue into the fundamental weirdness of a circle, which would seem to be the simplest of all shapes." Rowan was entranced; no one had ever taught jhm math this way before.

Sa Osten reached high to draw a vertical line down through the center of the circle, then a horizontal one crossing it to make the large square into four smaller ones. She shaded in three of them, leaving the upper right one blank.

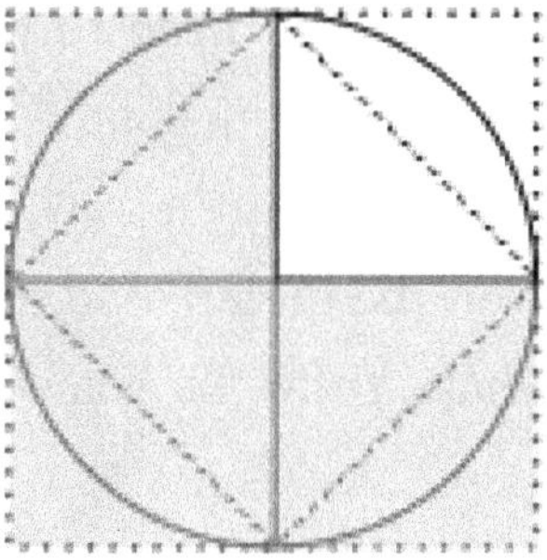

"Given that each of the four smallest square is r^2, this shows the Gyspans' guess at the circle's area, $3r^2$. Let us now place the corners falling outside the circle into the circle's unshaded quadrant."

Rowan nodded excitedly—*of course*! That would show the amount by which it differed from the circle's actual area.

"The first corner is easy." She erased it, and as if it had been a puzzle piece, shaded it in so it was touching the circle's center. "That leaves only the biconvex shape unaccounted for. Doesn't it look like a sleeping eye?" She tilted her head, saying, "Or maybe more of a mouth." She pursed her lips, and the class laughed aloud.

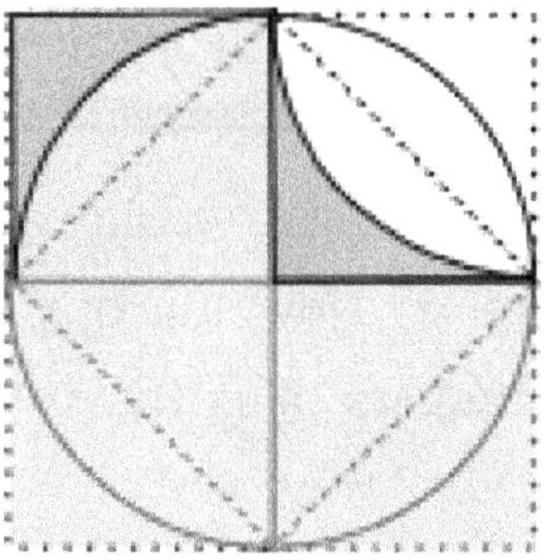

"So, what is the difference between the area of these convexities and the two orphaned square corners we still have to place? You have all the information you need to work out the problem, so get to work." Rowan's pencil flew, but jhe made some careless mistake or other along the way, and the answer didn't make sense. However, jhe understood the larger lesson, and carefully copied the shape from the board into jhr notebook.

"If the value of pi had simply been three, this line I've drawn to represent the eyelid, or the meeting of the lips, would remain closed," the Sa summed up some minutes later. "But as the ancient Hellenics realized, pi is actually a bit larger than 3, and a very strange little bit that turns out to be, for I could tell you its digits all the suncircle long and right through to Sunreturn, and be no nearer to finishing it than when I started. Some professas ask their students to memorize the first 20 or so. Don't worry, I'm not going to do that," she added, as a few students looked nervous. "You can look it up, if you're interested."

"But the eye—" Rowan blurted.

Sa Osten fixed her eagle gaze on Rowan. "Yes?"

Rowan gulped. "It's like it's starting to open, right? Because of the extra bit more?"

"Well done, Rowan-dyu," said the Sa, etching out a very thin curve on either side of the eyelid. "Now, this opens an eye into a very bizarre aspect of numbers, a portal to another world, which we will enter," — the bell rang as if on cue — "tomorrow. Class dismissed."

After geometry came the day's emphatic downside: Ethics and Modern History, taught back-to-back by Sa Krusi, an ancient stick of a professa who'd taught all their parents and probably some of their grandparents too, or so at least the students liked to imagine. Rowan endured the wearisome lessons as best jhe could, craning jhr head to see if the tower light, just visible from one window, had begun to change to orange yet. Time had never passed so slowly as on those dark and dreary forenoons.

Evenings, Rowan and jhr sibs gathered around the fireplace to talk and roast nuts or make popcorn, before tackling their homework. Dana came by now and then, infesting the air with noxious pipe fumes and flowery speeches. Fortunately (from Rowan's perspective), Dana was busy with other friends this year, most of whom had already been accepted into the Akademy. They could often be seen behind the steamy windows of a café they favored, talking incessantly while pounding on the table for emphasis, and laughing uproariously at each other's jokes.

Urged on by Orry, who'd contracted a serious case of hero-worship, Erkanni became a frequent visitor to the house. Everyone liked Erkanni; well, everyone other than Dana. "Not that thrice-poxed lout again!" Rowan had once heard jhm mutter upon hearing the Islander's distinctive voice in the hallway — which was one more reason to welcome Erkanni to the family hearth. The feeling appeared to be mutual: after getting a taste of Dana's snobbery, Erkanni took to calling jhm "fortune's child" and would address jhm as "m'lord," with a mocking flourish.

Orry would ask Erkanni question after question about sailing the archipelago from the far northern reaches, and Erkanni would answer in a lilting Islander accent.

Once Erkanni said offhandedly, “Do you know, we saw some Syowyans in the Ronne Sea last summer.” Syowyans were Outlanders that lived on the far side of Terraus. Centuries ago, they had regularly raided Nuathan towns, but had not been seen in living memory.

“You *did*? in one of their ships?” Orry, of course, was thrilled. “Hah, Rowan, you sure look scared! I bet you’re remembering one of Grandmother’s tales.”

Erkanni told them, “Truly, it was like something from out of the old stories: their prow was carved to look like a dragon’s head, and they had row upon row of oars, as well as brightly painted sails. But they looked peaceable enough, and paid no attention to us.”

“Still, I don’t like the sound of that,” said Dialfi, looking up from a book. “On the Ronne Sea, you say?”

“Yes,” said Erkanni. “They were sailing this close to the wind,” tilting a hand, “bowled over like you wouldn’t believe. They were headed right out into open ocean. The way their ship handled the waves — oh, it’s like nothing built in Nuatha.” Rowan saw with disgust that Orry too was fired up with admiration for the barbarians.

Under Orry’s coaxing, Erkanni’s stories came to resemble the well-embroidered tales that Anno and Kiril had told them in years past. There had been the harrowing storms while crossing the Ross Sea, the sturdy lapstraked *Nioren* showing the virtue of timbers that breathed like a living whale. On the volcanic island of Toreo, those lucky enough to get shore leave had seen the famous fire dancers. At Getz, they had spent several glorious days exploring the capital, where Erkanni had won many victories in a succession of wrestling matches and drinking contests, or so it appeared in the telling.

"I beat you arm wrestling just last week," boasted Rowan.

"It won't happen again, now that I know your tricks," Erkanni answered.

"Oh yeah? How about a rematch?"

"Not tonight; all this sweet cider I've had weakens the blood. I'll let you hold your title a bit longer."

The Ynglings were fascinated as well to hear Erkanni's account of a childhood spent on the farthest reaches of Nuatha. "Truly is Faraday called the Summer Country, for there we see the sun all winter long, even if only for an hour a day. In winter, though, the waves can grow high as mountains, and then we have to move to the lee village until the storms abate. Back on the windward side, we find all sorts of debris washed up on shore, streamers of kelp and huge tangled logs, rope welded into fantastic knots, strange objects from ancient times, that no one knows the use of."

"Like that pendant you always wear?" asked Orry.

Erkanni pulled it out to show them a battered rectangular ornament. "Yes, but this has been handed down in my father's family since before the Exodus."

Orry fingered it with awe. "Do things from shipwrecks wash up, too?"

"Sometimes they do. Before I was born, there was a terrible shipwreck right off our beach. The efts and young imagoes devised a daring rescue. Many of the castaways ended up settling there, and many were the children born out of that wreck. That was how my own father came to the village, in fact."

After school, students would go swimming off the rocks beyond the wharves, taking advantage of the heat the sea yet held for a bit longer. Often the mist would roll in to muffle the lights and sounds of town, but there was still a dim glow from the North and streaks of phosphorescence in the water. It was a dreamlike world, where water was the source of both light and warmth.

Erkanni, being from the summer country, was a marvelous swimmer, and could paint a long trail of luminescent coils and rolls before suddenly surfacing to spout a great jet at someone.

"*How* do you hold your breath so long?" Orry begged to know.

Erkanni laughed, "Well, if you want to know the truth, my father was a selkie."

"A what?"

"A seal that can turn into a man — do you not have them here, on the mainland?"

"No! I never heard of that!" cried Orry in astonishment.

Rowan and Dialfi grinned at each other. They sometimes forgot how young Orry really was.

Orry was thinking hard, treading water that lit up jhr face in a bright glow. "But wait — I thought you said your father had been shipwrecked."

Erkanni lunged out of the sea to sit on a rock above the barnacle-line, wet and regal. "No, I said that he came to the village because of the shipwreck. As my mother and the others mounted the rescue, they saw a great dark seal out there braving the surf. He swam over to carry lines for the lifeboat and steady it from the worst of the waves. Afterwards, on the beach, he climbed out of his pelt and stood, a tall and splendid man — much like myself, only of course a bit broader. And for love of my mother, he left the sea and came to live in the village. That sort of thing happens now and then, where I come from."

Orry asked eagerly, "So are many Islanders part selkie?"

"Oh, indeed, it runs through our blood from way back. We're never quite comfortable on land; and besides that, we're very hard to drown." Erkanni uncurled from the rock and dove into the warm sea with hardly a ripple, and Rowan could almost imagine that a seal was slipping along that twisting luminous path, far below the surface. At school, Erkanni was quite the clown, always attracting a crowd of amused spectators, but was a bit calmer when it was just the Ynglings. Yes, there was undoubtedly something of the seal in Erkanni, something playful, but also elusive and of another element; something that despite all the clowning made Rowan feel oddly protective.

In the midst of all this activity, Rowan found time to scour all the libraries in town for information about gnomad writing. But all jhe could find was a few tattered books on the primitive people who followed the seasonal migrations of the caribou, with no mention of any writing. Could people who traveled through all kinds of weather really be expected to have books? It was all very discouraging.

Once, browsing the stacks, jhe ran into Dana. "Great Gaea below, Rowan, what are you doing here? did the ocean run dry, or did you take a wrong turn on the way to the beach?"

"Something like that," Rowan answered, intent on jhr search.

"So, I hear your great archaeological find turned out to contain nothing but the chicken scratchings of gnomads."

A pox on Orry! thought Rowan. Jhe'd been blabbering about the book to jhr friends, and of course the rumor had eventually made its way to Dana. "Pretty much. Like you said, nothing that scholars would care about."

Hearing such a mild response, Dana looked curiously at Rowan, then took a step closer to see what books jhe was looking through. "Oh, this is too perfect! You've set out to become a scholar of gnomads, haven't you?"

"For once in your life, Dana, could you just see your way to minding your own business?"

After a few more episodes of fruitless searching among the library stacks, Rowan put the casket and its contents out of jhr mind to immerse jhmself in the pleasures of town life. Sometimes, Rowan thought jhe saw Dialfi looking askance when jhe and Orry went out after supper for a game of Olioli.

But the book of mysterious runes wasn't going anywhere; there'd be time enough to tackle translating it when the darkness set in for real.

Chapter 10. The Kymran

Relations between the Kymrans and the scientists are never easy, however dependent each is on the other. The scientists pursue their holy quest to endlessly increase knowledge, ever on the verge of the next great discovery. Never satisfied, they always dash on to the next question like children on a treasure hunt. Meanwhile, the Kymrans look after the animals and crops, the cooking, the plumbing, the electric, all the routine work without which the place would collapse, and which, if they thought about it at all, the scientists would think beneath their notice. Likewise, the Kymrans refuse to see how the whole enterprise of science actually does matter. It has made possible the antibiotics that preserve their children's lives, revealed the wondrous true meaning of the stars, and, not least, provided a refuge from the coming cataclysm. Am I the only one who can see both sides?

— Kassandra Morgan-Ávvu

One evening, Orry burst excitedly into the living room where Rowan was halfheartedly working on some math problems. "Guess what? I've found you a gnomad!"

“Really?” Rowan threw down jhr wet brush, then wiped at the resulting ink spatter using a sleeve.

“Heis, don’t be such a slob, Rowan.” Orry handed jhm a pristine handkerchief from jhr pocket. “So I saw this kid working at the docks, loading stuff, running a crane and all that.”

“Why would they hire a kid?” Rowan asked.

“I wondered the same thing,” said Orry, who’d have loved to work there jhmself. “But I think it’s only that jhe doesn’t look big enough to be a full-grown eft. Jhe’s really weird-looking, with orange hair and no eyelashes, or none that you could see, wearing one of their funny hats. I bet jhr head only comes up to my chin. I mean, jhe’s even shorter than *you*, Rowan.”

“Yes, Orry, we’ve all noticed how tall you’re getting, and how handsome—”

“But the point is, Rowan, jhe’s a real, live gnomad. You should talk to jhm — jhe’s easy enough to spot.”

It might be easy to spot the gnomad, as Orry had said, but talking with jhm turned out to be another matter. By running out of school as soon as the last bell rang, Rowan could make it to the wharves before the stevedores had finished for the day. From a distance, Rowan watched the short and wiry figure laboring at the cranes and handcarts down on the shipping docks, bright hair poking out from beneath a colorful, flat-crowned cap. The others gathered in small knots of activity, but jhe always seemed to work alone. When a long whistle blew the end of the workday, the stevedores would make their way up from the docks, most of them heading towards a street full of pubs. The gnomad never went with them, but melted away like the ghost of a minnow into a nearby maze of alleyways.

Rowan hesitated to approach jhm. That bubble of stillness around jhm was part of it; but most of all, jhe feared discovering that the gnomad would be unable to make sense of the runes. It was tempting to keep hope alive a bit longer.

"Poor Rowan," said Orry, when Rowan had come in shaking jhr head once again. "Gnomads are so difficult to engage in *conversation*, aren't they?" Orry still liked to tease Rowan about the interaction with the young trader, that Mar had broken off.

Rowan grabbed Orry's head with one arm and bent jhm over, knuckling jhr scalp. Orry yelped, "Okay! okay, already!"

Ignoring Orry's plight, Erkanni asked, "What's this about gnomads?"

"See, Orry told me there's one working at the docks."

"That would be Yrssu."

"You *know* jhm?" Rowan stared at Erkanni.

"Sure — Yrssu sailed with your uncle this past summer, same as me. Why are you so eager to meet a gnomad, anyhow?"

Rowan hesitated, and Orry said mischievously, "See, Rowan has this thing about gnomads—"

"I do not!"

"Jhe's not some sort of a sideshow, you know," Erkanni said with disapproval.

So Rowan began to explain about the casket and book of strange writing.

Erkanni whistled through pursed lips, thinking, then said, "All right, let's go talk to jhm. I should warn you, though, now and then Yrssu can be a bit prickly."

Erkanni led the way to a row of buildings whose wooden shingles were silvery with age where the dingy paint had flaked off. An old woman sitting in a scrap of sun in the courtyard scowled at them as they headed up a rickety staircase.

They knocked; the door opened a crack, and a sliver of face peeped out. The door opened a bit wider. Yrssu neither invited them in nor came out, but stood blocking the half-open doorway, looking at Erkanni. Rowan sensed that this reticence, disconcerting as it was, constituted an alien mode of courtesy.

Erkanni broke the silence. "Eh, now, Yrssu, how fare you?"

Yrssu nodded curtly as if to say "well enough."

"Here are two of our Captain's nevvies, who are wanting to make your acquaintance: this is Rowan, and that there's Orry."

Now Yrssu turned to look at them, and said to Rowan, "You were watching me these past days, neh?"

A bit embarrassed, Rowan answered, "I wanted to ask if you might be able to read these — we think they are gnomad writing." Jhe held out the sample page jhe'd brought.

Yrssu didn't look down at the paper, but held Rowan's gaze. "Gnomad, you are calling us, but what we are calling ourselves, is Kymran."

Erkanni said, "You never told me that, Yrssu!"

"You, my friend, were never calling me anything but my own name. —*Gnomad*, I am guessing that is some kind of Nuathan idea of a joke."

"I don't know anything about that," said Rowan. "But would you take look? They're copied from a very old book. We don't even know if gno— if your people still use writing nowadays."

Yrssu gestured angrily at the paper in Rowan's hand. "What use would we *gnomads* be having for writing, eh? A gnomad is a sorry fool of a creature, like that Ghéppa roaming the alleyways with his drum, hunting for garbage and scraps, spouting nonsense to all who will listen, and alike to all who will not listen."

"Hey," Orry nudged Rowan. "Why don't you tell jhm about our gnom— I mean our *Kymran* ancestress?"

"Ancestress?" Yrssu looked sharply from one to the other. "Now you are claiming to have Kymran blood in your veins?"

Rowan thought that perhaps Grandmother's poetic words would attest to the improbable truth. "A Kymran from out of the Waste danced with our grandmother's grandfather at the Autumn Fair: Rilla with hair of yellow flame, who came riding on a windnose white as driven snow. We are her great-great-grandchildren."

"Indeed?" said Yrssu. "So many greats is it taking, to make such a small drop of your blood." With that, jhe shut the door and latched it emphatically.

Rowan crumpled the page into a wad and shoved it into jhr pocket.

"I'm sorry," Erkanni said. "Yrssu's usually not quite so difficult."

"It doesn't matter," said Rowan. "Probably jhe couldn't read it, anyway."

The next day, bored with Sa Torin's rambling lecture, Rowan found the crumpled page in jhr pocket. Furtively jhe smoothed it out on the desk. Maybe jhe should try again to do frequency counts of the letters, even if there were so many of them. But what help would that be, when jhe didn't know which sounds were most common in the gnomad tongue? And jhe'd still need to know what the words actually meant, for which jhe'd need a speaker of the language — one a good deal friendlier than that Yrssu person. Rowan heaved a gusty sigh.

Erkanni leaning way over into the aisle to look, whispered, "Hey, are those the runes?"

Rowan jumped, and glanced at the Sa, who fortunately was busy at the chalkboard.

Undeterred, Erkanni said, leaning over even farther, "Come on, let me see."

"Have you two finished your essays so soon?" asked Sa Torin. "In that case, I will be happy to take them now." He walked over and collected them. Rowan's only had a few sentences, but Erkanni's looked as though it might indeed be done.

Sa Torin lingered at Rowan's desk. "I wonder, what is this that is so engaging your attention?" He picked up the page of runes.

"Hey!" protested Rowan, barely suppressing the urge to grab it back. "That's mine!"

"On the contrary, sirrah, anything you place on the desk during my class is by definition classwork, and rightfully belongs to me. If you wish to discuss the matter further, you may see me after class."

Sorry, mouthed Erkanni, as the Sa stalked back to lock the page in his desk.

After the bell rang, Rowan waited for Sa Torin to finish taking assignments, thinking unhappily how the last student to have been late to Choir had been required to memorize all the modes, even that horrid Locrian.

At last Sa Torin called jhm over.

"I apologize for misusing class time, and won't do it again," Rowan said in a rush. "Now could I please have my paper back?"

Sa Torin sat back in his chair. "All in good time. As it happens, there was another matter I wished to speak with you about, Rowan-dyu."

"There was?" Rowan was puzzled. The Sa spoke as if he were about to ask a favor.

"I understand you made an archaeological find this past summer."

"Oh, that was just some old gnomad thing," Rowan figured this would quench his interest.

Instead, Sa Torin looked intrigued. "Yes, that's what I'd heard: a casket of gnomad provenance." A strong suspicion came to Rowan that Dana was behind this sudden interest: not because jhe thought it was of any scholarly value, for jhe'd never let Sa Torin have the credit for bringing it to the attention of Akademe, but merely to upset Rowan.

Sa Torin continued, "Might you be so kind as to bring this object in and show it to the class? I'm sure your fellow students would like to see it, and I flatter myself that I have rather an eye for primitive art."

"I don't have it here in town. My grandmother is very protective of it, see, and won't let it out of her sight."

"I see." The Sa thought a while, drumming his fingertips, then opened a drawer and got out the page of runes. He laid it on the desk and gazed curiously at the strange markings.

Rowan's heart began to pound. But there was no way the Sa would make a connection between this and the gnomad casket, was there? Jhe fervently hoped no word of the runes had drifted to Dana. As long as Orry had kept jhr mouth shut . . .

Sa Torin asked disdainfully, "I suppose this must be some sort of code you're using to pass notes?"

"No, it isn't," Rowan began indignantly, then thinking better of it, stammered, "or, well, not exactly . . . but I won't bring it to your class again, I promise you that."

"Good. I won't stand for that sort of nonsense, do you hear me, sirrah?" He handed Rowan the page by way of dismissal.

Chapter 11. Foiling Sa Torin

And so I consign this testament to the Earth.
— Kassandra Morgan-Ávvu

Rushing into class just ahead of the bell, Rowan was surprised to see a substitute sitting at Sa Torin's desk. She told the class, "Your teacher has gone to pay a visit to the family of a student who is in the running for a prestigious scholarship to the Akademy." Glancing around the room, she added, "I'm told this student has a sibling in this class." Heads turned to stare at Rowan, who hardly noticed. Jhr mind was racing. Would a professa really visit a farm way up in the hills, just to talk to a student's family? Or could this have something to do with Sa Torin's interest in the casket?

Thinking Rowan silent from embarrassment, the substitute said kindly, "I presume you are the sib, then? I hope you yourself will apply to the Akademy, one day." Rather to the young teacher's puzzlement, the class burst into laughter at the notion of *Rowan* trying to become a scholar.

Under cover of their jeers, Rowan rushed out of the room.

The sub yelled after jhm, “Where are you going? Come back, this instant!” but jhe raced down the hallway towards the staircase.

Erkanni told the sub, “Don’t worry, I’ll bring jhm back,” and was gone before she could protest.

Rowan’s first thought was to run to the house to radio Yngencloven and warn them to hide the casket. But no one answered. They must all be working outside; or else the radio was broken again.

So Rowan tore back along the streets towards the train station. Cutting around a corner, jhe nearly ran into Erkanni. “There you are, Rowan! Listen, you shouldn’t let those clowns get to you.”

“It’s not that,” Rowan panted. “I think Sa Torin has gone to take the casket!”

“The casket? But you said it wasn’t anything scholars cared about.”

“He was bugging me about it the other day. I’m pretty sure Dana’s been putting ideas in his head; Dana was his favorite student a few years back.”

“That I can easily imagine,” snorted Erkanni.

“Come on!” Though jhr lungs were aching from the unaccustomed exercise, Rowan set off running again. Erkanni followed.

They burst through the train station gates, then stopped short. Sitting on a bench was Sa Torin, dressed in a finer suit than he ever wore to the Collegium, nose in a book. Silently, they backed away. Rowan said, “Maybe if we got on at the last moment . . . .”

"Too risky. Students on the train, this time of year?" Erkanni thought a moment, then said, "We've got a little while before it leaves, right?"

Glancing at the posted schedule, Rowan nodded.

"Okay, come on!" Erkanni led the way down to the wharf, and skidded down a steep ramp to a floating dock where a crew was hard at work unloading barrels from the net of a crank-crane. Among them was the unmistakeable form of that troublesome gnomad. Rowan stopped short. "What do you want with *jhm*?"

"You'll see." Erkanni went over and spoke in Yrssu's ear. The gnomad gave a quick nod of assent, and spoke briefly to the foreman.

They ran back towards the train station, Rowan's legs by now weak as jelly. Town soon did that to you, all that sitting and studying for hours at a time. When they were still a few blocks from the station, Erkanni yanked at Rowan's arm. "This way!" Yrssu was already headed down the side street that dead-ended in a woody hillside.

"What? Why?" panted Rowan, but was too winded to argue. Yrssu led them to a bushy place near the top of the hill, beside the train tracks. As they sat there catching their breath, Yrssu crouched down and put an ear on the tracks. "It is all right; we are in good time," jhe told Erkanni.

"For what?" demanded Rowan.

Erkanni grinned. "Hopping the train. It'll slow down here, so it should be easy to climb up the back."

Rowan peered down the empty track. "Have you stolen rides like this before?"

"I? No. But you do it all the time, right, Yrssu?"

The gnomad shrugged. "The trains are running this way and that, and sometimes they are running where I wish to be going."

"And they never catch you at it?" Rowan asked skeptically.

"No," said Yrssu, deigning to speak to Rowan at last. "They might catch *you*, thumping on the roof with your great boots."

Rowan ignored this. "Why are you helping me, anyway?"

"My friend has said you are wanting to keep these runes from a scholar, is it not so?"

"So you hate scholars, then? Along with boots and people whose great-great grandmothers were gnomads, I mean Kymrans?"

Yrssu gazed calmly at Rowan. "I could well believe you have more than a drop of our blood, for you are of no hulking height, and *dikalzhamat* like the winter sky. As for scholars, they are too much akin to skua-birds for my liking."

"Skua-birds?"

"They are swooping down to poking their long beaks into everything, whether it is concerning them or not."

Rowan laughed, picturing Dana as a gawky skua. "I don't much like scholars either," admitted Rowan. "And the runes are no business of Sa Torin's."

"What business are they of yours, Rowan Yngling?" asked Yrssu, looking at jhm piercingly with those strange, ice-blue eyes within their pale lashes.

"I already told you, I want to read them. They're a message from the distant past, some kind of a warning."

"You said nothing of this before."

"You didn't give me much chance," retorted Rowan. "So can you read them, or not?"

Yrssu's face was inscrutable, and jhe declined to answer.

"Hey," said Erkanni, jumping up, "I think it's coming!"

It wasn't as easy as Rowan had been led to believe to climb onto the moving train. After the first cars had lumbered by, Yrssu in a motion too quick to parse scrambled up as though mounting a staircase. Erkanni swung up after jhm with a sailor's easy grace, but Rowan in a heart-stopping lurch missed a handhold, and dangled just above the wheels. They hurtled around, faster and faster, with a sound like flashing knives. Erkanni reached down to grasp jhr hand and hauled jhm up with surprising strength. "Thanks," Rowan grunted, resolving to do better the next time. Jhe leaned back to catch jhr breath, already envisioning all sorts of possibilities: weekend forays into the highlands or down the coast, quick visits home — well, maybe not those, since Mar and Far would ask where jhe'd gotten the train fare.

Up on the roof, the wind was bracing. The sun poured out from behind a cloud bank, making Yrssu's hair shine like copper. Rowan looked around at the faded countryside illumined by shafts of sunlight, and laughed with delight.

During the scramble up the train car, Rowan's sleeve had gotten stuck above jhr elbow. Yrssu stared at the scar the casket had seared into the flesh of jhr forearm, amazed and somewhat disturbed. "How do you come to bear this mark?"

"You mean Emru?"

Rowan's casual use of the gnomad word further astonished Yrssu. Though jhe enjoyed turning the tables on the arrogant gnomad, Rowan was also very curious to find out what the symbol meant, so jhe was grateful when Erkanni said, "Does it mean something to you, Yrssu?"

"It means 'danger foretold.'"

"Heis, Rowan, no wonder you beat me at arm wrestling!" laughed Erkanni.

But Yrssu did not laugh. "How did you get this mark?" jhe asked Rowan.

"It was on the metal casket that held the runes," Rowan explained. "I was scarred saving it from a fire."

"And how were you coming to have this casket, at all?"

So as the train chugged steadily up into the foothills, Rowan told Yrssu about how they'd found the treasure of family legend. After a while, they lay down out of the wind, and dozed off to the rumble of wheels on track.

Much later, Rowan sat up suddenly, afraid they'd missed the stop; but they were just in time. They slipped off as the train slowed near the top of a rise, and took a short cut through a patch of forest bordering Yngencloven's northern pasture. Yrssu halted to stare at a ring of stones. "That's where the traders camp every fall," Rowan told jhm.

"A journey-wheel," breathed Yrssu, looking at Rowan with increased respect. So traders stopped here, did they?

Maybe there was some truth in this tale of the far-off great-grand-dam, at that.

"Come on!" urged Rowan, and they raced through the pasture to arrive well before Sa Torin in his fancy suit could have walked there from the station.

Their breathless forms hurtling into the farmyard aroused much astonishment. The family didn't waste time when they heard what was afoot. They weren't about to let some insinuating professa swoop in and snatch the gnomad treasure on a mere whim.

Far pointed out, "if it *does* turn out to be of scholarly worth after all, Rowan and Dialfi should be the ones to bring it to the attention of Akademe."

Grandmother scurried off to get the book, while Far went over to the radio. He took off the cover, and hesitating only a moment, unsoldered a component and stuck it in his shirt pocket. "No, it wasn't broken this time," he told Rowan over his shoulder, "but it is now! We can't let Sa Torin suspect that you warned us of his visit." He put the rosin core flux to heat, and its delicious piney scent began to pervade the room. Going over to the odd-jobs chest, he yanked out a heavy wooden drawer, and dumped its contents out on the table. Resistors and capacitors with their varicolored stripes and dots rolled and clattered every which way. Far began fishing through the pile as if looking for a particular component.

"If you would ever just sort those properly—" Mar complained.

"Well, maybe today I will!" Far said, laughing. "It'll make me to look the busier at this task."

Mar looked askance at his antics, but said, "I guess I'd best be knee-deep in sheep, then," and hurried off to the barn.

Then Rowan saw Anno standing in the doorway to the kitchen. She must have come back from the mountains quite recently. She stood there watching the scene with astonishment, a soapy cup forgotten in her hands. Erkanni was staring right back; Rowan elbowed jhm irritably. The family hadn't been expecting visitors, and if jhe'd had any manners at all, Erkanni would not have looked at an obviously new imago, informally dressed as she was.

Grandmother bustled back into the living room with the casket and a packet of papers as well. "I finished copying it just the other day, luckily! Solder it good and tight, mind you, before you rebury it." Rowan nodded. "Off with you!" Grandmother pushed them out the door. "We'll act the country bumpkins for Sa Torin, and lead him in a merry dance. I've heard enough about *him* to know what tune to play!"

Rowan led the way to a little outbuilding. While jhe shut and bolted the door, and got some items down from a shelf, Yrssu took out the book. Jhe began to page through it, tilting it to the light that came through a slit between the thin boards. It certainly looked like jhe was reading it, and Rowan hoped it wasn't just for show.

Erkanni asked, "Who was that?"

"What?" Rowan said distractedly. Jhe was trying to light a cold stove, a touchy process when you were in a hurry. If only there had been an electric hookup in the shed, jhe could have soldered the casket shut in no time. Grandmother was right: reburying the casket was the safest plan. Jhe peered anxiously out of a knothole, but here was no sign of Sa Torin coming up the road just yet.

"That young imago, in the doorway?" Erkanni persisted.

"Oh, that's my cousin Anno. You've heard about her — Narv and Matti's daughter."

"What did she look like, as an eft?"

"Hmm?" Rowan was blowing on the flames, trying to get the bigger sticks to catch, and old ashes flew around jhr face.

"Did she look like you?"

Rowan coughed as smoke wafted into jhr face. "Not that I ever heard."

"She's beautiful."

"Then she definitely didn't look like me." Rowan put the iron in to heat, and shut the stove door with a clang, and glared at the Islander. "Ready to head off on your ordeal, are you?"

Erkanni laughed, and said expansively, "Even an eft must take notice of such loveliness."

Rowan wished Erkanni would stop blathering. If Sa Torin should come while they were still there! Not that he would be likely to go around opening doors in the farmyard, but the sooner they were away, the better. Rowan checked the knothole again, then pulled the iron out of the fireplace to see if it was hot enough.

The iron sizzled when Rowan spat on it. Jhe turned to ask Yrssu for the book, and caught sight of Erkanni's pendant. That was why it had reminded jhm of something: it looked like the little object that had been in the casket with the book. "Look!" jhe said, holding it out. "It's like yours, only less beat up."

Erkanni was fascinated. "You're right. I've never seen another one."

Rowan wrapped the book and device painstakingly in the heat-resistant cloth, and tucked them inside the casket. Then jhe carefully soldered it shut again. Jhe made sure that no moisture would get in to harm the venerable runes, not even were it sunk in the pond.

Just then, Grandmother exclaimed loudly from the vegetable patch, "Oh, dear, we weren't expecting company, let alone a distinguished visitor, and me deep in the muck! Come, come; sit on the porch a spell while I get myself decent. Oh, heavens no, not the back porch, come around to the front; it's more proper, though not what one such as yourself would be accustomed to, to be sure. Askve, Askve! (Now where has she got to)?" The loud voice faded as they went around to the far side of the house.

"Come on, she's giving us a chance to get away!" Rowan said. Grabbing a spade, jhe led the way to the cover of the woodlot, where a creek-bed would take them straight up the mountainside.

"How far are we going to go?" asked Erkanni. "There's not much daylight left, you know."

Rowan stopped short. "We have to bury it somewhere safe, the higher up the mountain, the better."

Yrssu suggested they bury it in the stone circle.

"But people know that's a gnomad place!" objected Rowan.

"It will be safe there," insisted Yrssu. Jhe was so adamant, that in the end Rowan acquiesced.

At the stones, Yrssu walked around the circle, studying each stone carefully. One stone was a slightly different grain and color from the others. Pointing out a cleft-shaped rock high on a nearby mountain peak, jhe had Erkanni pace out twelve strides in its direction, then Rowan, and last of all jhmself. Oddly enough, no tree barred the arrow-straight path into the forest. They dug a deep hole beside the knotted roots of an ancient oak, and again gave the book into the Earth's keeping.

They rode the evening train back in the ordinary fashion, there being no charge in the downhill direction, and made it back to Adare with no one the wiser. As they parted ways outside the station, Rowan told Yrssu, "Come by our uncle's house any evening you like, and we can start reading the copy Grandmother made of the runes. We always have a fire going in the evenings, and lots of food. It's the big red house on Stella Hill just off Smoot's Alley, with a corner tower and a flying owl weather vane. You can't miss it!"

It took several days for Far to put the over-enthusiastically dismantled radio back together, so it was some time before Rowan heard the full story of how jhr family had tormented the hapless Sa Torin.

The first thing Grandmother said, tapping it out in dashdot, was, "So that was Orry's famous Erkanni, the selkie of Faraday."

"Jhe's not really a selkie, Grandmother," Rowan tapped back. Sometimes it was hard to tell what Grandmother believed.

"And a gnomad, too! I do wish we could have met them properly. Oh, come to think of it, I never got a chance to give you the rest of the runes! You'll have to wait until Midwinterfest."

"It doesn't matter, Grandmother. It's not like we've made any headway translating the first batch."

"But isn't that gnomad going to help you?"

"I don't know; I hope so." Since that day's adventure, Rowan had heard nothing from Yrssu. "But tell me, how did things go with Sa Torin?"

"Oh, therein lies a goodly tale. Let's switch over to speech, expense be damned." There was a click, and the alphabetic tapping gave way to a distorted but recognizable voice, full of laughter. "First, we had him sit out on the front porch a long while, in the newest and least comfortable chair, while we cleaned ourselves up. Oh, yes, we'd made good use of the time before his arrival. Your mar's hair was that full of straw, and as for the stench of ram, I don't believe she's got rid of it even now!" (A muffled exclamation from Mar came over the wire, amid Grandmother's hearty laughter.) "Well, and you saw your far rummaging through the capacitors; he was a sight to behold, wiping his fingertips daintily on a doily, with his hair all on end from sifting his fingers through it for thoughts, and his face all streaked with dust. And me caked with mud from the poor turnip garden — I shouldn't have trod in it, but that black glop had been tempting me deliciously, ever since the thaw. I can't remember when we last had so much fun!"

"But what did you say to Sa Torin, about the casket?"

"Oh, well, after a good deal of washing, we finally acted like we thought we were clean enough (though we were far from that), and sat down with him, and accepted all sorts of advice on Dialfi's behalf, about manners and such among the scholars. We brought out the tea things, but took our time preparing it, to give you plenty of time. Oh, and we asked all sorts of questions about life at the Akademy: do they really sleep on beds made of stone to make them long to get up and study; are there electric lights in every room; can it be true that they drink their coffee out of a communal pot using long pewter straws? I'm sure I can't remember all the nonsense your far dreamed up. That Sa must think Dialfi is a changeling born into a family of imbeciles!"

"That would fit his opinion of me, at any rate," said Rowan.

"And all the while the poor Sa Torin was trying to drop a hint about the casket. He didn't want to mention it directly, or show undue interest. And we headed him off every time, oblivious to his meaning, while he twitched and itched in that awful suit. At last he couldn't stand it any more, and out it came.

"'I happened to hear how an old copper coffer was found in this vicinity,' says he. And it occurred to me to be overeager to show him (a fine inspiration on my part, if I do say so myself!). So I jumped up and ran to find it; I clattered about looking, and at last came back sadly empty-handed, to confess that it had gone missing. The Sa's face fell; I wish you had seen it! I explained ever so sorrowfully, and at great length, how I had been keeping it on the top of the wardrobe, but I must have moved it – maybe back at All Howls when I'd rearranged the furniture to confuse our resident ghosts? No, I was absolutely at a loss; I couldn't think what I had done with it. When I invited him to help me look, he perked up, and helpfully turned over my whole apartment looking for it. Ripped the seat of his pants in the process, but I didn't mention that; after all, I didn't want to embarrass the poor fellow (though now that I think of it, maybe I shouldn't have let him ride the train back like that, what must people have thought of that gaping hole in the nice suit, Rowan?). And the whole time, he was trying so hard to hide his disappointment . . ."

Orry had come into the room some time back, and was rolling around on the floor in fits of hilarity that threatened to engulf Rowan as well. When Rowan could get the words out for laughing, jhe asked, "And what happened after that?"

"Well, do you know, he gave up at last. I believe he saw he'd better be getting back to Adare before he had to ask to spend the night with us. To console him as he left, I said we'd set the old goose to looking for it, being as she's a rare hand (or should I say wing) at finding lost objects; why only last summer she'd found my favorite mud-clogs out beyond the raspberry patch, and brought them to me, wearing one on each foot, and walking as solemnly as a scholar with hands behind back . . ."

Truth be told, Sa Torin was a bit bottom-heavy, and what's more the grey suit he'd been wearing had been just the shade of the goose in question. "Now that was going too far, Grandmother! What if Sa Torin had guessed you'd been teasing him all along?"

"Yes, your mar was rather annoyed at me too; she started banging the pots in the kitchen the way she does. But oh, you should have seen the way your far's shoulders shaking, as he sat working with bits of the radio strewn all over the table. Sa Torin never noticed anything, I promise you that. My, he is a piece of work, and no mistake! I hope they usually turn them out better at the Akademy, or what can we expect for our poor Dialfi?"

"Oh, Grandmother!"

Chapter 12. Let the Translation Begin

If this message ever washes up on Time's windward shore, it will be thanks to the Kymrans, and to their language that they hold in such reverence.

— Kassandra Morgan-Ávvu

As night drew like an iris around the lens of the day, so the soul began to shrink to its winter dimensions, and seek the fellowship of the living room with its well-laden sideboard. Aunt Matti had no equal in cultivating that sort of comfort. The hanging lamps shone a warm magenta, ample illumination to set the phosphorescent ink of books and papers aglow. The earthenware pitcher of cider stood in its nook by the fire, mismatched mugs ranged round. A marmalade house-cat stretched out luxuriantly on the hearth. Another, shadow-grey, graced the window, an exquisitely curved statue.

Rowan looked out at the street yet again. Orry asked sympathetically, "Still no word from your gnomad?" Rowan shook jhr head.

“What gnomad is that?” asked Dialfi, coming in from the dining room with a harassed look. Jhe began sifting through a stack of papers from a desk drawer.

Rowan and Orry glanced at one another. Lately Dialfi had been so busy with schoolwork and scholarship applications that there’d been no chance to tell jhm about their exciting lead. Nor had Rowan seen fit to mention the Sa Torin escapade.

“Well,” began Orry, “I noticed this gnomad eft working at the docks, and Rowan’s been trying to make jhr acquaintance.”

Dialfi said distractedly, “Good, good.” Having found what jhe’d been looking for, jhe headed back towards the dining room, where jhe added the papers to carefully organized arrays on the table.

“You’re not even interested in the book anymore, are you?” said Rowan, following jhm.

“What book?”

Rowan was sorely tempted to sweep the neat piles of papers right off the table. “Oh, never mind.”

Dialfi waved jhr arms in frustration. “I’m sorry, Rowan; it’s just that I’ve been filling out yet another mind-numbing form for yet one more remotely possible scholarship, and the essay questions are ludicrous, but I’ve got to answer them with all my heart as my whole future is at stake.”

“I’d better leave you to it, then.” Rowan turned to go back to the living room.

Dialfi put the papers down and really looked at jhr sib for the first time in days. "The *book*; of course I know what book. Tell me."

Rowan said, "This gnomad Orry found, jhe's going to come over and look at the runes."

"And jhe's not drunk or crazy or anything, either," called Orry from the other room.

"That hardly qualifies jhm to translate an ancient text," said Dialfi drily. "When is jhe coming?"

"I don't know, exactly," admitted Rowan.

Just then, a clatter came from the porch. Rowan ran to the hallway, but it was only Erkanni, coming in from Olioli with a wide grin and dripping-wet hair. Rowan went back to jhr station at the window.

Some time later, a series of muffled thumps came from the vicinity of the front entrance. Aunt Matti's voice could be heard greeting unfamiliar company. Rowan told jhmself it was sure to be no one of interest. Footsteps came down the hallway, and Aunt Matti ushered Yrssu into the cozy living room.

Rowan and Orry jumped up to greet jhm, and Erkanni clapped jhm on the back. Dialfi came over and shook hands. Rowan thought to offer jhm a mug of cider, but the gnomad waved it away. From a pocket jhe brought out a small cloth bag, wrapped round at the top by a beaded string. Jhe shook a few small, pointy seeds into an open palm, and offered one to each person in turn, each time announcing "I am Yrssu," so that they instinctively replied in kind with their own names.

They held the seeds awkwardly, unsure what they were meant to do with them. "Tivel seeds, good for beginnings," explained the gnomad. “Taste, but do not swallow.” The seeds were spicy and bitingly fresh. Following Yrssu’s lead, they spat them into the fire. Then, as if some boundary had been crossed, the gnomad held out both hands for the mug of cider.

Yrssu sipped at it unhurriedly, while taking in the big room with all its curious furnishings. These Nuathan efts looked mighty comfortable, sprawled as they were on various couches and window seats, drinking hot drinks, cracking nuts, peeling fruit, reading books, and writing with glowing, white-tipped brushes on dark paper. Strange people, to make their pens out of the wrong end of a feather. The sib whom Yrssu had not met before was wearing the flat, blue cap of an advanced student, and working away assiduously amidst great stacks of books and papers. It was clear that jhe was older than the others, with an air of great dignity for an eft. But then again, many things were different here in the land of the *Siéntu*.

Rowan brought out the stack of pages Grandmother had copied, and watched anxiously as Yrssu picked up the first page. It was still a bit creased from Rowan’s angry crumpling, the day they’d first met Yrssu. The gnomad tilted it to catch the lamplight. Rowan held jhr breath, but all Yrssu said was, “Bad handwriting, this. The strokes, they are strangely formed.”

“You can make sense of them, though, can’t you?” Rowan asked. It had certainly looked like jhe was reading them, that day at Yngencloven.

Dialfi said, “The runes may be so old as to be unintelligible. Most of the Anglic sections certainly were.”

“Our runes are not changing ever, for it is not like your slippery tongue,” said Yrssu.

“Aren't tongues supposed to be slippery?” Orry asked in confusion, touching jhrs between finger and thumb.

“It may be so,” Yrssu told jhm. “But I was speaking of Anglic.”

“Anglic isn't slippery!” Orry protested.

“Anglic, sure,” scoffed Yrssu; “used to be called Inglish, but cannot even keep its own name. Eh, you Nuathans, but you are not even remembering how it was the Colony that was called New Athens, and yourselves you called the New Athenians.” Erkanni caught Rowan’s eye with a grin. Yrssu was a piece of work, to be sure.

“An interesting suggestion,” said Dialfi; “I wonder what a specialist in ancient history would say about that.”

“Yes, Nuathans surely do love their *specialists*,” said Yrssu. “Yet you will be finding no Nuathan specialists in the runes.”

Orry muttered pointedly, “Nor any gnomad specialists, as far as I can see.”

Yrssu didn’t answer. Jhr eyes were tracking down the page of runes. Every so often jhe would raise jhr eyebrows as if surprised, then knit them again in concentration. Jhe was sitting plum on the floor, legs stretched out towards the glowing fireplace. Jhr damp socks exuded a scent of scorched and none-too-clean wool, an effect of which the gnomad seemed utterly unaware, and which everyone else did their best to ignore. Dialfi had cracked a window a while ago, and no one was sitting as near the fireplace as usual.

Eventually, Rowan asked, "How is it, Yrssu, that your people manage to carry books safely through all their wanderings?"

"We have no books. We are writing mostly on our walls."

"Walls? Then you have buildings?"

"Tent walls." Yrssu put down the rune-filled page jhe'd been studying, and gave Rowan jhr full attention. "You Nuathans are also People of the Book, is it not so? Where are you keeping your Great Book?"

"The Humanual? It's on the mantelpiece." Rowan gestured at the Book proudly displayed in a glass case.

"Yes, so, all nicely shut up." Yrssu smacked jhr hands together, then spread them out. "We Kymrans are living within the Book, for its words surround us when we are in our tents. So it is, when we are outside, that we are seeing how the Book is written over the whole of the world, on the clouds and constellations, the aurorae and the waves that stand in the river, on the boulders shaped by the winds of ages."

"That's all well and good," said Orry, "but if you really can read this thing, why not tell us what it *says*?" For once, they were all grateful for jhr childish impatience.

Yrssu looked around at their intent faces, lingering on Rowan's. This one, who did not look like a *Siénttu,* stood with one hand unconsciously cradling the arm scarred by the mark of Emru. The gnomad nodded slowly to jhmself, and at last came to a decision. "It is beginning with time travel."

"What?" said Rowan, startled.

"Whoever is reading this book, so the writer says, is a traveler in time."

"A traveler in time, eh?" Dialfi mused. "Was the writer a philosopher, then; or a poet?"

"She is no poet, that is of a certainty," answered Yrssu. "A poet of my people would not trouble to write down such a thing, with no word play or rhythm, and lacking attention to the balance of sounds. This, it is bristling with dry facts and logical explanations, of the kind you Nuathans love."

"But the Humanual's chock full of poetry," objected Orry.

"To be sure," said Yrssu; "those parts that the Kymrans wrote."

"Your people wrote part of the Humanual?" asked Dialfi skeptically.

"Yeah, give me a break," Orry said.

Yrssu answered calmly, though Rowan was starting to gather that this covered a fierce pride. "So it was, and so I shall tell you, that long generations ago our two peoples lived side by side."

"We did?" asked Rowan. It was true that, besides the Humanual, the Nuathans and the gnomads did share a common humanity – in contrast to the bestial Outlanders.

Yrssu continued, "You may have forgotten, Nuathans not being over-fond of history, how we and the *mammút* drew forth your farms in those ancient days, from out of bare rock."

"What's a mammút?" interrupted Orry.

"You know them as mehemoths, which would be another sample of your Nuathan humor, so I am guessing." They shrugged, uncomprehendingly. "—And though you Nuathans may have forgotten, we remember, we Kymrans, how the Sages had likewise drawn forth the mammút from out of the mists of time. Those giants were among the first creatures that had been lost, when humans began to overrun the Earth. And so were we then a lost people, but the mammút have led us back to our path. So they do even unto this day, however the snows of winter cover our way, and the winds blow contrariwise."

They were all amazed at this outpouring of strange eloquence. After a moment Dialfi asked, "What do you mean, Yrssu, when you say that the Sages drew forth the mehem—the mammút?"

"I mean," answered Yrssu, "that they created them anew, when only their ancient bones remained to tell us of their passing. From out of these bones the Sages spun threads so tiny that no eye could see them, and these threads spun yet finer threads, that in turn wove the stuff of life of the mammút."

"Wow," breathed Orry; then, after thinking about it, "No way. Not even the Sages could make mehemoths out of old bones. Could they?" jhe appealed to Dialfi.

"I wouldn't have thought so, but what Yrssu says does make a certain amount of sense," Dialfi answered. "Listen, this is all absolutely fascinating, and I don't want to miss any of it, but," jhe gestured to an open textbook, "I really, really have to get this work done, or I'll be up till the Dawn Trill. Maybe we could put off the translating until tomorrow?"

"I've got a better idea," said Rowan, who wasn't about to wait any longer to hear what these runes said. "Let's just let Yrssu look at it, without any more interruptions."

Yrssu peered again at the wrinkled page. "The beginning is full of standard turns of phrase, but there follow many odd and difficult words."

"Well, maybe your runes do change over the centuries," suggested Orry.

"No, these words were never part of our language." Jhe stabbed at several with annoyance. "I think they must be from the Anglic."

"How about just writing them out with normal letters, then," suggested Dialfi, looking up briefly from jhr textbook with a resigned sigh.

Yrssu muttered something about the presumption that there was anything normal about Anglic letters, but set to work transcribing them above the runes. Rowan helped, as it was clear the gnomad had little acquaintance with written Anglic.

Erkanni looked over, and pointed to the phonetic rendition of one of the words. "*Fohn* — that's what my father called this pendant."

"Really?" asked Rowan. "Hey, Dialfi, remember that little rectangular thing that was in the casket with the book?" Rowan reminded jhm. "Erkanni has something that looks a lot like it."

Curiously, Dialfi examined the pendant. "Where did you get it?" jhe asked Erkanni.

"From my father. He had it from his, and so on, going back farther than anyone can say."

"What could they have been used for, I wonder?" said Rowan.

"Most likely they had some ritual or religious significance," answered Dialfi with a shrug.

Erkanni was still looking at Yrssu's notation. "And that word, 'flotsam,' means something washed out of a boat by accident — as opposed to jetsam, which is thrown out when you're sinking."

"What strange words," said Rowan. "I can't imagine why you'd need to make the distinction."

Orry looked indignant. "They're two utterly different nautical circumstances, Rowan."

Erkanni added, "And the salvage rights differ: jetsam is finders-keepers, but flotsam must be returned to the owner of the ship, if possible. Where I come from, we have all sorts of words that I've never heard you mainlanders use. Maybe we're just more fond of hearing ourselves talk."

Yrssu had meanwhile been studying the page, mouthing words under jhr breath. After a moment more, jhe read slowly but steadily:

> Whosoever you be, and however far away, know that you are a traveller in time. Reading my story, you will be exclaiming, "She breathes and lives even as I, though the cold wind of another age stirs the dust of her passage."

Yrssu paused, and Rowan cried, "You *can* read the runes! I knew it!"

"You did not," said Orry.

Yrssu went on:

Writing is a wonderful and miraculous creation: with a few scratches of oily lamp-soot, using a feather plucked from Hermes' foot, I can speak in your ear across the gulf of untold centuries. That is, I can be doing so if people have taught the skill of writing to their offspring, generation after generation, and if the language has continued sufficiently unchanged. ["There is your dry Nuathan style treading hard on the heels of poetry," said Yrssu.] If this be not so, and I have no reader, then I am speaking all unknowing, into the empty darkness. ["Or perhaps it should be 'black emptiness,'" said Yrssu.]

My name is Kassandra Morgan.

"Did you just say Kassandra?" Dialfi asked, startled. The others looked at jhm questioningly, and jhe explained, "The scholars have a saying, 'It's in Kassandra's Saga,' meaning no one knows the answer to something."

"But what is Kassandra's Saga?" asked Rowan.

"Like I just said, no one knows," Dialfi said with a grin. "Maybe an alternate account of the Catastrophe, or the Founding, or so some say. In any case, it was lost long ago."

"So this could be a famous lost work?" said Orry in great excitement. "And we'll all be famous for finding it?"

"More notorious, than famous, I think," answered Dialfi. "One gets the impression that Kassandra's Saga was dangerously unreliable, or mistaken, or heretical, or something like that. So maybe it was not so much lost as allowed to fade into obscurity."

"Cool, a forbidden book!" said Orry. "Read on, Yrssu!"

Yrssu nodded, and not without a sense of self-importance, continued:

> So it was, and so I shall tell you, that I found myself a bit of flotsam from the wreckage of my former life, cast up against a faraway shore.
>
> When my mother died, they shipped me off to this forsaken place at the wrong end of the earth. I barely even had time to say goodbye to Sarah, or Josiah. Never mind that Sarah's family was ready to take me in; they'd been looking after me for these last months, helping me through the nightmare of starting high school at such a time. I'd never have survived without them, above all without Josiah. I wonder how long it will be before I see them again.

No sooner did I arrive, than they took away my fohn, and gave me a lot of inoculations. What disease are they thinking I would catch in this isolated and frigid place, I wonder? They even burned all my clothes. All that is remaining of my old life, then, is a compass my father gave me before he left for good (as useless as can be, here), and this notebook for all weathers that I found in my mom's lab. They would assuredly take the notebook away, too, if they were guessing the sort of thing I am going to write in here. But I will write in the tongue of my father's people, that no unfriendly eyes may discover my secrets.

Needless to say, I hate it here.

When Yrssu stopped reading, they were too awed to say anything at first. They were hearing the thoughts of someone from who knew how long ago, perhaps the first ever to do so. Reading her words, they were indeed travelers in time. Like a musician whose performance evokes in their audience that peculiar quality of intense and amazed silence that is the highest form of praise, Yrssu felt well repaid for jhr efforts.

Then the questions and speculations began to fly round the room, as did Rowan, unable to confine jhmself to a chair. "Who could she be?" asked Rowan, and before anyone could answer, “Did you guys notice what she said about writing in her father’s tongue?"

“Hopefully it wasn't too slippery," muttered Orry.

Yrssu laughed, and Rowan said, “Don't you see, she must be part Kymran, just like us!”

“What kind of a place *was* she sent to, where they confiscate stuff, and burn your clothes to welcome you there?” Orry wanted to know.

“Some kind of an orphanage?” Erkanni suggested.

“Why would an imago be sent to an orphanage?” wondered Rowan. “Kassandra calls herself ‘she,’ so she can’t be an eft!”

“That is strange,” agreed Dialfi. “I suppose she could have added that fancy introduction later, after her Change. From the style of most of it, it sounds like it was written by someone no older than Rowan or Orry. I wonder what she means by a ‘high’ school.”

Just then, Aunt Matti put her head through the doorway to say, “It’s almost the Tolling, my hardworking scholars.” They glanced guiltily at their abandoned homework. “Time to wrap it up for tonight.”

Rowan turned to Yrssu. “Can you come again tomorrow?”

“I will come.”

Rowan fell asleep that night to the sound of running rainwater. Jhe dreamed of a ship rolling in dark starlit waves. The people aboard were on some sort of journey, but whether this was in the distant past or in time to come, jhe could not afterwards say. Jhe retained only the sense of desperate, heart-pounding urgency.

Chapter 13. The Translating Continues

This place is so weird. Parts of it look like an antique farming village. But the livestock are housed in metallic barns that look like tin cans sliced from top to bottom, and laid cut-side down. The housing for humans is similarly ugly. I suppose it must make for a drier habitation than in the old days, when people had to do the best they could with chinked wood and whatnot.

When I first got here, there was an oddity that I couldn't quite put my finger on. Then it came to me that no one went around with the familiar bent-head posture, gazing at their screens. They walk around looking at the sky, or the ground, or each other. It's kind of unsettling, but after a while you get used to it. Josiah would like it, I think.

Another strange thing about this place is how the sun is never very high in the sky. There's always a vague feeling of dawn or sunset, beginnings and endings, and the rich colors are endowed with mysterious, otherworldly significance. The ocean is a silvery blue streaked with dark shadows; the varied and fantastic shapes of clouds are underlit by ever-changing hues of rose, yellow, violet; everything seems half in darkness, even when the light falls full on it.

— Kassandra Morgan-Ávvu

"Wow," breathed Orry, expressing an awe they all felt. Kassandra, who had lived and breathed, struggled and loved, even as they did now, was speaking to them across the gulf of centuries. Yrssu, who'd given voice to the mysterious runes, wore a look of quiet pride.

"It's like actually being there," said Dialfi. Jhr textbook lay abandoned on the floor. "It almost seems as though—" Dialfi stopped short.

"As though it really is the long-lost and unfairly maligned Kassandra's Saga?" prompted Rowan.

But Dialfi only said, "I want to hear more before I speculate."

"I thought gnomad runes weren't worth a scholar's attention," teased Rowan. Jhe had played an integral role in the translation, by looking up all the archaic Anglic words at the library.

"A scholar should always be open-minded," Dialfi declared.

"I thought that was heroes," said Rowan.

"What's the difference?" asked Dialfi, only half in jest.

Through many an evening thereafter, they labored over the translation. Yrssu with a bit of chalk and slate would rewrite any runes that jhe was uncertain of, slashing out the strokes with deft jerks of the wrist. The scratching sound of the chalk was oddly comforting, bringing back memories of childhood art work and easy problems in arithmetic. Rowan watched closely, for jhe was determined to learn how to read the runes jhmself.

This proved much harder than jhe had imagined. Seeing jhr interest, Yrssu insisted on teaching jhm the strokes with a proper writing instrument. This turned out to be the wrong end of a feather, sharpened and split a little ways up. In Yrssu's hand, the strokes flowed out effortlessly in smoothly curving streams, but try as jhe might, Rowan could not satisfy Yrssu's notion of their correct formation. Still, it improved jhr ability to recognize the runes.

A further complexity was that only a subset of the words, mostly archaic Anglic, were written out phonetically. The majority were written in a way that Rowan at first found ridiculously unwieldy. Each word or phrase had its own elaborate symbol that bore little or no reference to its sound, so there were thousands upon thousands of them. Rowan thought such a style of writing must be cumbersome to learn.

Yrssu explained that children passed the time while herding by scratching out runes in the snow or on muddy stream-banks, and studied the tent-writing by flickering firelight. It served them well, for even Kymrans of distant tribes, who could not follow one another's speech, could communicate by means of the runes. Perhaps that was also why the runes had managed to remain unchanged over the centuries.

Though Yrssu and Rowan, with some help from Erkanni, did most of the work on the translation, Dialfi too was drawn into Kassandra's account. While determined not to fall behind in school, jhe would keep one eye on the proceedings from a built-in perch high in a corner of the room, which jhe favored as if it were an aid to lofty thought. Jhe would descend laughingly to dispute the interpretation of rune-strokes with Yrssu, citing expert knowledge of Grandmother's handwriting, if nothing else.

"Look at this, Dialfi." Rowan had climbed halfway up the ladder to Dialfi's perch with the latest bit jhe and Yrssu had been working on.

> It's so much quieter here than where I lived before: no bunker-builders boring their way into the foundations of abandoned hirizes [?]. No riot-trucks clattering and shuddering down the street, or protesters chanting in the pervasive rhythm of "dinn, dinn, dee-dee-dinn!" No endless foot-traffic on the pot-holed streets: the jostling people with their carts piled high with cheap groceries; bikes and skuters[?] weaving every which way, while the old grannies and harassed mothers of small children shout and wave their fists; the rare, brazen limmozeen[?], curtains pulled tight on the side and rear windows, muscling its way down the middle of the street, as people pound on its hood and hurl insults and the occasional tomato.

Here, it's so peaceful that you can hear the wind ruffling the feathers of bird wings. But there aren't any songbirds – just screeching gulls and evil-looking skuas.

Rowan asked Dialfi, "Where do you think Kassandra was talking about, that she used to live? The capital wasn't ever like this, was it?"

"No," answered Dialfi, much puzzled. "It doesn't sound like any place I've ever heard of."

As the initial excitement of being able to read the runes wore off, Rowan became frustrated at how often they'd decipher a short entry only to discover it to be a meandering complaint about the unfriendliness of the local children, the uncommunicativeness of the adults, or the awfulness of the weather.

"Just look at this." Rowan showed Dialfi the fragment jhe and Yrssu had been laboring over most recently, full of flowery words that had cost jhm many hours of searching through old Anglic dictionaries.

My mom loved all kinds of weather. She thought it was the one thing that reminded even the most insular city-dweller that the wide world still exists out there, beyond our control. The blizzard that forces people to go on foot again, and see each other face to face; the heat wave that puts out the power, and drives people to sleep on rooftops, and see the blazing stars that have always watched over our sleep. And if those stars are now diminished to a sprinkling of faint pinpricks, she would say, it is we and not they who have changed.

"It doesn't even make sense," Rowan groused; "all this about the stars shrinking, and waves of heat."

"It's amazing that you and Yrssu are managing to read as much as you are, Rowan. Try not to be discouraged. The Anglic part did say we had to read the 'Tale Entire.'"

Still, however hard they worked on the translation, there were parts they just could not make proper sense of. In an entry about a school essay that had gotten a poor grade, Kassandra declared that her mother, at least, had always liked her writing. Though it started off well enough, the passage had then descended into a thicket of what they assumed must be scholarly terms.

"Oh, Kassandra, what a way you have with words," she'd told me; "I suppose it must be in your blood."

"You mean from Dad?" Kymrans love the written word, the more striking the better; and they revere poets no end. The Avúu family were disappointed that their brilliant son had become something as staid as a geologist, even though he would tell them he was reading the greatest book there was, the Book of the Earth itself. He made it sound like poetry, too, the vast stretches of time written in the rocks and ice, the history of life on Earth and all that.

"Yes, certainly," my mom had answered (she was always careful never to say anything mean about Dad), "but those of us who study fruit flies aren't so bad with words ourselves. Researchers on mice or worms tend to choose boring, utilitarian gene names, like YAP or GLI, but we called the fly versions yorky and gleeful. We've got a long history of giving imaginative names to fly genes. Ken and Barby are mutants that lack external genitalia. Tinman mutants have a defective heart. Then there's Hamlet, which affects the 2b cell lineage. The best scientists are playful, knowing that everything comes down to stories in the end."

When Rowan and Yrssu brought this very strange passage to Dialfi, jhe explained that scholars had long used fruit flies to study all manner of basic biology. "I've heard that there's a tradition of naming their genes based on stories or sly jokes, the better to make sense of them and remember them. Although nowadays, we often don't understand the references anymore."

"Jokes are creatures of the moment," commented Erkanni, "and even the Kymrans' runes cannot be conserving them for all time."

"Of course not," agreed Dialfi. "But Rowan, you did get the Hamlet reference, didn't you?"

"No," Rowan said grouchily. Jhe'd been missing a lot of sleep lately, with all this translation work.

"Two-B or not two-B, that is the question?"

Rowan groaned.

Finding this unexpected penchant for stories interesting, Yrssu had wanted to know what was a gene. Dialfi explained they were parts of those same threads the Sages had used to bring back the mammút from old bones, that ran the machinery of life in every creature's cells. When Yrssu asked what a cell was, Rowan listened as well, never having realized how fascinating this microscopic world could be.

In the midst of this, Aunt Matti came in to tell them it was rather late. She smiled at Erkanni and Yrssu. "It's nice to have some new faces about this year. Your old friend Dana never seems to come by anymore."

Rowan told her, "These days, Dana spends jhr free time guzzling coffee with a bunch of other stuck-up windbags, the sort who think it's a great achievement to be invited to pay full tuition at the Akademy."

Looking amused at this description, Dialfi nevertheless rose to Dana's defense: "Well, jhe may feel awkward with me these days, not knowing whether I'll make it there myself."

Rowan and Orry walked out into the drizzling night with Yrssu and Erkanni. The dark streets were quiet. Bright lights shone out from many windows, where people could be seen chatting and laughing, playing musical instruments and games, the sorts of things people did to raise their spirits in the winter. It was customary to keep no particular hours during the season of darkness. As long as a lamp was lit in the entryway, you could knock at any door, and be sure of being offered a cup of tea and some sweet rolls. In this way, many friendships blossomed in wintertime.

A lone figure clattered past them, and Yrssu grumbled, "How the people of Adare do love their boots. *Clip-clop, clip-clop*, tapping at the road like ponies' toes."

Yrssu really had a thing against boots. Rowan glanced over at Yrssu's feet and saw jhr footwear was thick and padded as a cat's paw, bulging out between crisscrossed laces.

Erkanni began to whistle in time to the receding steps, some chanty or other, and Orry joined in, slapping jhr palms against jhr thighs. Yrssu had to smile at their impromptu duet.

As they reached the alley leading to jhr back steps, Yrssu pursed jhr lips and let out a soft, high-pitched whistle. Crouching down, jhe held out a hand and greeted a small, whiskery face. It sneezed, then scampered off into the shadows.

"Was that a *rat*?" Orry asked, aghast.

"She's a bold one," said Yrssu approvingly. "Comes up to share my dinner, most nights." Orry shuddered. Rowan was inclined to agree, but told jhmself the little face had not been so very different from an otter's.

After seeing Erkanni home, Rowan and Orry walked back through the lamp-friendly streets. The tower lights were slowly shifting from magenta to deep blue. Orry said, "Did you see the way Yrssu touched that rat — ugh! And do you think jhe *ever* bathes? You have to admit, jhe's a bit of a savage."

Rowan bristled. "No more than your precious Erkanni!"

"What's that supposed to mean?"

"All those little braids, jingling with shells?"

"That's how Islanders wear their hair," said Orry.

"And the way jhe plays Olioli, leaping from one rooftop to another like some kind of a lunatic—"

"Ha, Rowan, you're just mad you can't keep up with jhm!" With that, Orry scampered off; but Rowan caught up with no difficulty, and beat jhr sib to the front door by a house-length at least.

Chapter 14. At the Research Station

While outside the winds tear through primeval darkness, inside the station's capacious greenhouse a miniature sun glows with light and warmth. There, in damp exuberance, grow vanilla, coffee, limes, bananas, cinnamon, cacao: all the precious fruits of a hundred centuries of agriculture. In the corners, hives of honeybees throb with golden life, and their denizens pollinate the flowering crops with diligence and fairy-like precision. And there are other inhabitants of this improbable Eden as well: garter snakes dart through the undergrowth, tiny spring peeper frogs hop among the branches, and salamanders hide under dank logs. The biologists came up with ecological arguments for their presence — such as the need for diversity to make an ecosystem stable — but love of creation was surely the real reason, as further evidenced by the persistence of some volunteer dandelions that no one has had the heart to eradicate.

— Kassandra Morgan-Ávvu

As the autumn wore on and the load of classwork increased, Dialfi could no longer devote so much attention to the unfolding translation. Jhe suggested that rather than leaping up to show jhm the latest burst of progress, they could complete each of Kassandra's entries in full before reading it aloud to the group. Accordingly, whenever a new passage was ready, they would all gather round the fireside and listen while Yrssu read it aloud.

> Much as I resent having been bundled off to this isolated research station, I have to admit it has kind of a familiar feel, probably from all the late evenings and early mornings Mom brought me into work with her. It must be the same the world over: the late-night camaraderie and buzz of coffee-fueled marathon efforts, the sudden bouts of playfulness, the mix of accents and languages. Above all, there's the touching faith that much of value can be learned by asking good questions, which was basically my mom's religion.
>
> What's more, the people here were my mom's colleagues from her younger days. The way they talk about the world reminds me of her, too. This hurts, but I guess it's better than not being reminded at all.
>
> My guardians, Ingrid and Karl, were old friends of hers. Ingrid studies the growth of

plants and lichens at extremes of temperature and latitude. Much of her work takes place in the greenhouse, though she says she does a fair bit of fieldwork in the summer. Karl's work is all on computers. He goes outdoors as little as possible, preferring to experience weather and climate conditions at the remove of remote sensors that have amassed mounds of data.

I have to say, even after living here for all these months, there are things that I just don't get about this place. I can understand how a research station in the middle of nowhere would have peculiar needs, and develop customs of its own, but it seems more than that, somehow. They take themselves so very seriously, even though all they're doing is measuring flow-rates and thicknesses of ice-sheets, air and sea temperatures, fish die-offs – and all while the world is going to ruin around them. What do they imagine is the point of all that?

Then there are all these rules: no fohns, no radios, net[?] access strictly reserved for research purposes only; no lights at night except in windowless rooms. Ingrid and Karl say that would be apt to get the place noticed.

Noticed by whom?

And so what?

Those piecing together Kassandra's account wondered the same thing. But the next entry did nothing to answer those questions, instead being a vivid description of a winter harsher than any they'd heard tell of, even in the Helluland where Far's hardy relatives lived.

I arrived here in the midst of summer, and coming from a northern winter, it didn't feel too bad. Now, though, I'm beginning to see what a place I've been exiled to. It's the University of Shikággo's old joke about how hell really does freeze over, come true in spades. All the old-timers have been saying what a mild winter it's been. I wrote this off as teasing the newcomer, until I saw the records in the Climate lab.

We've just come out of three weeks of snow storms. After you scrape off a centimeter or so of frost from the inside of the windows, there's still nothing but blankness to see outside. Still, it's been such a long time since I've seen the sun that it no longer seems dark, what with the snow, the full moon, the racing clouds, and, on the rare occasions when it's clear, so many stars that the skies of home seem like a tawdry imitation.

Tunnels run everywhere, so hardly anyone has to go outside during snow storms. Exploring this warren kept me from going completely stir-crazy. That's how I met Mary, who looks after the kennels.

"You're Valerie's kid, huh?" Mary introduced me to a bunch of dogs and fluff-balls of puppies in the dog-yard, then to Baldri, who I assumed must be her son. Now that the weather's cleared, we were able to go out for a sled ride.

Baldri's all right, friendlier than most of the kids around here. They're all younger than me, and are pretty much a tribe of their own, having been born here and neither knowing nor caring much about the rest of the world. They act like I'm the one who's a freak and want nothing to do with me. Maybe it's just a small-town mentality, but it gets old fast.

These dogs sure love to pull the sled. They eat up the ground like it's the best ice cream ever, and go on and on, for hours. Racing over the brand-new snow, under the blazing stars and the Aurora's shimmering curtain, I was madly, wildly happy. It didn't matter that my eyelashes froze together, that my eyeballs, throat, and hands ached with the cold and my feet were blocks of wood. For the first time since coming here, since Mom and all that, I was glad to be here – just here, and nowhere else.

The mountains were drowned in snow up to their black peaks, and glaciers curled down their flanks. Never could I have imagined such immense and terribly slow rivers of ice. But mostly what we saw was an endless expanse of gently undulating whiteness, extending from horizon to horizon. We rushed over it like the wind, whooping and whistling and urging the dogs to ever greater speed, and carved wide curves in the trackless snow. The dogs too had been cooped up all those weeks during the snowstorm, and although we'd planned to halt for a thermos of coffee and some chocolate-chip cookies tucked in an inner pocket of my parka, we didn't stop once until pulling back into the yard. Mary yelled at us for overworking the dogs and made us slather their sore paws with some sort of stinking ointment. But she forgave us when she saw the palms of Baldri's driving gloves worn almost

> through from trying to hold back the eager dogs.

"It's weird to think of dogs pulling a sledge," commented Orry. "Do your people do that, Yrssu?"

Yrssu shook jhr head. "We are using caribou for that. Our dogs are for herding, like yours."

Orry laughed. "How does a dog herd a mehemoth?"

"They do not," Yrssu answered gravely. "The mammút would never permit such a thing."

The next entry, though short, generated a lot of discussion. Yrssu began:

> Lately, with the returning light making everyone more talkative, I've been wandering around asking questions of anyone I can find. I don't usually get much out of the scientists, who are wrapped up in their various tasks—

"What can Kassandra mean by 'scientist'?" interrupted Dialfi.

"Do you not use that word?" asked Yrssu. "It is coming up a lot in the diary; it means someone who studies the sciences."

Dialfi said, "But we already have a word for that: scholar. Or 'sage,' if we are talking about a very great scholar."

Yrssu answered, "We also have this word 'sage.' But we use it only for wise people."

"As do we," said Dialfi, rather nettled.

"When my people speak of you Nuathans," Yrssu continued, "we are calling you the *Siénttu*, the scientists. I do not know why your Anglic is so very changeable." Jhe shook jhr head, and went on reading the passage aloud.

> Nor have I learned much from the station kids. But the laborers, who are all Kymrans, tell me all sorts of things once I greet them in their own language. (They get a kick out of hearing about my dad, one of their own who went off to college in Shikággo to become a scientist.) They say they were promised steady jobs and a home for their families, but not told about all the rules and restrictions. They are pretty much cut off from the civilized world, and even from the scientists here, for the most part. They hadn't even heard about the new limits on air travel.

"Air travel? What's that?" put it Orry.

Yrssu shrugged, rather irritably. "That is what the words say. Or else, 'movement through the sky.'"

"Could it be sailing?" wondered Orry.

"No." Yrssu began reading again:

So I told the Kymrans what's been going on lately: the thousands killed and the millions displaced by storms and rising water in the past year alone, from Bongladesh to Floridda; the huge inland fires that have destroyed forests and farms across wide swathes of North Umerikka and Ostrelya. How the survivors of all these disasters are stuck in makeshift camps behind hooked wire and electrified fences, and no one has any idea where to put them all, how to feed them or give them work. Even Kaskadia's started turning them back.

Rowan said, "Hey, Dialfi, doesn't it sound like this could be about the Catastrophe?"

"It does," Dialfi admitted, "but that was what, some seventy-odd generations ago? Even the runes can't be *that* unchanging."

Yrssu did not dignify that piece of ignorant slander with a reply.

Chapter 15. Futures of Long Ago

Until I started running simulations, I had no notion of the severity of the problem. Have you ever watched a large ship coming into port? Even when it's moving very slowly, and its engines have been turned off, its great weight makes it coast on and on, with awesome power, crushing anything in its path.

— Kassandra Morgan-Ávvu

They read on through the darkening days. Rowan neglected jhr schoolwork shamelessly, doing just enough to keep the teachers at bay. Yrssu had plenty of time to devote to the effort, as this late in the fall there was little work to be had at the docks. The others eagerly awaited each new passage they deciphered.

It's hard to believe I've been here nearly a year already. Even after all this time, it still feels like I'm an outsider, almost as if there's this big secret that everyone but me is in on. That's got to be nothing but paranoia, right?

I've been spending a good deal of time this spring in the climate modeling lab, where Karl all but lives. It's a flickering cave lined with banks of computers from floor to ceiling, that Ingrid jokingly calls his Den of Augury. No wonder, given the way Karl talks about it. "People used to read omens in the flights of birds and the disposition of entrails, in the movements of the stars, in all manner of natural phenomena. Are these not the same signs we use as input for our simulations? How animals are changing their preferred diets, how birds are migrating later and later each fall; cycles of sunspots and slow wobbling of the Earth's axis all affect our calculations. We're not as far removed from ancient ways as we like to think, even if we use digital oracles nowadays."

"Hang on," Orry interrupted. "What in Gaea's name is prognostication? And that other word — oggery, orkery? Can't you stick to proper Anglic, Rowan?"

"Augury," corrected Rowan, a bit touchily; jhe'd worked hard on the Anglic words from that entry, and was rather proud of the result. "It means foretelling the future, by means of indicators--only 'prognostication' has a better ring to it.

They are too proper Anglic words, even if *you've* never heard of them. Kassandra's just being poetic."

Dialfi said, "I sometimes wish Kassandra would say things more plainly."

Seeing they were of a mind to talk, Yrssu resignedly sank down onto the hearth. Jhe skewered an apple, and began to roast it, turning it this way and that above a patch of coals. "Kassandra is trying to writing poetically, in imitation of the Kymrans," Yrssu told them.

"When are you going to recite some of this famous poetry for us?" asked Erkanni.

"Anglic cannot be carrying Kymran poetry it its coarse net of words," Yrssu said with visible, though perhaps unconscious, scorn.

"Yet you manage Kassandra's writing well enough," Erkanni argued.

"I already have said that Kassandra is not not writing poetry, however she is at times making the attempt. And Rowan is having a skill for turning Kassandra's words to sense in Anglic, without losing all their virtue," answered Yrssu.

Rowan blushed at the unexpected praise. "I take what Yrssu tells me, and the strange words Erkanni knows, or that I've found in the Dictionary of Archaic Anglic; then I turn them over and over, thinking about them, until it's as though — oh, you'll probably just laugh."

"No, we won't." Dialfi shot a warning glance at Orry.

"I start to hear a whispering in my ear . . . or more like a wind blowing over bare ground, an empty rustling sound . . . and that's when I know the words are about to come right."

“Hmm,” said Dialfi, looking skeptical.

“Hmm,” echoed Orry, talking jhr cue from Dialfi. “And I still don’t get all that stuff about foretelling the future.”

Dialfi answered, “Oh, that’s clear enough. Kassandra’s doing computronics, like we use to forecast the weather or the tides.”

“But she makes it sound like magic; and you said we don’t believe in magic.”

Dialfi said, “No, it's just using what you know of current conditions and rules for how the world works, and extrapolating the system forward. It’s like an educated guess, except that with computronics, your assumptions are explicit and therefore more correctable.”

“Is *that* all?” Orry said, disappointed. “It sounded so much more interesting.”

“Just you wait,” said Rowan. Jhe held up the scar seared into jhr forearm. “Danger foretold, remember?”

Yrssu continued:

> School was not really working out, academically or socially. For a while I tagged along after Ingrid, but when she ran out of non-critical experiments for me to help with, Karl starting bringing me to his lab. He said it would be the most appropriate education for this day and age, and that I might well contribute something of value, if I worked hard enough at it. He gave

me a tutorial in modeling, the same as they used to start new graduate students with. Then he got me set up playing with simulations, first simple toy ones, then increasingly complex and involved.

It's addictive, the modeling; I've sometimes spent all night on it without noticing how the time passed. I suppose it makes me feel like I have some sort of control over this mess we're living through. Zing, I give central Afrikah back to the creatures of the jungle. Zap, I see what happens if low-lying cloud-cover increases over the tropics. Can I find a way to keep the monsoon over southeast Ayjha going? To keep the Sahaira from getting even drier than it already is?

I dial Earth's temperature up a bit, and hurricanes begin to appear over the oceans, spinning like tops, fueled by the warm, wet air rising. More evaporation brings unheard-of rainfall to some places, but in patterns I can't understand, brings extreme drought to others. When all the warm, wet air meets a cold front, it can make for heavier snowfall as well. It's crazy! But this snow melts in a great whoosh faster and earlier each simulated spring, causing floods followed by long summers of drought as rivers run dry. So far I haven't found a single scenario where the temperature goes up by more than a few degrees, that doesn't lead to awful consequences.

Today, I asked Karl if things could go into a runaway greenhouse effect.

"Like on that hell-hole Venus?" he answered. "Unlikely. But nothing is certain, given that the rate of change is so much faster than anything our planet has ever experienced, and there are so many feedbacks we're barely beginning to understand. Right now, we think the worst-case scenario is it gets too hot for anything but microbial life over much of our planet's surface."

I told him that wasn't very reassuring.

"More likely there will be widespread deserts, but also newly tropical regions at higher latitudes, and forests nearly to the poles. We know from fossils that it was forested here some thirty-five million years ago, when the continent was just as far south as it is now; and I don't mean dwarf willows of the tundra, but actual woodlands of birch and beech. Though you'd still have months of total darkness, so the plants and animals would have to cope with that. So whatever ecology established itself would be different from anything we have now."

I tried to picture the profusion of life spreading out and engulfing this barren continent, a place without a single tree, where bits of lichen clinging to pebbles were a cause for wonder. We recall with disbelief how we used to curse the heat up north; the sizzling summers and stifling autumns and winters that never came. Somewhat guiltily, we cheer on the creeping exposure of new rock, month by month, the waves of tundra spreading ever further southwards. And meanwhile, much of the rest of the living planet is frying and drying up and washing into the sea.

It's just bad luck, I guess, that all that fossil carbon was waiting underground, so immediately useful and so ultimately deadly.

Dialfi interrupted, "*Fossil carbon*, are you sure that's what it says?"

Yrssu answered, "Fossil, that is a stone whose shape says it was once alive. And Rowan was telling me the other word should be rendered 'carbon.' It means," Yrssu pointed at the glowing hearth, "what those pieces of wood will be looking like tomorrow morning, when they are grey dust, or black, crumbling lumps."

"Ash, do you mean — charcoal?" Dialfi asked eagerly.

Yrssu nodded, and went on,

We've spun the dial on Earth's thermostat and it's wildly out of control. Millennia of unavoidable warming lie ahead, for temperatures have not yet begun to level off from the gaseous carbon already added. And there are so many positive feedbacks: hot air holds more water which holds yet more heat; melting ice leaves dark rock and dark water that absorbs more heat and melts yet more ice.

People hope an effective way may yet be discovered to scrub carbon from the air. Yet the oceans have absorbed so much of the excess themselves that even if we did, they'll be off-gassing carbon into the air for centuries to come, swamping whatever heroic efforts we make.

No, this carbon has to be locked away in the rock before the climate can return to normal. Green plants breathe it in, and if after dying they do not rot or burn, they may fossilize slowly into coal, as did the great primordial forests of the eponymous Carboniferous. Meanwhile, in the oceans planktonic creatures, coccolithophorans and their ilk, snow it down to the bottom of the sea in vast drifts of carbonate shells. Both are exceedingly slow processes even when life is flourishing; and conditions now are far from ideal. The land is deforested, desertifying, flooding, and paved over; the oceans impoverished of nutrients by loss of upwelling and disruption of currents. Worse, all the gaseous carbon has rendered the oceans so acidic that many sea creatures can hardly build their shells. Erecting another edifice like the White Cliffs of Dover will be impossible for a long time to come.

In short, everything points to greater extremes of disaster for humankind rather than any amelioration. Most scientists here at the station believe we have crossed a threshold to a hotter planet, from which there will be no returning for millions of years – forever, as far as humans are concerned. Even so, if only the burning of fossil carbon could stop, then slowly, slowly, but surely as a huge ship coasting into port, the planet would start to cool again.

"But this is incredible!" Dialfi broke in, unable to contain jhmself.

Rowan could guess what had Dialfi so worked up. "You're thinking of the Fourth Commandment again, aren't you?"

Dialfi nodded. "If fossil carbon had been somehow connected to the Catastrophe — assuming, for the sake of argument, that this text does date so far back — then it might account for that strangest of all the Commandments."

"Then do you think there were so many stoves and furnaces in the world that they warmed everything up too much?" Orry asked.

"No, of course not," said Dialfi. "But if we let Yrssu keep on reading, maybe we'll be able to make sense of it."

"You're the one who's been interrupting jhm all night," retorted Orry.

So Yrssu resumed:

> I had never been able to believe it could be as bad as my Mom said. After all, the world outside our windows hummed on the same as ever, and didn't fall apart: the same ordinary, imperfect, beautiful, painful place it had always been. I figured once things got bad enough, people would fix them.

But I saw now that things could break too badly to be fixed.

What happens to a world where unpredictably changing weather patterns wreak havoc on agriculture and forests over vast swathes of the globe? Where the glaciers and slowly melting snow no longer feed the great rivers Ganjees, Bramaputra, Indus, Irawadi, Mikang, Yongzi, and Yellow, upon which upwards of two billion people depend? Where one tempest or firestorm after another strikes in the same place, before it's had a chance to recover? People will unite against a common enemy with noble courage, but in the face of a world turned upside-down, when they are hard-pressed to keep themselves and their families alive, they are apt to look for scapegoats, build walls, hunker down, and proceed to tear each other apart.

I gave it my best shot, looking as hard as I could for a way we might still fix things. I even ran simulations of what would happen if the whole world stopped emitting gaseous carbon today. Of course it was totally unrealistic: no more cars, trucks, trains, or container ships; no planes at all; no more coal-fueled power plants, not even to provide air-conditioning. No more heating or cooling of any sort by fossil fuels: no gas stoves; no propane refrigerators; none of that. No backup generators, not even for hospitals. Never mind how, or why – I only wanted to see how quickly it fixed things. One of the other researchers shook her head ruefully when she saw what I was up to. "Yep, we all try that scenario, sooner or later."

Much to my consternation, it made virtually no difference to the warming; not for thousands of years at any rate. How could that be? I must have done something wrong; I checked and rechecked my inputs, but everything was as it should be.

Then I understood. People have added so much gaseous carbon to the atmosphere that it will be a long time before the planet finishes reacting to what is already out there. All these projections you hear about what temperatures or sea level may be like in 50 or 100 years can lull you into thinking things will settle down after that. They won't. Even if we didn't burn another drop of fossil carbon, everything is going to keep getting worse, for a great many centuries to come. I hadn't understood this. And I know I'm not the only one.

Rowan glanced over at Orry, who was looking suitably stunned. As for Dialfi, jhe was scribbling furiously in a notebook. At breakfast the next morning, jhr eyes were smudged with the marks of a sleepless night; but would only say that jhe wanted to make certain of jhr inferences before telling them.

Chapter 16. The Cosmic Riddle

It's an old, old story; perhaps the oldest in the cosmos. Could this be the reason the stars are so eerily silent?

— Kassandra Morgan-Ávvu

Rowan and Yrssu plunged into translating Kassandra's diary for all they were worth. The Catastrophe had always sounded like a singular event. Now they saw it must have been a long, drawn-out period without a clear beginning or end, those living through it not knowing how bad it would get.

> We're headed deep into the heart of winter. Unlike last year, I know what we're in for. The sun barely lightens the northern sky at noon, even when it's not choked with clouds. Recently, to escape from cabin fever, Ingrid, Karl and I went out for a walk. We hadn't gone far before the sky began pulsing with a faint greenish glow, that grew to a psychedelic display in fuchsia, gold, and violet: the Aurora Australis.

I'd never seen it so brilliant before; the clips on the net don't do it justice. You have to be under it to really understand what it is, flashing and leaping across the canopy overhead. We sat down on a hillside to watch, cozy, despite the bitter wind, in our bright-red, one-piece survival suits.

"Truly a paradise," murmured Ingrid.

Karl nodded. "And it's all changing faster than anyone thought possible."

Ingrid the botanist rhapsodized, "It's true: not only lichens and mosses, but even grasses are spreading farther south than anyone expected for centuries to come. The wild caribou are already managing to forage on the mainland, too."

I knew about that, and also that some of the Kymrans had followed them, though none of the scientists seemed aware of this. "Maybe things have started changing so fast because they gave up on Climate Control," I said. Climate Control had been a last-ditch attempt by the Union of Countries to stave off the worst of the warming: filling the upper atmosphere with reflective particles, fertilizing the open ocean to drive plankton blooms that would sequester carbon at the bottom of the sea, that sort of thing.

My mom had not approved of such rash measures. She'd explained, "It's like when you twist the hot and cold knobs in the shower too quickly, and go from burning to freezing and back again. They're unlikely to improve matters, but could easily worsen them – especially if at great expense they do manage to ameliorate the heating for a while, but then give up. " She'd gone on to me how weather was a fundamentally chaotic system, and as such its behavior over anything but the shortest term was impossible to predict. "But that's not a bad thing, you, know, Kassandra! It's actually quite wonderful, because it means we live in a universe that is both fundamentally rule-driven and deterministic, yet whose future will always surprise us."

With all my heart, I wished she were sitting here with us, under the astonishing display of the aurora. The tears rolling down my cheeks were an admixture of missing her, and of her missing the beauty overhead.

Ingrid mused, "Yes, we're doing well enough here, but everything just keeps getting worse down north, doesn't it?" People at the research station always say "down north," with faint but unmistakeable superiority. "Rivers drying up and monsoons failing, widespread food shortages, refugees pouring from the most desperate to the less desperate places, military takeovers of one democracy after another."

I said, "What about that uncontained outbreak in Jingjinji?" To their startled stares, I added, "Everyone's been hearing about it; it's no secret."

Karl glanced at Ingrid. "The clandestine radios are getting out hand."

She just shrugged. "Better that they know what's happening."

All at once, her clinical tone was more than I could take. "Why? Why should we know what's happening? No one ever does anything about it but talk, talk, talk! All you smug scientists down here tabulating the gory details of melting ice and dying oceans, why don't you actually do something, instead of studying it to death?"

They looked at one another, disconcerted. Karl began to speak, but Ingrid cut him off with a sharpness that surprised me. "What exactly are we supposed to do, Kassandra, at this late stage? We did try, you know; for decades we tried desperately to sound the alarm, and set the world on a different course. Your mom tried with all her heart and might, you know she did, Kass. Your dad, too. We all did."

"And none of it made any difference, did it?" I said bitterly, sensing that Ingrid had stopped Karl from saying something altogether different, something that might have helped me. The feeling of being utterly alone, a perpetual outsider, which had abated somewhat during the months of working in Karl's lab, returned in full force.

"No, it did not," admitted Karl, gently and with a sorrow in his voice I'd not heard before. "At first our warnings were too alarmist to be worth listening to; later the situation was still too uncertain to merit the painful switch to sustainable energy. What a dirty word that always was, sustainability! A pie-in-the-sky ideal for starry-eyed dreamers! Just consider the fact that sustainability was always ridiculed as an impossible standard, and you will begin to glimpse the insane nature of the world-view we've been up against."

Ingrid added, "Really, it was failure of political will that made it impossible. Leaders preferring to grandstand and appeal to fantasies and fears; people allowing themselves to be thus deluded instead of shouldering the burden our times required. Deep down, most of them knew what choice they were making, I think. Knew that by doing nothing to change our course, they were ensuring their children's lives would be much harder, and their grandchildren's unimaginable. What must it be like to come of age in such times?"

I did not know how to begin to answer that.

Karl said, "Perhaps people will get back to living as hunter-gatherers, in the end. They might even be the happier for it; it's the lifestyle that our evolutionary history has fitted us for, after all."

"So that's your hopeful vision of the future, then?" I asked. "That's the best you scientists can come up with?"

Ingrid said, "Some kind of balance must be restored, Kass; the Earth simply cannot support so many of us. We're only facing up to reality, here; we're not cheering it on."

As soon as Yrssu had stopped, Dialfi asked, "Is that all you had to read for us tonight?"

"What do you mean, all?" said Rowan indignantly. "We worked really hard on that passage!"

"I know, but you could do a just bit more, couldn't you?"

A gaping yawn gripped Yrssu for long seconds.

"Maybe if you had some coffee?" coaxed Dialfi, bustling off to get a bit from Uncle Narv's precious store.

Thus fortified, Yrssu and Rowan, with the others alternately helping and dozing, worked on, into the blacknight. When the lamp shone out with the salmon-pink of early morning, Rowan awoke the others who'd drifted off one by one. Dialfi sat up slowly, rubbing jhr eyes, whereas Erkanni the sailor was wide awake in a moment. But only with difficulty did they manage to prod Orry out of the deep sleep of childhood.

Ingrid and Karl have been very busy lately, and the level of clutter in our living quarters has gotten worse than I've yet seen, which is saying something. The kitchen table and counter are crowded with several days' worth of dishes and pots that we shove out of the way to make room for the current meal. Karl doesn't seem to notice things like dishes one way or the other. Ingrid notices, but not so much as to distract her from more important things.

Tonight, though, Karl was in a conversational mood. Pushing a crumb around on his plate meditatively with one fingertip, Karl brought up the Sphinx.

"Hey," exclaimed Orry, sitting up straighter, "It's our old friend, the Finx!"

Karl went on, "Do either of you know the answer to her riddle: What creature goes on four legs in the morning, two legs at midday, and three legs in the evening?"

"One of those lizards that's so good at regenerating their limbs?" suggested Ingrid.

"Riddles aren't meant to be taken so literally, my love," chuckled Karl. "No, the answer is us humans, who crawl as babies, then stand up and walk on two legs, and finally hobble with the aid of a cane. Or consider it from an evolutionary point of view: we progressed from quadrupeds to bipeds, and what comes next?"

"Hobbling with a cane doesn't sound like progress," I objected.

"Perhaps the cane could be a metaphor for technology," said Ingrid.

"Technology: our glory and our downfall," agreed Karl. "It all started with the taming of fire – the road to hell if there ever was one, and paved in the traditional manner."

"How terrible that our ancestors thought to protect themselves from wild beasts," said Ingrid sarcastically, "and to increase their food sources by cooking."

I added, "And to tell stories by firelight, instead of just going off to sleep. Oh, and let's see, making pottery, forging metals, all of that."

Karl said, "Yet the cumulative effect of all these wonderful developments has been overpopulation and the destabilizing of ecosystems we depend on, to wrecking the very climate itself. It's a cruel snare that's been laid for us. We're curious and clever enough to glimpse the glories of the cosmos, only to find that we've engineered our own collapse."

"Yet perhaps we blame ourselves too much," said Ingrid. "Most planets with life develop stores of fossil carbon, that any intelligent species will eventually exploit to fuel an industrial revolution. We're probably just the latest instance of a tragedy played out countless times, in the unwritten history of the cosmos."

I thought about that. "What about an intelligent species that lived underwater?"

"That's an interesting thought," said Karl. "Yes, marine life might offer an exception to the rule: worlds peopled with dolphin-philosophers, or seal-poets, who never had the misfortune to tame fire."

"But we won't be getting any radio messages from the likes of them," pointed out Ingrid.

Karl shook his head. "Exactly. Of all the species who did develop technology, has there ever been a single one who answered the Sphinx's riddle?"

I was puzzled. "I thought the answer was us, growing up and growing old."

"But we have not grown up as we must, not yet," said Karl. "We cannot afford to behave like heedless little children anymore, we who are become so mighty. We who have been designed by natural selection to be prodigies of selfishness, whose highest instinctive generosity stops at family and tribe, must learn to think on a global scale, and consider the consequences of our actions for the millennia yet to come, to match the extent of our impact. How to grow up at last: that is the riddle we must answer, on pain of extinction." With that, Karl began to stack the dishes.

Chapter 17. To Walk in Darkness

As the research station includes representatives from all corners of the Earth, I've been amusing myself lately by imagining what an interesting mix their descendants would make. Skandinavians make up a substantial minority, being pre-adapted for this crazy place in that they actually enjoy snow, cold, and hardship. Then there are lots of Chilayans and Argentinians, a contingent of South Afrikahns, a sizable group from China, and of course plenty of already-mongrel Umerikkans like me, as well as a sprinkling of others from every-which-where. There's enough genetic diversity among them to make a creditable Ark, despite the small population size.

I'm guessing that any hypothetical distant descendants would likely be darker in skin tone. For one thing, the Skandinavians have quite a penchant for exposing as much skin as possible, on these fine spring days we've been having, and the others have taken to emulating them. Given the persistent local gap in the ozone layer, natural selection would surely favor the spread of whatever pigments existed in the gene pool.

The Kymrans, though, who work outside exposed to the elements, cover up against wind, cold, and sun alike. Assuming they remained a separate group, they could end up being the palefaces around here.

— Kassandra Morgan-Ávvu

Yrssu's orange hair shone bright in the lamplight, as jhe bent over the desk putting the finishing touches on the latest passage. They'd been working on it for several weeks. Rowan couldn't wait to read it aloud. The others had been so busy lately that only jhe and Yrssu knew what Kassandra had discovered about the odd little research station, where she'd been unwillingly brought after her mother's death.

Rowan ended an essay with a flourish, an effect destroyed in the attempt, as jhr sleeve sweeping over the wet ink smeared it. Jhe scowled at it a moment, then went over to sit by the fire, where Yrssu was beguiling the normally aloof cats. Orry and Erkanni were playing a lively card game on the couch.

"These cats remind me of mammút," Yrssu said. Rowan smiled at the ludicrous comparison. "Yes," Yrssu insisted, "for they live among people with dignity, as equals. I had not been guessing you Nuathans kept any such creatures about."

They spoke at length of the peculiar qualities of various animals; the ways cats smiled with their eyes but dogs with their cheeks and tails, the way rats' hands looked so very human when they ate; and went on to debate the relative virtues of ponies and caribou as riding animals, a discussion made the more vehement by each having had no experience of the other's favorite.

Orry and Erkanni started another round of cards. Rowan called up to Dialfi, “Aren't you done studying *yet*?”

“Not yet,” came the muffled reply from the high perch.

“Oh, come on; you know you always sail through the midterms, Dialfi!”

“Those of us chasing elusive scholarships can't afford to do less than spectacularly.”

“Fine, go ahead and study all night if you've a mind to, even though the next passage is full of the most amazing revelations about the Founding. It can wait, of course.”

“It will have to.” Dialfi said without even looking up.

Rowan sat down in the window seat again. “Yrssu, do you ever miss your homeland?”

“Kymrans say *Ang tarn arra kern*; meaning it is all right, even when it is not feeling so,” said Yrssu. “Sleeping in these houses of stone, with their thick walls, not hearing the wind, is very strange to me. It is like having one eye shut all the time. And when I am going out of doors, I find this town very noisy – like that city that Kassandra talked about, that *Shikággo*.”

Rowan said, “That's how I always feel, when we first arrive from Yngencloven.”

“It makes me want to curl into myself, like a snail in its shell; but I have no shell.” Yrssu sighed. “You Nuathans, it seems you are doing indoor things always. Studying, going to hear music, dancing.”

"What else can we do in the dark of the year?" Rowan asked, surprised.

Yrssu explained how among the Kymrans, people spent long hours out under the winter stars. Their tents were not large, and the dung fires made them uncomfortably stuffy. Also, in the Inner Waste, it did not rain so much as on the coast. So they shunned the lamp light and let their eyes adapt to the lights the heavens provided. The full moon, when it came out, seemed to them a blazing noon. But here in town, Yrssu felt fenced in by the regimen of lights and bells, and longed for open spaces where you could hear even the softest sigh of wind through the fir branches. "We call that wind *suf-souskh*," jhe said wistfully. "This place, Rowan, sometimes I am thinking it will be turning *me* to stone, in the end."

"I know what you mean. When spring comes, I can't wait to get out of Adare."

"Come outside now, then!" cried Yrssu. "I will show you!"

Rowan was glad enough of the excuse to follow Yrssu out into the night. Still, as they headed out beyond the cheerful, lamplit streets and up into the hills, Rowan found jhmself losing jhr nerve. Then again, Kassandra had been out in just such a dark winter night with sled dogs, in the deep snow no less, and had greatly enjoyed it.

As they got beyond the range of the streetlights, Rowan could see ragged clouds racing across an obsidian sky studded with stars. There was a half moon hanging just above the horizon, eerie and green, shedding little useful light. There was not much else to see out there, only blackness stretching out dizzyingly in every direction.

On the wide top of the largest hill, where they'd had the Opening Ceremonies, and where the Maypole would be raised come spring, they lay back against an accommodating boulder. Side by side they looked up, out, into the night. The unseen, the unknowable, loomed inescapably huge. Rowan thought about the plight of those in Kassandra's world battered mercilessly by the indifferent laws of physics; about the cold empty vastness of space, the incomprehensibly large distances the Humanual said lay between neighboring stars, and the even more staggering distances that separated galaxies. Suddenly, all jhe wanted was to be back in the light and warmth around Matti's hearth, comforted by the companionable chatter of friends, ignoring all that lay outside that tiny circle of solace.

Far down below, the lights of town shone from another world, one that seemed to have no more to do with them than did the stars. Rowan saw now that the lamps sprinkled through the town were the merest illusion of control over the great reigning darkness; nothing but an elaborate hoax that people had dreamed up to ward away a terrible truth written across the great width of the heavens. The reality was that there was nothing but this aloneness, this terrible exposure in the face of an unimaginable, indifferent, and everlasting night. Having seen how insignificant those little lights really were, it would be no comfort to return to them, either. Panic swelled in Rowan's throat and jhr breathing came shallow and quick.

Yrssu pointed past Rowan's nose to the right, then higher up: "See, there is the Albatross, and the Helix, and over there is the Great Ship, *Argonavissu.*"

"We call that the Sail," Rowan said faintly.

Yrssu, who had been watching Rowan closely, said, "When the weirding takes hold of you, there is but one thing to be doing." To Rowan's dismay, jhe launched into a strange, wailing song. It kept coming back to a falling cry, *wo-rae-da, wo-rae-da,* that invoked all the horror Rowan was sensing. Jhe almost hated Yrssu for it.

And then Rowan was pushed through to the other side of the awfulness; and the night and darkness held no more terror. Jhe gazed up at the wide bowl of stars ringed by the black silhouettes of firs, and breathed deeply. Never had jhe felt so free, not even in the height of summer in the mountain pasture.

"What does it mean, that song?" Rowan asked.

"It is about how we have two souls," Yrssu answered; "and one is always flying to a different place, far from the other. This is what is making the Kymran wander from place to place, for the two souls never will stay together for long."

"Do Nuathans have two souls as well?" Rowan wondered.

Yrssu shrugged. "That I am not knowing."

"Right now, I feel like I could walk up into the mountains, and never come back."

At this, Yrssu laughed. "I was not thinking that one of you would take to the winter air so easily."

They lay there in silence, gazing upwards. Rowan caught a strong waft of unwashed Kymran, but out here it wasn't so bad; it was even rather comforting to be able to smell one familiar person in the vastness of the world.

After a while, Rowan asked, "Where you come from, Yrssu, is there as much snow as Kassandra was describing, that day they went out sledding with the dogs?"

"Perhaps not so much, no." Yrssu looked thoughtfully at Rowan. "My people remember, though you Nuathans have no doubt forgotten, how the whole of this land used to be covered by kiloms of ice, right up to the tips of the mountains."

"But Yrssu, that can't be right. The Humanual says that Gaea raised the land 'from beneath the waters.'"

"Ice *is* water, is it not?" Then Yrssu began a sort of chant, "So it was, and so I shall tell you, that the world has always begun and ended in ice . . . ." Yrssu told how the world had countless beginnings and endings, with long intervening epochs of mildness, times of cool and pleasant water, and rolling mists and falling dew. Other times, the ice and snow had held sway; and the winds poured relentlessly down a dark hole at the world's center, bringing their chill tidings of the blackness of space, onto the very ground where mammút now grazed and caribou, and scattered bands roamed under blazing stars at the top of the world. "In the pictures we make of the stars, we read hints of the oldest stories, ones that people were telling in the beginning of time, back when first they learned speech."

Rowan objected, "But, Yrssu, in those days people lived far to the North, under different stars; stars that we have never seen."

Yrssu looked at jhm in surprise. "You are right, Rowan Yngling. I had not thought of that." Jhe continued, "Winter is the time for storytelling, and also for traveling. It is then that you can go easily over the ground by sled or by skis."

"What are skis?"

"Skinny little boats you tie onto your feet, that are floating you over the deepest snow." Seeing Rowan's skeptical look, jhe added, "It may not be as much as in Kassandra's day, but south beyond the mountains we are getting more snow than you have ever seen. Without skis, you would be up to your chest in it, freezing and cursing."

"But what's wrong with traveling in summer?"

"It is too hot and fly ridden, and people have scattered to their summer camps and are harder to find. Then, spring is too wet and muddy, and autumn is too busy with the roundups and harvest."

Rowan hadn't thought the Kymrans grew anything. "What do you harvest?"

"Meat, of course. The yearlings." Yrssu looked toward the high peaks of the Shield that separated Nuatha from the Inner Waste, hanging black against the clear, starry sky. "By now that will be all finished, and people will be gathered in the large winter-camps by the deep-flowing springs. The soothsingers will be telling the histories, and everyone but the oldest efts, who must watch the herds, will be gathered about the great fires eating and playing games and making gifts for their family and sweethearts. It is a good time of year, the early winter."

"You must miss it very much. Yrssu, what made you come to Nuatha?"

Yrssu looked away. "That is a story for another night, I am thinking."

Then Rowan took a deep breath, and voiced the hope that had been growing in jhm. "Sometime, Yrssu, would you show me the Waste?"

"Nuathans are not welcome there." Yrssu looked Rowan over critically. "Almost you could pass for one of us. – But you know nothing of how we live."

"I could learn!"

"Do you think it so easy? Children can lasso a caribou almost before they can walk; they are always practicing on each other. They strap on their first skis the winter after they come out of the cradle. Older children sew all their clothes and gear, and guard the herds in the bitter night of winter, going many tens of kiloms through wind and storm, fighting off the beorn and wolf as need be, staying warm in hollows of snow."

"What about the mammút?" Rowan asked eagerly.

"Yes, their ways take a good deal of learning, too." Yrssu's eyes grew distant. At last, jhe said, "There is so much that I cannot begin to tell you, that I know as I know how to breathe. Surely it the same for you, here among the *Siénttu*."

"I've never really felt I belong here," Rowan said softly.

"That does not mean you would find a home among my people," replied Yrssu, "any more than I have found one among yours."

Chapter 18. The Secret Colony

In those days, people swarmed like ants through all the lands, devoured the honeyed fruits of Earth . . .

— Exodus I: 8-9, The Humanual

On the last evening before the Ynglings headed home for Midwinterfest, they had gathered as usual in the living room. The entryway was crowded with luggage, from Orry's neatly lashed duffle to Rowan's overflowing rucksack. Birch logs burned brightly in the fireplace, and Aunt Matti had laid out an especially fine spread on the sideboard, meat pastries and potato rolls and fishcakes and all manner of little cookies.

What with the ordeal of the midterms, there had been no reading of Kassandra for many days. The delay had been hard on Rowan; the passage that awaited them was extraordinary. Now, with everyone settled expectantly about the fireside with their mugs of cider, Rowan and Yrssu held a whispered consultation.

"What's the matter?" asked Dialfi. "I thought you'd had this passage ready long since."

"Oh," Rowan told jhm airily, "it's just that we're deciding how to pronounce all these tricky place-names and whatnot."

Dialfi got up from the couch. "Well, if you need more time, there's something I have to look up at the library."

"No, wait!" cried Rowan, jumping up in dismay. "We're ready, aren't we, Yrssu?"

With a faint grin, Dialfi sat down again. Then, in the purple blacklight, Yrssu began to read aloud that night's passage, the last they would hear from Kassandra for several weeks.

I keep talking to the Kymrans whenever I get the chance, as part of my ongoing, and so far futile, quest to figure out the truth about this place. They don't seem to know either, but at least they don't give me the feeling they are shutting me out, the way the scientists do.

At the end of my second summer here, I still feel so much an outsider. The rapidly shortening days give me this panicky feeling that I'm running out of time to find my place. I can't go on like this, carried like flotsam by currents I don't understand.

Earlier today, I was deep in conversation with a plumber when Karl happened by. He took me by the elbow and led me towards the house, muttering, "Damn it all; I'd forgotten about that father of yours."

"Don't tell me that's another one of the station's crazy rules, that I can't talk to the Kymrans."

Sitting down at the kitchen table, he clasped his hands behind his graying head, and leaned back to gaze at the ceiling in a classic "thinking man" pose. I think he's still a bit shy of me. "Not exactly. It's just that we're not accustomed to outsiders, here."

"Are the Kymrans outsiders then?" I demanded.

"The workers? No– or, well, more or less; they're only here while we get things up and running. –Although lately, there's been some talk of whether we should reconsider their long-term role."

I was puzzled. "Isn't it up and running already?"

Karl looked away "What I mean to say is, there are good reasons for the rules that you find so onerous, whether or not you understand them."

Keeping a smooth face, I looked down at my hands clenched in my lap. "I'd understand perfectly well, if somebody would just explain what's really going on around here."

"Yes, well, that's been a bit difficult. You're a special case, Kassandra—there weren't supposed to be any more people joining us, you see."

"What, never? This is a research station, not a lifeboat on the Titannik!"

Karl grimaced. "It's been so hard to know how to talk to you, Kassandra. You're too young to be classed with the adults, but unlike the children who've grown up here, you know a great deal about the outside world. Well, I suppose there's no help for that . . . " He broke off, staring at the wall. Karl's one of those skinny, intense thinkers who has two states when it comes to talking, off or on. If I could just get the spigot into the "on" mode, I might actually learn something at last.

Karl took out the bourbon from the bottom cupboard, and poured himself a glass. Good; that might do the trick. He took a good swallow, and wiped his mouth with the back of his hand. "Kassandra, your mother – well. We were very good friends at one time. Even after she decided to leave the station, her work remained of the utmost importance to our goals."

"Fruit flies?" I said skeptically.

"She uncovered a conserved genetic basis to the timing of reproductive maturity," he said. "But never mind that. She reached out to us at the end, Kassandra, and we could hardly refuse, under the circumstances."

The 'circumstances' being my mother dying of pancreatic cancer. "I never asked to come here!"

"Ingrid and I are .very glad that you did, Kassandra," he said gently, "regardless of the complications that have ensued. You are one of us now, for better or for worse. I think, in time, you will find it much for the better."

"What the hell is that supposed to mean?"

Karl sighed. "Look, I'd have explained everything a long time ago, but it's been tied up awaiting a decision from Council all these months. . . oh, damn it all, I've had enough. After all, what can they do to either of us, if I just tell you? They certainly won't send you away once you know, will they? No, of course not!"

I held my breath. Karl took another sip of the whiskey. “So. This station, we’ve been isolated for quite some time, independent as it were, working on things, officially and, well, not so officially. At first, we were just another one of these polar research institutes that the various countries scattered around the continent, partly as placeholders for their geopolitical games. But little by little we’ve evolved into something much more.”

"How did that happen?" I asked as casually as I could.

“To tell you the truth, I’m pretty sure it started with the dogs – when those clueless bureaucrats up north decided to ban the dogs from the whole continent. It was just so idiotic. Dogs did less damage to the environment than gasoline-powered vehicles, even if they did get fed on seal meat! Those of us overwintering at Rothaira got to talking, then; you know, just sitting around over beers and whatnot, talking about our various governments’ shortsightedness and incompetence, and how much better things were in this wild alternate reality called Antarktikka, where there were no passports or money or any of that stuff, just people getting to be human, doing science, living life. I mean, even the clocks were shown up as purely imaginary constructs – we could have been on Washintun time, or Lundun time, or the time of Timbuktu, for all the difference it made. It made us realize how off track things had gotten from what really matters. But whenever we tried to go back and warn them about the melting or over fishing or heavy metals or destruction of the ozone layer or destabilization of deep-sea methane clathrates, or what the computronic models foretold about global warming, we couldn't make ourselves heard against the roar of trivia."

"People just never want to listen to that depressing stuff, do they?"

Karl shook his head. "Not enough to make a difference. So at last, we realized we had to make a fresh start, far away from all the craziness. We're calling it New Athens."

Yrssu couldn't resist interrupting jhmself to point triumphantly to the pair of words. "I told you that was the original name! You Nuathans who are forgetting so much!"

"New Athens?" I asked blankly.

"That was my idea," Karl said with shy pride. "It's to honor our intellectual forebears, the ancient Hellenes. Do you know, Kassandra, they intuited the existence of this continent without ever having set eyes on it? They assumed there must be a vast southern land to balance all the northern lands, and oddly enough, so it proved to be. Antarktikka, they named it: 'against the Arctic'; and later, when it was still undiscovered, people called it Terra Australis Incognita, The Unknown Southern Land."

"See," interrupted Rowan, "that must be where our word Terraus comes from!"

"It took us 2000 years after the ancient Hellenes' guess for people to actually reach it. To their great disappointment, they found the last continent to be completely uninhabitable; a frozen hell, as you so aptly call it. Yet this 'frozen hell' will be our salvation.

"And the changes are all happening so much faster than we expected. The western ice sheets are eroding before our eyes, and the mighty glaciers dammed up behind them won't hold out much longer. At the rate cracks are opening to melt water, even the massive ice sheet in the East may crumble into the sea before too long. They've had to abandon Amunsen/Skott, Vostokk, Dome K, Mosson and others along the coast, but we've hung on, here in our sheltered bay.

"Meanwhile, the lichens and grasses keep spreading south year by year. The caribou are already thriving, and we'd soon be able to build up larger herds of sheep and cattle, except that it would get us noticed by the damned bean-counters. Overall, though, it's been easier than you might think; these days especially, with government oversight getting more and more spotty.

"Even as we speak, the Second British-Nors Geomorphological Survey is hard at work setting up caches against future need while they go about their work. And of course, this is an obvious place for several comprehensive seed banks, ostensibly for a quite different purpose than the one we intend. Then there are the strategic reserves that a whole different set of bureaucrats thinks they're in charge of. In short, we've been secretly storing food and equipment for a long time, under all sorts of pretexts."

I sat very still, doing my best to hide my astonishment and shock, hoping the long-awaited monsoon of information was not yet over.

"Sooner or later, Kassandra, the world out there is really going to break down; I mean, completely. We mean to ride that out as best we can, and save as much as we can from the coming flood."

"What, in this little place?" I have to say, I was not impressed.

"Oh, this station is only the colony's jumping-off point." Karl waved his arms, looking more excited by the moment. "One day we'll board the ships that will take us to our real home, our anarchic allotopia, to the other world that turns out to be closer than we ever imagined."

Anarchic allotopia, no less. Karl was definitely in full swing. "Where, exactly, are you talking about?" I asked, wondering wildly if this could have anything to do with that possibly habitable planet they'd recently discovered in Alfa Sentarry or thereabouts.

Karl answered, as though it was blindingly obvious, "Mainland Antarktikka. After the great melt is over. I wish I could see with my own eyes how it will be one day, the mammút wandering through the lush grasslands, the rocky earth greening, the barren world coming to life. There's a mountain ash that Ingrid planted long ago, that flourishes under glass at Mikmurdo base. Someday, that tree shall breathe the open air. And such a moat as we'll have – no one will be able to touch us!

"But everything depends on how things progress in the next decade or two – the climate, the politics, the inevitable wars for ever-scarcer resources. If the world warms too quickly, oil-starved nations might break all the pacts to go prospecting, and that would spell trouble for us. (It was touch and go a few years back, with Oil Borealis wanting to start operations in the Weddell Sea, but luckily the ecoterrorists managed to chase them off, though at a heavy cost, poor bastards; and no one's dared to try since). Yes," Karl mused, "the next few years will have the trickiest shoals. Still, if we can just manage to get through them, your grandchildren will not want for schooling, medicine, or food."

I sat there, not knowing what to say. Either Karl was completely off his rocker, or – the alternative, I could hardly grasp.

Dialfi broke the stunned silence. "This is absolutely *astonishing*! We've never had an eye-witness account of the Founding."

"It is, isn't it?" Rowan said, gratified to see they were properly awed by the evening's revelations. "It goes right back to the Catastrophe and the Exodus and everything."

Dialfi continued, sounding more troubled than pleased, "But if the Founders knew that fossil carbon had caused the Catastrophe, why did they not say so plainly? The Fourth Commandment states, 'You shall not burn the heat of a thousand summers in a single winter, nor take more than the fruit of the season, lest the core of the world-tree become rotten.' Why in Gaea's name would the Humanual leave out the real reasons behind such a law, and justify it with rank mythology?"

Yrssu grumbled, "Rank mythology? You Nuathans have no sense of poetic truth."

"That's not so, Yrssu. I once heard a bard tell of the Exodus." Erkanni sang a few haunting phrases: "Ember Wavedancer led them through starfall and moonrise, the great ships fleeing the dying lands.'"

"Wow, you sing really well!" said Orry.

"All selkies do," Erkanni said modestly. Yrssu shook jhr head at this nonsense.

"Then what happened?" Orry asked.

Erkanni said, "I forget the exact words; but it was something about Layf Life-giver and the mehemoths Audumla and Gefion, whose stamping strides awoke volcanoes that melted the rivers of ice into rivers of water, and the rain of ash helped bring the land to seed."

Rowan laughed. "Yeah, and their mighty dung piles must have helped bring it to seed too."

Erkanni said in mock amazement, "Gaea below, did our Rowan just make a joke?"

"It happens, every so often," answered Dialfi. "The thing you have to understand about Rowan is that jhe's fundamentally too joyful to have much sense of humor."

Rowan glared at them both. "So, *anyhow*, if this diary really does date back to the Founding—"

Orry interrupted, "What is this *Founding* you all keep talking about, anyway?"

"Oh, you know, Orry," said Rowan, "how people came here fleeing the Catastrophe." Orry still looked blank, so jhe added, "Don't you remember the Nine-fold Pestilence? It's recited every Sunreturn: 'They loathed to drink of the river'? And the locusts swarming over the crops, the hailstorms smashing them to pulp, and the plague, and the cyclones?"

"Oh, and the frogs!" Orry exclaimed. "So the Founding was when they found Nuatha."

"Don't be silly, Orry; it's not that kind of found, like finding your mittens!" Rowan said, exasperated.

Dialfi said, "See, Orry, it's one thing to find land, and quite another to found a civilization."

"What's the difference?" asked Orry, obstinately.

"The difference is that we're reading from the book they left us, and not just living on the land they delivered us to. Through the Humanual and our traditions, we have an unbroken connection to our past, and to the earlier civilization that gave rise to the Founders."

Orry objected, "Well, if our Founders were so great, how come they wrecked most of the world then?"

"They didn't, that was all the others," said Rowan. Jhe intoned, "Hear, now, and listen: for this is the account of the Exodus and Founding:

> In those days, people swarmed like ants through all
> the lands, devoured the honeyed fruits of Earth;
> The deepest oceans combed of shell and fish.
> As locusts take no heed of future wants,
> But fill their greedy bellies past all need,
> So they laid waste the wide and pleasant world
> And made a meager mite where wealth had teemed.
>
> With fumes of ceaseless toil they filled the air,
> Burned deep-buried wealth of summers past,
> Made kindly sun a torment; turned fertile field
> to scrub land bare; made a rocky waste
> of valley green and hidden forest glen,
> The marshes cracked, the waste and desert spread.
> They felt the world turned hard against them then.

Rowan hesitated, forgetting the next verse, but Dialfi had meanwhile taken the Great Book out of its case on the mantelpiece, and went on:

"The seas lapped up and up, and drowned
the shining cities; towers crumbled down,
War, scourge and savage might held sway.
of billions lost, a remnant found new land—"

"See?" Orry pounced on the word. "They found it, just like I said. I still don't see why they don't call it the Finding."

Rowan rolled jhr eyes, but no one troubled themselves to argue any more, for it was very late, and they had to catch a train in the morning.

Chapter 19. Midwinterfest

Those of us from the northern hemisphere found it confusing enough for spring to arrive in November and winter in May. Still worse was the awkward timing of the festival of light observed each December, by pagan, Abramist, Hindu, and atheist alike. To celebrate the transcendence of the human spirit over worldly darkness at the height of the southern summer was absurd. Antipodeans that we are, we simply turned the calendar on its head to realign our habits with the seasons. So November once again heralded winter, and everyone was happy; everyone, that is, except the sprinkling of Aussies, Kiwis, Chileans, Argentinians, Batswana, and South Africans, who called us hidebound northern chauvinists.

— Kassandra Morgan-Ávvu

The ascending train puffed slowly through the hills rising from the Adare Valley towards the Victoria range, whose mountains formed one end of a coastal shield fully three thousand kiloms long. A thin layer of snow coated the foothills, casting light in the starry darkness, while far over the sea, a brooding, reddish glow was slowly fading from the undersides of clouds in the North. Now they were in the darkest part of the year.

Rowan, Dialfi, and Orry dozed during much of the journey. Aunt Matti supplied them from her bottomless basket of comestibles, while Uncle Narv slipped them the occasional tip from his flask of grog. The familiar, comforting pattern wrapped them in its quilt-folds for another year.

Far was waiting for them at the depot with the big sleigh and a bundle of rugs still warm from the hearth, and they flew over the icy road with silver harness bells ringing like stars, or at least the way Rowan imagined stars must ring. As they came through the door at Yngencloven, such a confusion of hugs and greetings clogged the entryway that it was some time before they managed to sort themselves out, put away cloaks and bags and mysterious bundles, and at last to sit, holding warm mugs of Grandmother's pungent fruit soup, under the glow of the great lamp lit only upon special occasions. They were home, and everything smelled right, even the dust. Snatches of song that came from the kitchen meant that Matti had already taken over the cooking. The tall spinning wheel in the living room hummed its graceful dance with Mar's eloquent fingers, her treadling foot keeping time. The porch door banged, and then came the sound of Far knocking each boot three times before sitting down to take them off.

Anno was sitting demurely at one end of the couch. Rowan peeped at her surreptitiously. There was no denying it; she was utterly different. Her face was rounder, and her eyes had that slightly wounded look that the eyes of the newly Changed always seemed to have.

She was clothed in loose white robes that hid a good deal; no doubt her new form took a lot of getting used to. Rowan was just as glad that it be hidden a while longer. An uncle much younger than Far had become a man when Rowan was little, and had come to the May fair with worn, grizzled cheeks. His eyes had been restless and sunken, his figure gaunt. Rowan hated the thought of ever Changing, and hoped for a good many decades yet before jhr time came. There was no telling, for everyone's clock ran differently. Anno's efthood had been shorter than usual, cutting off that precious time of moving through the world with only oneself to care for. At least she'd turned out to be female—unlike men they often enjoyed an extended old age.

Anno smiled at Rowan, and Rowan, somewhat ashamed of jhr thoughts, came to sit by her. Anno grasped Rowan's hand, paying no mind to jhr slight start at the touch, and said, "Little couz, it *is* me in here, you know." But the smile was not as carefree as of old, and there were new lines, that spoke of suffering, around her mouth.

Doing the round of evening chores with Orry, Rowan listened with contentment to the sighing and shifting of cows beyond the small circle of lantern light. Several calico barn cats, old friends of Rowan's, graciously offered their bony heads to be caressed. In the roomy warmth of the hay-smelling barn Rowan took deep breaths until jhe was seized by a fit of sneezing. Everything was just the same as always, despite Anno's change. If Rowan had guessed how many long years were to pass before they would again be so gathered, jhr heart would not have been as light.

The next few days were a blur of preparations. It seemed to Rowan that the recurring customs linking the years together suggested that time itself could be reshuffled, so that each Midwinterfest came right after the last, with the intervening months falling away. Imagine how it would feel at Grandmother's age of nearly 150 years old, to look back on all the holidays!

Under Matti's tolerant eye, they jostled together to bake in the warm kitchen, their feet scritching in spilled sugar, their clothes covered with flour, filling the huge stoneware oven and all the countertops with tray after tray of cookies, from the delicate cones of krumkacka to buttery sunbuckles, nut-filled sandymen and pungent, chubby gingerbread people. Rowan got yelled at for licking jhr fingers and for eating too much of the dough ("Behave yourself, or Cinderclaws will put coal in your stocking!" Orry told jhm), and, as always, Grandmother refused to let anyone else make the kringerl, saying she did not know what they would do when she was gone, for they were a hopeless lot when it came to pastries.

When they'd had their fill of baking, they made candle lanterns in tissue covers, and paper snowflakes to put in the windows. Gathering in the living room after dinner, they told family stories of relatives long dead whose legends lived on: the old uncle who as a child watching the sheep alone had seen, so he said, a leather-clad kobold disappear right into the side of the mountain; the great-great-grandfather who had in a rage of grief broken the bull's neck with his bare hands after it killed his wife; the distant cousin who had swum a hundred kiloms across the open ocean when her sweetheart had sailed off without her, and had been rescued by a pilot whale. Rowan wondered if jhe would ever do anything that jhr descendants would tell of long after jhe was gone. Then jhe wondered about all the people stretching back whose stories had been forgotten. This business of remembering was like building a sand tower of drippings that collapsed as fast as it grew. Then again, perhaps the stories were lived over and over, within a family. Any of them might be the spitting image of some ancestor or other, with the same quirks, the same passions. Who alive could say it wasn't so? So maybe the world itself remembered the stories, as people lived them over and over.

At one point, Rowan slipped out of the warm kitchen and stepped outside. It was a clear and bottomless black sky, so cold it took your breath away. The majestic procession of stars shone steadily through the flickering streamers from the aurora. This was what the Kymrans in their caribou-skin tent villages were seeing, far to the South. Jhe pictured it as Yrssu had described it: efts guarding the herds against marauding wolves; parties of men tracking lost animals and hunting the fearsome, snow-white beorn; small children playing at lassoing one another as they pranced, fingers curled by their foreheads to simulate antlers, while their mothers gossiped and drank coffee.

The day that opened Midwinterfest, the family gathered in the living room and sat solemnly while Far got out the Humanual and found the right page. He read the somber passage from Exodus, that spoke of the violence people had inflicted upon each other, their fellow creatures, and the planet itself, before they had learned to restrain their fearsome power and greed. It was painful to listen to, but admonished them that the only way to keep from falling back into the terrible ways of the past was to remember what had been done, by people little different from themselves.

One of the most poignant readings told of the now-vanished cousins to humans.

The great apes evolved long ago, from the five-handed monkeys who scampered in the canopy of the endless forest that in those days covered much of the Earth. Apes were larger than monkeys, and like us were large-brained and without tails; yet unlike us, hair covered their bodies, and they walked on four legs, and were male or female from birth. They had large brains and clever, tool-wielding hands; and faces that showed their feelings with a grimace or a gentle smile even as we do; and they also lived in tribes, and raised curious, mischievous children up through their long and heedless years. The apes were our closest relatives, and walked the Earth with us for long ages, until like hapless siblings in a vicious dynasty, they fell victim to the most brutal and ambitious claimant to the throne.

These were the names of the four non-human apes: shy Orangutan,

with its long orange hair; huge Gorilla, benign and broad-backed, whose dark hair was mingled with silver; clever Chimpanzee, smaller than us and bandy-legged, but immensely strong; and its sister species, the pleasure-loving Bonobo.

The apes were on this Earth until shortly before the Exodus, but now, save our lineage, are as extinct as the trilobites. They were our brothers and sisters, and we in the frenzy of our greed would not share this sustaining Earth with them; those who tried to make a space for them were too few and did too little, and now they are lost beyond hope of recall. We mourn their passing and accuse ourselves, the human race, of a great and irredeemable sin.

For we knew what we did, and would not change our ways.

After the reading was over, the lights were put out all over the house, both the electric lamps and the lanterns, the candles, the stove, and last of all the fire in the living room hearth. The echoing glow of the phosphorescent lamps slowly dimmed, eventually to die as well since there was no light to renew them.

Thus did the three-day Solstice ceremony begin with darkness, even as the world began with darkness, even as new life begins with darkness. All things come out of darkness, and all things must return to it. The moment of Solstice was a tipping point of the year's circuit, when they swung from a time of increasing darkness to one of increasing light, a moment of hope at the nadir of winter. By ancient tradition, therefore, the day leading before was spent in bleak darkness, in hunger, and in somber reflection. No lamp or candle would be lit, and the house waited cold and dim. There was no need to cook, for they would fast, taking only a scanty meal of cold fish, seaweed, and water to remember their ancestors' hardship in the early days of the Founding. There was little talk, but each went jhr own way, thinking on the deeds done in the past year; what might be bettered, and what was best forgotten and forgiven.

In the afternoon of the next day, whose unchanging darkness was marked only by the faint ticking and tolling of the clock, they gathered again in the living room, and Far began the chant traditional for the day of the Midwinter solstice. The ancient and renowned song cycle had, as Grandmother reminded them every year, been sung at winter solstices throughout the world stretching back to times even before the Exodus. It began with high notes that Far could only reach by singing very quietly, in the gentlest of tones:

Comfort ye.
Comfort ye, my people.

As the melody descended, so Far could sing the soothing words more strongly:

Seek ye comfort in our new refugium.

And cry unto all,
that our struggle is accomplished,
and our iniquity
is pardoned.

After that, Narv with his deeper voice rumbled out the joyous song about valleys being uplifted, and the seas and dry land being shaken, that told of the legendary geological upheavals in the early days of settlement. Rowan listened to the old, familiar words with ears newly attuned to their meaning, thinking of Kassandra and the Colony and how it must have been for them in those days. How it would have been to escape, while the rest of the world they had known was being flooded and destroyed.

Then it was time to rekindle the flame. Some used electric sparkers, but the Ynglings preferred a slower and more ceremonial way. Mar got down the box where the fire hammer and anvil were stored, together with a wad of lichen (the kind called gaffer's beard) that they had carefully set aside before the autumn rains came. Beginning with Grandmother, the eldest, they tried in turn to strike a shower of sparks from the stone anvil with the sharp-edged hammer, at first just making a show of the lovely lights (like the first suns in the dark of the newborn cosmos, Rowan had always thought), then after everyone had vied to make the greatest possible shower (Orry energetically scattering the sparks far and wide), they lit the fire in earnest, carefully catching the sparks on the threads of lichen, feeding the tiny flame with bits of chaff and twigs as the tendrils of smoke rose up, and puffing gently on it, adding the larger sticks while arguing over the best way to place them and whether Rowan was blowing too hard or not hard enough, until finally it was crackling mightily and they could place the traditional yew log, and sit back in the lovely flickering light and breathe the aromatic scent, evocative of all the past Midwinters stretching back as long as Rowan, or Grandmother for that matter, could remember.

Mar and Far began the song of rekindling, and after the first verse they all joined in. In town, people would go to hear the Midwinter song cycle performed by practiced musicians, and it was always broadcast on the skywave, too, though in outlying regions the quality of transmission was poor. Rowan had heard it in Adare one year. The blending of all the instruments and voices was awe-inspiring: the bowed viows and reedy sloons, the cimbalachord, buzzing krumporns, clarion silverhorns and the great barrel drums with their padded mallets making distant thunder. Still, the Ynglings liked making the music themselves, even if they had to do without the instrumental accompaniments. Anno had played the clavichord for them in past years, but said she was too out of practice to do it justice this year. Her poignant mezzo was a welcome addition, for this might be the last year of Orry's piping child's voice, so tall was jhe growing—

O thou that tellest good tidings Nuathan,
get thee up into the high mountain.
The glory of summer's sun
is risen upon thee.

(Of course, the sun would not really rise for another couple months. But the year turned a corner at Midwinterfest; from now on they could be assured that the darkness was on the wane.)

This year, they also performed the part of the song meant for new imagoes. Anno was brought to a place of honor by the hearth, dressed in pale blue and with a crown of rosemary resting on her dark curls. Grandmother, Matti, and Mar began the Song of the Fire, whose wild and disturbing strains Rowan had only heard once or twice before:

But who may abide the day of its coming?
For it is like a refiner's fire . . . .

The notes swirled up and around, like smoke blown by the wind from a bonfire, only to fall back towards the hard earth. Anno listened with a remote and inward look.

Next Far and Narv joined in to sing a plaintive, echoing song that made shivers run down Rowan's spine:

O Eft,
Where?
Where art thou gone?
O grave,
Here is a victory.
The sting of Change is death,
Yea, the sting of Change is death,
For we all shall die.

Rowan dared to glance at Anno and saw tears running down her cheeks; Far's and Mar's were wet as well. After that, Rowan kept jhr eyes firmly on the floor.

Then Narv sang the Mystery in his deep baritone. Grandmother valiantly took the part of the trumpet with her small reedy-pipe, playing with swaying body and one eye shut.

Behold.
I tell you a mystery:
Though we were born to live eternally,
We shall all be Changed.
For this incorruptible must put on corruption,
And this immortal must take on mortality.
We shall be Changed,

And here, Narv sang a note so out of place, so surprising and out of tune that Rowan opened jhr eyes, sure he had made a terrible mistake. But the next moment he resolved it; so maybe it had all been part of the music, part of the change that was at first unimaginably wrong-feeling, but somehow, so the song insisted, could yet be made right in the end.

We shall all be Changed.

Grandmother on the reedy-pipe repeated the triumphal run of notes one last time. Then the imagoes clustered around Anno, and held her, and patted her on the back; and Rowan felt very small and insignificant, and most of all, very glad to remain an eft for a long time to come.

The cousins were gathered in the attic bedroom. At last, Rowan found the voice to ask Anno what it was like, Changing. They all listened to Anno's quiet, halting words. "Not for nothing is it called the Small Death. It's nearly impossible to describe, or even to quite remember, all but some vague impressions. And much of what I do recall, I'm forbidden to speak of. They say it's a mystery, each one must face it in ignorance, and it is well that a veil of darkness falls over it afterwards."

"But the monks must know," said Dialfi.

"The monks . . . I suppose so."

Orry asked, "How did you know when it was time to go away?"

"Everything feels different, like someone else has gotten inside you — it's all prickly and wrong. And you can't seem to stop talking, all sorts of nonsense, whatever comes into your head." She broke off, staring at the intricate patterns in one of Mar's rugs. "The monks take care of you through the worst of the physical change . . . it's not very comfortable, everything is achy and strange, but there's nothing to be done and you just have to get through it somehow. Oh, I don't know how explain it to you! Sometimes my skin still feels too thin, there is so much beauty suffused through the world, and also so much pain. It's all closer to the bone now. The monks taught us all sorts of things to help us adjust, but still . . . ."

"Like what?" asked Dialfi curiously.

"Oh . . . how efts are complete to themselves but imagoes need one another."

Orry snorted, and Anno added, "No, I don't mean like that, I mean like in marriage, where two people join their souls into one—"

This time Orry laughed aloud, and made a crude gesture. Rowan slapped at jhr hand, but Orry said, "Come on, tell us the truth, won't you, Anno: the imagoes always act like it's so serious and dreadful to become one of them; but isn't it kind of fun, too?"

Anno smiled sadly at Orry. "For many, it seems to be so. For myself, I fear I may never again find such easy joy as I once had, in Kiril's company."

"What happened with Kiril?" Dialfi asked softly. Rowan had wanted to ask this too, but had been afraid of hurting Anno. Now jhe saw that Dialfi had done the kinder thing, by giving Anno a chance to speak of her boon friend.

"Kiril . . . that was another life, a story that happened to someone else. We had so many adventures together; shoulder-to-shoulder we faced the world, ready for anything. It was as easy as breathing, as rolling out of bed on a fine morning. . . I thought it would always be like that. Even though you hear the whispers, the tragedies, you think it is different for you, that you have a bond like no one else, a bond that can withstand any shock, adapt to any Change. Yet the pair we made does not exist anymore, except in my flawed memory."

"I don't understand," said Rowan. "Why would the Change make so much difference?"

"I just don't know how to explain it to you. It was a bit like losing your sense of balance; it was a kind of blindness, and then a new kind of sight, with different shades than you'd seen before. The old bond was dissolved; our names turned to ashes in the other's mouth. There are things one cannot choose, it seems."

"Do you wish you had never paired with Kiril then?" Rowan made bold to ask, remembering Far's injunction to them about boon friends.

"I do not." Anno looked off into the distance. "I only wish it could have lasted always."

After a long sleep, they awoke to the third, and more lighthearted, day of festivities. Matti had laid out a generous spread of food on the side table, that would be replenished throughout the day. There would be caroling, and conversation, and games like Marco's bluff and Hide & Beckon, in which the imagoes joined as eagerly as children, even Anno with her newfound dignity.

The efts had brought boughten gifts from Adare. They gave Mar a small silver coffeepot to replace the one that had been in service for so many years that it looked like a porcupine, with all the screws plugging its many holes; and gave Far an electric headlamp that pleased him very much, to ease his winter chores. For Grandmother they had a fancy music box whose tune they'd happily argued over for a whole afternoon. To Anno they gave a small book of poetry. It brought tears to her eyes when she first looked into it; but then seeing their distress, she laughed through the tears.

The homemade gifts from the farm-bound imagoes were no less appreciated. Mar had woven them capes in dizzyingly complex patterns of pewter, chalk, midnight blue, forest green, all the sober colors of town in winter. Far had made funny little wooden carvings for them, as he did every year: Dialfi got an owl, Orry a seal, and Rowan a little tusked mehemoth, much to jhr delight. And Grandmother had the rest of the runes copied out for them.

While the others went off to work on supper, Grandmother and the three youngsters curled up on the couch with a big patchwork quilt tucked around them. But this year, instead of Grandmother telling them a story, they began at last to tell her about what Yrssu had helped them to read of the runes.

"The book was written by someone named Kassandra, who lived in the days of the Founding," Rowan began.

"Right in the middle of the Exodus, and the Catastrophe, and everything!" Orry put in.

"Goodness, that must have been exciting," said Grandmother.

"I think it was more awful than exciting," Rowan told her. "Their whole world was falling apart, before their eyes." Their voices tumbled over one another like leaping mountain streams in their eagerness to tell her all they'd learned: just how cold it had been in those days (Rowan quoting Kassandra, said, "Whiteness of snow and ice stretching as far as the eye could see, with not so much as a blade of grass"), the chaotic and dangerously overpopulated world the colonists had left behind, and their determination to solve the problem of how humans were to live in the world without destroying it.

Grandmother, as though feeling for the words deep in the cupboard of her memory, intoned, "The day will come when our world will again face a great change, as the future and past mingle like criss-crossing waves. Ordinary events will spiral outwards towards great consequence; terrible sins may be redeemed; and great struggles won, or else utterly lost."

They stared at her, then Dialfi asked gently, "That didn't come from the Humanual, did it, Grandmother?"

In her regular voice she said, "I believe I heard it long ago, from Granny Rilla, who would have had it from the gnomads."

"Kymrans, Grandmother," Rowan corrected her. "They don't like being called gnomads – didn't Granny Rilla ever tell you *that*?"

Chapter 20. Laying Low

The audacity of this little research station! In the guise of cutting costs, the station has become almost entirely self-supporting in terms of both food and energy, all the while keeping up with their research. The original reason for coming here was to study the changing climatic conditions of the high latitudes, and that turns out to be highly relevant for the Colony's own survival. The glaciologists keep the modelers abreast of rapidly evolving conditions, and the modelers continually update their simulations of climate. Lately, they've also been dabbling in geopolitical forecasts, though only for in-house consumption.

Meanwhile, the molecular botanists are developing cold-tolerant crops that grow well in low-angled light. Yet the fisheries scientists insist that the sea will be our best source of food for a long time to come. They are thinking not only of fish and the seaweed, but also of krill. They've worked with the station's engineers to build huge filter pumps that collect it in shimmering masses, figuring that what supports the great whales could likewise—

"Since you are not raising your hand, I take it you agree with the decision of the Thirty-Fourth Convention, Rowan-dyu?" Sa Krusi's voice broke through Rowan's absorption in the passage Yrssu had translated over the holiday.

Sa Krusi had been droning on about some apparently significant constitutional convention or other, from hundreds of years ago — Rowan could never keep them all straight.

"I had almost dared to hope that what you were reading with such absorption was your notes concerning the Ferelist Convention of the forty-second century." Sa Krusi took a rumpled sheet of paper from his desk, and dangled it disdainfully from his finger and thumb. "Your most recent essay, Rowan-dyu, displayed a similar lack of respect for your studies. The hastily contrived and poorly thought out arguments, and the outright tautologies contained therein, were not of such a value as to merit the effort required to sift them from the smears and smudges."

Rowan writhed uncomfortably in the hard seat.

"You come from a worthy family," the Sa continued. "If you do not wish to belie their hopes in you, you must stop sleepwalking through your life, and set your mind to serious endeavors. For a start, you may restrict your daydreaming to some less important part of your day than my classroom."

After school, Rowan evaded a sympathetic Erkanni by going out a side gate. Shouts and laughter rang out from the nearby schoolyard, and chattering students streamed past, as jhe stood under a bright yellow streetlamp reading the rest of the passage. Yrssu's handwriting in Anglic was stubbornly unconventional, and Rowan found it almost as much trouble to decipher as the runes.

. . . .figuring that what supports the great whales could likewise sustain people.

The engineers for their part have been hard at work turning out other marvels of robust technology. These include geothermal heating for homes and greenhouses, simple engines that can run on anything from firewood to dung, wind turbines able to generate electricity or run machinery even in the midst of katabatic gales.

The lack of soil is one of the biggest obstacles. Most of the tilled fields go to make hay for the precious mammút, remnants from a rewilding experiment that was defunded some years back. Difficult as it is to keep them fed, they're expected to be essential terraformers over the long term. The Kymrans take especial delight in them. They also look after the herds of caribou, which thrive on lichen and moss. Originally brought by Norwegian whalers, they've run wild on some of the nearby islands for over a century, and seem quite at home here.

Last night (if you can call it night, when the sun circles us endlessly like a wolf on the prowl), a ship nosed its way into the harbor. No one had sighted it until it was nearly here, what with the low-hanging clouds and drizzle. All summer we've watched the horizon with fearful eyes, as distant ships go by towing tall, ungainly oil rigs towards the Weddell Sea, praying none come close enough to—

Dana stepped into the pool of lamplight. "You look deep in thought, Rowan; I almost didn't recognize you."

"Next time I'll have to try harder, then. What do you want?"

"From you of all people, Rowan, what I want, in a word is — intelligence!"

"Funny." Rowan's eyes were drawn down to the page again.

"What is it that has you so absorbed, anyway? Could it be an assignment from Sa Krusi?" grinned Dana. "I heard about your richly earned dressing-down; I only wish I could have been there to enjoy it in person."

Stung beyond endurance, Rowan burst out, "Sa Krusi has no idea what he's talking about. Serious endeavors! I guess it's a serious endeavor to be translating a lost document that dates back to the Founding. Yrssu's been helping us read it."

"Translating. . ." Dana looked blank for a moment, then chortled, "Ah, so that's what you and that scruffy gnomad have been playing at together. Translating a document from the Founding that just happens to be written in gnomad gibberish; that makes perfect sense."

"I'll have you know, Dana, that Dialfi takes our translation seriously."

"Actually, it was Dialfi I wanted to ask you about," said Dana, amending jhr tone somewhat. "I wondered if jhe'd had any word about a scholarship yet."

"If so, jhe's not said a word of it to me," answered Rowan.

"The Akademy would be remiss indeed not to offer such a scholar full aid," said Dana sympathetically. "I know it's been a difficult couple of years on your farm—"

"We're fine," snapped Rowan.

"Of course, of course." Dana held up jhr hands and backed away. "Well, give jhm my best, and all that, will you?"

Rowan read the rest of the passage Yrssu had given jhm.

> . . . praying none come close enough to discover our hidden refuge.
>
> After the initial panic, it turned out to be one of our own ships, returned from its final voyage to the outer world with a last set of supplies.
>
> There was a solemn mood throughout the Station, and many stopped their work to watch

the cranes swing load after load onto the dock, and to help cart them away. You could hear snatches of the new anthem, "Arise ye Sapient", being sung here and there. The effort to sound cheerful and brave was palpable and strained enough to have the opposite effect, on me at least.

As we stood there in the pouring rain, watching the unloading of the ship, I groused to Ingrid, "What noble settlers we are after all, bent on infesting the last virgin wilderness. It'll be Wee Cabin on the Plains all over again: make way for the railroads, and goodbye to the buffalo."

"Now, Kass," Ingrid answered, "It's not at all the same. It's been over 30 million years since this place had a terrestrial ecosystem, and we're going to bring it back – just like we did the mammút." Her voice was almost like a prayer. "We humans can be creators as well as destroyers."

"You sound like those Gaea worshipers." I said. Ingrid looked puzzled, so I explained, "Haven't you heard? Gaea is to be our new deity: the first one ever to be scientifically vetted and verified."

"Oh, that. Well, I suppose it's an improvement over the old gods," said Ingrid.

A squall blew through and obscured the harbor, and flung the rain into our faces. It seems like for my entire life, the end of the world had been just around the corner.

I have finally learned what those inoculations were about, back when I'd first arrived at New Athens. I ought to be furious for what they did to me, without so much as a by-your-leave, but I suppose, retroactively, I more or less consent. I mean, it actually sounds pretty cool, why these scientists decided to change everyone. And my mom's research provided the key!

They make no small plans, these New Athenians, I'll give them that. In order to restructure society to one "more befitting the human spirit," as Ingrid put it, they have found a way to upend gender roles and demolish sexism once and for all, or so they fervently hope. They have genetically engineered themselves, every last one of them. It was a sort of initiation rite for anyone joining the Colony. Developmental biology being what it is, the effects fall not on them, but on their children and their children's children, to the umpteenth generation. My own children, should I ever have any, will be like these Colony children, these so-called *efts*.

Efts: how can I possibly describe them? Girls without the giggles and shrieks; boys without the swagger; as tall as adults, and as knowing (save in one regard), with the unthinking arrogance of adolescents, but none of the hormonal mayhem. New creatures for a new world, inventing themselves before our eyes.

What the change is, basically, is a lack of any identifying sexual characteristics until puberty. Their kids truly have no idea if they will be male or female (I'd assumed it was just that they were being raised at the extreme end of a parenting style that de-emphasized gender). On top of that, puberty is delayed by quite a bit. The kids will grow to adult size, strength, and brainpower while remaining in their indeterminate state for several decades. As an added bonus, lifespan will probably be extended, and aging delayed.

Many in New Athens believe this will allow for a much more equitable and rational society, where people can just be people and women will no longer be subordinate to men. This tweak in human reproductive biology has the added benefit of shortening the period when people can have have children to a mere decade. The scientists expect this will stave off overpopulation of their icy paradise. However, some evolutionary biologists argue that natural selection may gradually extend the reproductive period, absent social regulations.

They'd better be damned sure they made a good choice. Because they have just willfully created a new species of *Homo sapiens*. They are calling it *Homo novior*, the newer human. Whether it's an improvement remains to be seen.

Chapter 21. Refugees

We are triply isolated here in New Athens: by geography, speciation, and finally by this quarantine. Sometimes I wonder, though, who are we protecting, and what purpose it really serves.

— Kassandra Morgan-Ávvu

With the holidays over, the far side of winter took them well and truly in its grip. Now came the bleak, uphill slog when the excitement of town had worn off, and spring seemed an impossible dream. The unrelenting night became, for some, nearly intolerable. People concealed or exhibited their growing instabilities, according to their natures. For those without the distraction of work or studies, it was a time for obsessive hobbies, for losing oneself in books or drink, for sleeping around the clock.

Most evenings after supper, the household would gather to listen to news on the skywave. While the radio droned and hissed, Uncle Narv would sit in the big armchair and puff at his sweet-smelling pipe, muttering remarks. He'd been kept home by the storms, unable to take the *Nioren* on the usual round of short winter voyages. Though the loss of income didn't matter that much, he was restless.

Much of the news was bad, and growing worse. Many places, Adare included, had been poorly provisioned due to a series of fierce autumn storms. On top of that, fishermen were often confined to the harbor by the unpredictable weather. Folk were making do with meals of potatoes, lentils, turnips, and other such humble fare. Up in the hills, the snow lay deep, deeper than anyone but the oldest could remember.

Still more disturbing were reports that towns up-current of Adare were being harried by Raiders. This had not happened in untold generations. If they continued to make incursions, said the radio announcer, the Council would have to take action. Meanwhile, local coast guards were being hastily assembled, to keep watch for impending attacks.

When the news was over for the evening, Dialfi and Orry got out their books. For Orry too was studying hard these days, ever since Uncle Narv had mentioned that he had no room on his vessel for ignoramuses who didn't know the rudiments of trigonometry and navigation. But Rowan found it hard to settle down to work, with the strange news from the skywave still ringing in jhr ears. Jhe would go wandering from window to hearth to sagging bookcases and back to stare out at the streaming rain, until Orry looked up from jhr calculations and self-righteously asked jhm to go fidget somewhere else.

The rain had started not long after they'd returned to Adare. Rain, not darkness, was what made winter so hard; rendered it grey and cheerless instead of transcendent with the light of moon and stars and aurorae. The winter rains always fell heavily on Adare. Yrssu detested this weather, grumbling, "We might as well be fish, living and breathing underwater. Inland, all would be clean, dry snow, bright in the moonlight."

Things were not going so well in Kassandra's world, either.

Rumors from the not-so-clandestine radios have been spreading through New Athens. The virus first identified in Jingjinji has seeded itself across Yurip and the Umerikkas. It's been spreading like wildfire, as those fleeing crowded cities carry it to the countryside (a fool runs from his shadow, as the Kymrans say). I haven't been able to find out if it's reached Shikkággo.

Ingrid shakes her head and says, "It was bound to happen. People have been sounding the alarm for decades, with so many farmers and developers penetrating ever deeper into the wilderness and getting exposed to novel pathogens. They've had near misses before this one, and yet governments chose to spend more on building space missiles and attempts to find killer asteroids."

Karl said, "Good thing we're safely sequestered on the only continent likely to stay untouched."

"It may not turn out so badly, though," Ingrid replied. "Some countries seem to be handling it pretty well."

"Sure, those with totalitarian regimes."

"Not necessarily. A more telling division is between the ones whose leaders are willing to deal with reality, and those clinging to the fantasy that nothing has changed."

In fact, things have changed very quickly. We notice it even here in our remote refuge. Though it's high summer, with the autumn freeze-in not expected for a record-setting three more months, it's been several weeks since any ships have been spotted lurking on the horizon. They've all been called back to their home ports.

Everyone up there has been asked to simply stay home. Life is on a monumental pause, unimaginable a little while ago. A great stillness has fallen over the Earth. Even the voices on the radio sound different, somehow subdued.

Air travel, already reduced in recent years, is virtually nonexistent. Factories and coal plants are shut down across broad swathes of the planet, and oil production has shut down amid glutted storage containers. No one knows what to make of the wild stock market fluctuations. People in horribly polluted cities look up to see blue sky and mountains on a distant horizon for the first time in decades. Apparently there is a massive shortage of bicycles in the great cities! There are even rumors, later said to be false (but as the Kymrans say, the story that did not happen can be truer than the one that did), of dolphins swimming through the canals of Venniss!

As we follow these developments with growing astonishment, hope is arising that this pandemic might serve as an eleventh-hour wake-up call. With so much of what had been assumed unchangeable now turned upside-down, there is a massive outcry to rebuild with an eye to more just and sustainable way of life for all. Change that is so desperately needed is evidently actually possible. For the first time in my life it seems something might actually be done to make things better.

We all find it strange that a disease that apparently only kills a small proportion of its victims has brought people to question the formerly unshakeable foundations of modern greed-driven society. Ingrid says it almost makes her believe in a benevolent god.

Still, Karl remains skeptical anything good will come of this. "The level of disarray in some countries right now is staggering. Former superpowers in their death throes, a couple more states who've recently acquired nuklear weapons – I'm just as glad to be far away from all that."

As the winter wore on, supplies of various foodstuffs began to run low. Some fishing boats had been lost at sea and others coming back half-full, with the normal fishing grounds not yielding well. It wasn't the first time Adareans had had to tighten their belts in a lean year, and most people did it with good grace.

Some people, though, began to embrace a rather fervid form of Gaeaism. Defying the streaming rain, they gathered on street corners singing mournful hymns, and speaking of Gaea's chastisement and the need for repentance. Their presence became a regular backdrop to the daily walk to and from school, along with the rushing streams that flanked the steep stone streets and mud collected in hollows.

These people claimed the harsh winter was a punishment for too many having gone outside the proper bounds set by the Commandments. Rumor was that some households were furtively heating and cooking with coal, and after watching Far's dilemma Rowan found this all too easy to believe. They also accused fishing boats of seeking fish too far offshore, and warned they would be punished if they did not mend their ways.

Exasperated with this logic, Dialfi told Rowan, "Of course people seek fish further away when they aren't to be found close to home. Or do they think their Gaea wants us to starve?"

One afternoon Dialfi stopped to question a group of them. Something that had long puzzled jhm, jhe said, was whether Gaea was in charge of just the Earth, or of all planets with life on them? Did each planet have its own particular deity, in a vast, intergalactic parade stretching across the heavens?

They told jhm this was not an important question.

Well, then, Dialfi wanted to know, did Gaea favor human life over other life on the planet, or was all life equally valuable?

All life, they answered, was in Gaea's care.

Even the Outlanders? Dialfi wondered, somewhat mischievously, Rowan thought.

As much as any other animal, they answered. You scholars dearly love to split hairs and ponder the unknowable, but our duty is to obey the Commandments, whose wisdom we are not fit to question."

Dialfi shook jhr head at this, and walked on. "They would throw away our gifts of reason and judgement," Dialfi told Rowan angrily. "And on top of that, they seem to take such delight in suffering!"

"It has been a hard winter, though," Rowan said. It would be hard to say whether jhe was thinking more of Adare or of events in Kassandra's ice-locked world, which much preoccupied jhr waking thoughts.

Dialfi answered, "That's not the point. Life can indeed be harsh, yet its overwhelming characteristic seems to me to be *overflowing bounty*. Only think how vast the cosmos is, Rowan, with more scope for exploration than we'll ever reach the end of; how it's deterministic and therefore reasonable, with rules that may be discovered, and yet in practice quite unpredictable, so that it will always surprise us. It grows larger, not smaller, as we learn more! Only consider how the sun pours out its tremendous energy, its light and heat, upon the earth, far more than life could ever require, the cup overflowing day after day after day."

"Is that your version of Gaeaism?" wondered Rowan.

"Not at all, it's plain sense!" Dialfi answered.

Now that summer is passing into fall, everyone has breathed a sigh of relief. Whatever turn things took in the outer world, this year at least no ships would find our hidden harbor. Pancake ice has begun to form and coalesce offshore. Soon it will be hundreds of kilometers wide, an icy moat protecting us from any incursions. As the sea-ice freezes, pulses of super-concentrated brine sink down deep; I've seen the underwater movies. This in turn drives great rivers of cold, nutrient-rich water into the warmer and poorer latitudes, that eventually circle round to bring warmth to the poles. But as the world warms, this cold heartbeat will falter and stop, with uncertain but probably unpleasant effects on climate.

A few days ago, we began to hear a faint but persistent booming and cracking coming over the new ice. The children heard it first. It was like distant rolls of thunder; like a tall building that's been dynamited crumbling down; like glaciers being repeatedly calved into the sea. Once noticed, it became hard to ignore.

Whatever it was, it gradually got louder. In the last light of the afternoon, someone with a pair of binoculars sighted the ship. It was an ancient and battered icebreaker, with a red hull and a green deck, plowing relentlessly through the pristine field of ice that had just sealed off New Athens from the rest of the crazed and plague-ridden planet.

We stood on a rise above the little huddle of buildings and barns that was our whole world, our lifeline to the future, gazing out over the bleak and frozen shore. Our blood beat in our ears like the vanished surf of summer. Slowly the ship drew closer.

A group of ever-shifting composition stood on the hill above town to watch its progress. As if to reassure themselves, people told stories of other times icebreakers had come to the station, carrying essential scientific supplies or welcome additions to a larder grown monotonous with preserved and overly processed food, and once to evacuate someone with a medical emergency. Back then, such relentless progress through the ice must have felt like heartening proof that human will and ingenuity would conquer all obstacles.

By next morning's light, it could be seen that the ship was halted before the thicker nearshore ice, several kilometers off. Already, the water was freezing up behind it. As it began to back up, people looked at one another with tentative hope in their eyes. Had our wall of ice defeated it, after all, then?

We watched in silence, trading binoculars from one pair of hands to another. Now the reversing ship was slowing down again, so the water churned up behind it. Then it accelerated straight towards the shore to crash head-on into the ice. A crack opened up and it shot forward tens of meters, as the ice groaned and shrieked in protest. It reversed and hurled itself at the ice again, rhythmically, inexorably forcing its way into our harbor.

The short autumn day seemed to last forever. No one tried to get any work done; it was impossible to concentrate on anything amid the suspended pauses and sudden booms of a nautical battering ram. Where the ice proved too strong, they had yet another trick. The ship's bow rose high up into the air and hung there a moment at a crazy angle, before crashing down to shatter the ice with its weight. Water opened up ahead like a wound, brown water washing out over the blue-white ice. The sound came with a delay, like thunder.

In the dying afternoon light, even without the aid of binoculars we could clearly see the ramshackle ship rimmed with ice. It flew the flag of a country warped by generations of war. Ragged men patrolling the deck stared hungrily at the crop of buildings they saw rising along the rocky shoreline. By that time, people were hastily erecting a crude but strong fence around the main buildings, using the steep hillsides to advantage. We worked at it all through the long night, generators running noisily to power floodlights.

The dim light of the next day revealed that they'd halted a little ways down the coast, and set up camp on a wretched strip of stony beach, improvising shelters out of tarps and scraps. There were an astonishing number of them, and far too many children. We could hear the babies wailing, day and night.

The Kymrans wanted to go try to talk to these people, and bring them whatever we could spare, blankets and food and medicine. despite knowing how dangerous the virus is. It can hide for weeks under cover of mild infections before raging up to begin killing again for reasons no one yet understands. And we did not have enough to spare to create quarantine quarters for them that would let them ride out the coming winter. Already, it had strained the Colony's resources to the utmost to adopt the Kymrans as permanent members when it became apparent how volatile the situation was in the north.

The choice to refuse all contact with the refugees was stark. It was of course also colored by the scientists' grand plan to create a wholly new society, with the help of their cherished offspring. The incipient species *Homo novior* would be quickly extinguished by the incursion of so many old-style humans and the intermarriages that would inevitably ensue.

I had no part in it, nor did the increasingly restive Kymrans. But I will tell you truly, that is no excuse in my case; for I do not know what I would have decided had the responsibility fallen to me. It was an inhuman situation to face, and it may be that there was no right choice by any moral standards our hearts are capable of understanding. These are terrible times, and I fear what such choices do to those who must make them.

The winter cold and darkness were rapidly barreling down upon us all, and it seemed certain these people would attack. Yet, the days went by and nothing happened. At first, we thought their hesitation must stem from a reluctance to destroy precious infrastructure. Their position was desperate enough that our puny defenses and improvised weapons could not have been much of a deterrent.

Then, those keeping watch on the miserable camp reported that they'd begun to hear the dreaded sound of coughing. Again the Kymrans asked to bring them medicine and aid, arguing that it would protect all of us to do so. They were told this would be a foolhardy and futile gesture, doing no real good and possibly causing much harm. Any who approached the refugees would not be allowed back into the Colony. It was later found that a few, who had no families, had slipped into the camp bringing a few meager supplies they'd managed to cobble together. They did not try to return, and we never learned their fate.

In the middle of the night, about a week after the ship had first been heard, we heard unusual movements coming from the encampment, and voices raised in argument. Grimly, we prepared for a desperate attempt to breach the barrier fence. But it never came. By the grey light of morning we saw the camp was being dismantled. A few people were being carried on stretchers over the broken ice towards the ship, by figures stumbling with weariness or worse.

From the hill above town we watched the icebreaker work its way back out through the ice, the way it had come. A few cheered, but most stayed decently silent.

The long, arrow-straight scar in the ice was all that remained to mark the ship's passing.

Chapter 22. Endings

The Kymrans say that the greatest poem of all is silence.

— Kassandra Morgan-Ávvu

Late in the winter, the dreary rains abruptly came to an end. The temperature plummeted and the sea began to steam off great quantities of fog, as in the first chill days of early autumn. This cold was of another order, though: it took your breath away. It crept through the smallest crack to send tendrils of ice growing up the insides of doors, and windows blossomed with massive frost flowers. People plugged cracks and chinks with rags, opened wide the valves to the geothermal, and bundled in shawls and coats around fires that ate up the remaining supplies of firewood and other scraps at a frightening rate. The tightly sealed houses were stuffy, but fetid air and headaches were preferable to the ferocious chill.

Something in Rowan loved this icy weather, and the stillness it imposed. Time itself seemed frozen. The streets were deserted. School was suspended, there being no means to keep the high-ceilinged rooms warm enough.

Rowan took long walks down to the harbor and up into the hills. As long as jhe kept moving the cold was not unbearable. There were chunks of ice floating in the harbor, and slush washed rhythmically against the jetty with a strangely soothing sound. Thresh, thresh; thresh, thresh. Ice coated the branches of trees, and sprouted in fantastic encrustations at the downspouts of drains.

This had been Kassandra's world, thought Rowan, a world of exquisite clarity. It trembled with possibility, with sleeping potentialities. The dim light of Sunreturn muffled by thick clouds; the empty streets unreal, dreamlike. One windless day snow drifted softly down from the blank skies, and coated the black tree limbs as with a white shadow that fell from above, or as if light had been made into something of substance. That day, jhe had a strangely expectant feeling, as if any moment jhe might turn a corner and come upon Kassandra, breathing a white-puffed greeting. But there had been no trees in Kassandra's day, Rowan remembered; not a single one on the whole continent, save the ash tree under glass that Ingrid had planted.

They weren't making much progress on the translation these days. There were many evenings Yrssu did not come, and when jhe did come, jhe did not stay long. Rowan contented jhmself with asking for the definitions of the most puzzling words. Then, after Yrssu left, jhe would go upstairs, make a nest of quilts in the chilly bedroom, and read Kassandra's account as best jhe could, alone, from the pages densely covered with scribbled notes. The entries were much shorter, and the writing seemed more disjointed, though this could also have been an effect of their struggle to concentrate on such a difficult task during the worst part of the year for focussed thought.

> After the departure of the ice-breaking ship, we settled in for the long winter. All was calm for a time, then came that terrible day, when someone ran through the hallways of the main lab shouting about the end of world.
>
> We gathered round the radios in shock, as reporters spoke of strikes and counter-strikes. Entire cities snuffed in an instant. I heard their names recited, but cannot bear to list them.
>
> * * * * *
>
> One by one, the radio stations are falling silent. Their static tells a tale more terrible than any words could.
>
> The greatest poem of all is silence, say the Kymrans.
>
> * * * * *

It's over, five thousand years of growth and civilization. This tiny Colony of New Athens is all that's left, an infinitesimal spark in the great darkness.

I weep without ceasing for my father, and for all our people in the old country; for Sarah, for Josiah; for a world forever gone, and with it, the chance to set things right.

* * * * *

As the long tail of winter draws out beyond hope, beyond bearing, I wander aimlessly through the underground corridors. If I walk for long enough, maybe I can stop thinking for a while.

* * * * *

Today, I found my old fohn in a storeroom that happened to be unlocked. I guess such devices no longer pose any risk of discovery to the Colony.

I've been wearing it on a necklace, under my shirt. I keep hoping that somehow, through some miraculous configuration of sunspots or whatever, I will get a call from Josiah telling me what has become of everything I used to know.

* * * * *

Spring is here at last. Its glaring light and overcast skies portend a painful awakening, instead of the eternally young hope it is fondly supposed to signify. The unaccustomed warmth chills me. The blades of grass shooting up everywhere are horribly wrong. This is fucking Antarktikka! Why should it of all places be coming to life, when the rest of the world is dead or dying? It's all backwards and upside-down, and it hurts so much and I want to go back to being dead like I was all winter and I can't – I can't – I'm incomprehensibly alive.

Why am I here? I'm neither a scientist nor a proper Kymran, and still less am I a child of the Colony, that newfangled tribe arrogant in their ignorance. No, I'm the one who doesn't fit, the awkward piece, understanding nothing, understood by no one.

Now they had reached winter's bitter end, when the lessening of gloom in the northern skies only mocked the absent sun with a simulacrum glow. Sometimes, in the middle of the day, the sky cleared and brightened, its clouds underlit with violet, yellow, rose; and the people gazed upwards, hungry, so terribly hungry for the light.

The top of a flight of stairs were more rickety than ever, and slick with winter's slime. Rowan paused to look in at the window. In the candlelit room, Yrssu sat cross-legged on the floor, surrounded by a pile of hides and a smaller mound of several kinds of fur in scraps of varying size, head bent low over jhr task.

Rowan tentatively knocked at the glass. Yrssu squinted at the dark pane and got up to let jhm in. With only a nodded greeting, jhe resumed sewing.

"I'm sorry it's been so long," Rowan said. "I did stop by a few times, but you were never home, I guess."

"I guess not," answered Yrssu. Jhr voice felt rusty.

"I managed to read some more of Kassandra, on my own," Rowan continued, setting some pages down on Yrssu's table with a hint of pride. "All this cold weather we've been having; it's funny, but it's made me feel like she could come walking around a corner one morning and say hello. I even had a dream about it the other night. . . ."

While Rowan talked of this and that, Yrssu, head bent, kept sewing. It had been such a long, long winter, words seemed to have been leached of all sense or import. It was as though Rowan was jumping up and down and waving and shouting from across a wide gulf.

Yrssu had lived the last month or two in a haze, unable to sleep or to really wake up. Gradually, the dreariness of waking life had faded to shadowy irrelevance, while the vivid dreams of a vanished childhood sprouted and grew in jhm like a strange, wintry crop. So Yrssu once more journeyed over the windswept waste, amid the clamor of hundreds of bells and the rumbling calls of the matriarchs. Under the wheel of stars jhe'd been guarding the herd from wolf-pack and from the dread beorn, flying over the shushing snow with the other efts light as ghosts. And then when their shift was over, skiing home to the crowded, smelly, smoky tent to crawl under the soft caribou skins and sleep at last. There in the *Siénttu*'s town of stone, jhe'd once dreamed of long-departed Ullahu, great pillars of legs shifting between jhr knees as jhe rode on his neck high above the plain. Jhe'd awakened with cheeks cold and wet with tears.

Rowan watched as Yrssu deftly trimmed the hide using a small, sharp blade, and began pricking holes along one edge for a new seam. "What are you making, anyway?"

Yrssu spoke around a long piece of sinew dangling from the corner of jhr mouth. "Clothes fit for the South."

"You're leaving Nuatha?" asked Rowan in dismay.

Yrssu nodded, and stabbed hard at a tough place on the hide. Cocooned by those long black nights, jhe had come to see, dimly at first and then with increasing clarity, that the time the old stories spoke of was upon them. The snows of the far south would lie deeper and deeper, untouched by summer's heat, and the rivers of ice would flow forth once again and begin their slow and relentless seaward journey. The great forests and grasslands would be entombed in white death; animal and human would flee before the onslaught. For a time the wind-loving people would sweep over the abandoned farmland, and seem to triumph over the arrogant *Siénttu*. Yet in the end the Kymrans too would subside, and wither as grasses before the autumnal blast.

"What are you thinking of, Yrssu?" Rowan asked, softly.

"Ends and endings," muttered Yrssu.

Then Rowan spoke the phrase the Kymran had taught jhm back in the fall: "*Ang tarn arra kern.*"

The room came back, forming itself around Yrssu from out of shadows and nothingness, with its shabby walls that did not flap in the wind and bore no words of wisdom, and the bare, scratched floor that held no place for a fire. Yrssu held Rowan's eyes for just a moment, then looked away again.

Rowan cried in dismay, "Oh, Yrssu, you've been too much alone this winter."

"Darktide is dreamtide," Yrssu told jhm; "and we all dream alone."

Chapter 23. Mayday

I cast my thoughts into your far-off times, oh future reader, when our loss and grief will be but the echo of an echo. Is the world we left you once again a kind and gentle place? Is your air full of birdsong and the drone of insects, of the perfume of blossoms and apples and balsam fir, and every shade of green my heart aches to see again?

— Kassandra Morgan-Ávvu

And now, winter was well and truly vanquished. Light was a solid, vital substance as much as water or food; it was breath, life itself. It was a revelation, it was a rebirth, it was Gaea's love for her children poured forth in an ecstasy of excess. The long night of winter had ended. The people stretched out their limbs and drank their fill of daylight.

The golden orb of the sun shone forth again in naked splendor, hurting their eyes, which had learned to glean as much as possible from the rays of lanterns and lamplight. They had forgotten how red was red, how bright the sea and clouds, how wide the world outside the small circle of lamplight. Even though most households were scraping the backs of their cupboards, everyone was marvelously happy. So the world hurtled forwards, like a mountain stream suddenly undammed from imprisoning ice.

No one wanted to be indoors. Students did their work, or attempted to, under the blossoming trees and on the beaches. Despite the looming threat of end-of-term exams, they would abandon their books for raucous games of frisrugby ranging over the streets of town, for impromptu lessons in juggling and slackrope walking and cartwheels (there was a craze for learning acrobatics that year), and for a hardy few, early season swimming in the chill sea.

Erkanni of the balmy northern isles scorned to swim among ice floes, but had gotten hold of a sweet little gaff-rigged yawl, and in the bright days would flit about the harbor like a gull.

Many a sleepy afternoon, Erkanni would whisper across the classroom aisle to Rowan: "Wind's rising." As soon as school let out, they would set off across the crowded harbor, zipping neatly past various vessels at anchor and rowboats plying their way among them.

After a few tacks they entered open waters, where the sun glinted off the fractured wavelets like peals of laughter. They skimmed past swaying bell-buoys that rang out summons to rejoice. When they reached the part of the bay that was littered with a multitude of rocky skerries, Erkanni threaded them on a maze-like course that looked sure to end in disaster. Rowan soon learned to bite back the occasional shout of alarm as the rocks loomed up mere decims from the hull, for this only made Erkanni laugh at jhm and go closer yet the next time.

"Hard a-lee!" cried Erkanni, nearly pitching Rowan overboard. They missed the underwater rock, but smacked a large wave. Salt spray washed glistening over them both. Erkanni laughed and shook the drops from a multitude of braids, setting all the shells a-clacking.

One windless afternoon Rowan found Erkanni lounging on deck, improvising tunes on a battered penny whistle. Rowan made jhmself comfortable on a bundle of spare sail, watching a thundercloud-shaped column of gnats swirling upwards, like self-willed dust-motes. Rowan leaned back and closed jhr eyes, enjoying the reddish cast of the light through jhr eyelids.

"*There* you are, Rowan! Wuttieff are you playing at, lazing around like a lubber?" Orry suddenly appeared on the dock, arms on hips, feet planted shoulder-width apart, swaying in an imaginary swell.

"I am a lubber," pointed out Rowan. "And do you really have to go around swearing like a sailor?"

"Yes." Orry turned to Erkanni. "Uncle Narv asked me to tell you he'll offer whatever wages you think you're worth, for the rest of the month. You were one of the best workers he had last summer, he says."

"Sorry, but I can't oblige him."

"Why ever not?"

Erkanni stretched out luxuriously on the deck of the little boat. "No wages are worth giving up afternoons like these, when the sun is newly born and the world is coming back to life."

Shaking jhr head at such foolishness, Orry headed back to the *Nioren*.

At home that evening, Rowan found Dialfi rifling through the mail. Rejections to jhr scholarship applications had been trickling in all spring. Rowan had stopped asking how many more were pending some time back.

Among the bills and routine notices, there was an oversized envelop, with Dialfi's name and town address written in elaborate calligraphic flourishes. It bore a silvery waxen seal. Rowan watched as Dialfi carefully peeled it away, and extracted the letter.

Dialfi went pale, then color flooded back to jhr cheeks, mottling them in violent contrast. Jhe stared at the page, as though unable to take in the words.

Rowan said hesitantly, "Well, maybe you'll have better luck next year . . ."

"Next year?" Dialfi's smile was fit to rival the spring sunshine. "Next year I'll be wearing the blue. They've given me a Foedell Scholarship, Rowan!"

Confused, Rowan asked, "Is that good?"

"You bet it is. Foedells let you study whatever you please, you don't have to commit to anything in advance. And they cover all sorts of extras! expensive tools, a virtually unlimited electricity allowance, expeditions to faraway research sites, you name it." Dialfi looked down at the letter again. "There's so much to do, my head is spinning. Can you believe it, Rowan? I'm actually going to the Akademy!"

Rowan clapped jhm on the back, sharing in jhr triumph and relief. "Of course you are! The scholars can't be as smart as people say, if it took them this long to figure that out."

Mayday shone forth amid a late blaze of daffodils, and blue skies racing with clouds. As she did every year, Grandmother had joined them in town for the festivities. The highlight of the day was the maypole dance, a renewal of Nuathans' living promise to stay within the bounds of the Commandments.

In the fresh morning light Rowan's family climbed the broad hill above town to where the maypole stood, going slowly for Grandmother's sake. There was a haze of new growth on the skeletal branches of oak and beech, a delicate wash of color whose tardiness made it the more welcome.

Adare's maypole was as tall as a two-story house, with a huge cartwheel mounted flat at the top. Around the rim of the wheel hung dozens of long streamers that trailed out along the ground like the train of a wedding gown, longer alternating with shorter. Anchoring the end of each streamer lay a crown of foliage, twined with ribbons of gold and azure. Amid the sturdy greenery were woven all the early flowers that could be found: dusty-blue cornflowers, delicate irises and violets, wild primroses, columbines, sweet-smelling lily of the valley, and a profusion of little pink-tipped daisies.

At the top of the hill, the townspeople were milling about. Many of the younger folk went barefoot, and everyone was dressed in flimsy spring finery. While efts and imagoes stood around chatting, the children darted about like spirits of summer, their loose white frocks fluttering behind them.

The fiddles finished tuning and began a cheerful, rollicking tune, and with only a little rushing and jostling, the children found their places, forming two concentric rings at the ribbon's ends. Suddenly solemn, each donned a crown of flowers, took hold of a ribbon, and stood stock-still. The oldest ones, like Orry, stood by ready to sort out any confusion. Everyone else gathered round in hushed anticipation. The music changed to a more stately tune, and the May dance began.

First the children circled clockwise, in deference to the sun and the heavens. Then, as the music shifted, they turned on their heels as one, and circled widdershins. In accord with their dance, the ribbons twisted down the pole, and then untwisted again. This was only a prelude, the hopeful statement of intention; the actual weaving had not yet begun.

The music took on a deeper tone and more complex rhythm, and half the children moved towards the pole while the others moved outwards, transforming the ring into a four-armed cross. They circled in step, the ribbons winding smoothly down the pole.

Rowan, watching at the outskirts, was thinking how different the dance looked from the outside, how intricate and yet how simple. For many years jhe had been one of the child dancers, concentrating on getting all the steps just so. Now jhe could see what an exquisite pattern it made.

Rowan glanced at Grandmother and saw tears running down her cheeks. She gave Rowan a wavering smile, and whispered, "I can't help it; I cry every year. It's such an old, old dance, and the children so young, not really understanding what they're doing, and that's why they do it so perfectly."

The children again formed into rings, but this time the two rings faced opposite directions. Each child nodded solemnly to jhr counterpart, then skipped in time to the music, faster and faster, weaving in and out, past and through, lifting the ribbons over and under each other, laughing now as they dodged one another and nearly, but never quite, collided. The pattern of ribbons twisting down the pole recorded the fleeting motions of their dance. If the dancers did well, the weaving would be even and tight and beautiful, foretelling a good summer and a rich harvest — though this was only said in fun, for Nuathans were not a superstitious people.

The ribbons were only halfway woven when someone cried out. People were craning their heads and pointing down towards the harbor. Rowan glanced quickly, and saw a half dozen ships offshore, sails dark as winter. So the supply ships were arriving from verdant Getz, and most welcome they were in the hungry spring.

But more and more people were turning away from the dance to watch the ships. This was very wrong: nothing should interrupt the May Dance. And all this chattering and pointing was apt to break the children's concentration.

Sure enough, one of the smallest children dropped jhr ribbon and ran to jhr mother, followed by several others. The dance faltered, as several others slowed their steps, looking bewildered. The musicians paused, bows poised uncertainly in midair as the silence swelled. They hesitated too long, and so the choice was made. Never in living memory had the dance thus collapsed.

Everything was happening in a jerky and fragmented way, as if time had broken out of its usual course. Children were swept up by their parents, and people ran in every direction. Someone was shouting, and one word at last penetrated Rowan's muddled mind: *Raiders!* Not supply ships at all! Rowan's throat closed up and jhe couldn't speak, or even breathe.

Uncle Narv returned with Orry in tow, and spoke urgently to Aunt Matti in a low voice. Some people were racing down to town; others were climbing up higher into the hills. Under Orry's protests, Narv herded the family towards the far side of the hill.

Rowan craned jhr head back towards the water, where three ships of strange design were slowly coming into the harbor. They had high, triangular sails and black smoke billowing out of squat chimneys at their sterns. It hung over the water behind them like an evil fog. Orry was asking, *What are they doing? Where are the ranks of rowers pulling with all their might?* but no one answered. The Adarean coast guard was racing out to meet them, two brigs and a fireboat shooting its fountain high over the water, just like in all their practice sessions before the harbor had iced over. A bright flash burst from one of the brigs, and a few seconds later Rowan heard the boom of cannon rolling through the hills.

At this, Orry became even more wild to go down and join the defense. But Uncle Narv told them to stay while he went down to help. "You efts had better stay well away from these creatures — and Orry, goddammit, you are wearing ribbony flowers on your head and a dress, you cannot go fight the bloody barbarians in a dress, listen to your Grandmother, she at least has some sense; Orry you scamp GET BACK HERE YOUR FATHER WILL HAVE MY HIDE! —*ORRY*!"

Rowan hesitated for an instant that stretched out like a trembling line of spider-silk, then flew down the hill after Orry. Having flung off the flowery crown, Orry ran swiftly in the loose frock, whereas Rowan's stiffer garments impeded jhr movements, but jhe charged on as best jhe could.

The thunder of cannon was echoing among the hills, the one mounted on the promontory at the edge of town joining the smaller ones aboard the brigs in repelling the invaders. Jhe'd lost sight of Orry, but that must be where jhe was headed. Jhe hurdled down the cobbled streets after jhm, breathing hard with the unaccustomed exercise.

Smoke was billowing along the wharf-side streets and knots of people pounded by on errands of their own. The cannon were firing way out on the farthest dock, but Rowan knew nothing of artillery. There was no fighting nearby, only distant shouts. A fire engine pulled by horses clattered by, and Rowan almost joined them, thinking at least to do something useful. But jhe had to find Orry.

Just then, a group of Raiders rushed by, hooting and hollering like imbeciles in their guttural tongue, brandishing torches and heading for the old, tarry docks where most of the fishing fleet was tied up, at the west end of the harbor. Could they be so bent on mindless destruction? Rowan raced after them, joining a shouting crowd brandishing all manner of improvised weapons. The Raiders, armed with nothing but torches and not having expected such vigorous defense, fell back under the onslaught, and ran back towards the beach where their long rowboats lay.

"They're no match for us," Rowan exulted, as the crowd pounded along in pursuit.

"They're half-starved, must've had an even harder winter than us," someone grunted in response.

All at once, Rowan's ears felt strangely empty, and jhe realized that the thundering boom of the cannon had ceased. The town's bells began to ring out in joyous peals, echoes piling on echoes through the stony streets. The strange ships were sailing away, one of them much lower in the water than it had been. A thin sound of cheering drifted over the water from the coast guard, joining the nearer roars from the promontory. On the docks, too, people were jumping up and down, shaking their fists, and shouting until their voices cracked.

Rowan looked back uphill, to where the abandoned Maypole stood against the bright, cloud-racing sky, its unwoven ribbons flapping and tangling wildly in the wind.

That evening, townspeople poured into the streets in raucous celebration. May Day's outdoor parties usually went on all night, or what had until recently been night but was once again a full suncircle. The younger children, especially, relished being allowed to stay up and witness the sun's full path. But this year the jubilation over having fought off the dreaded Raiders was greater still.

The woman who'd fired the shot that had hulled one of their ships had been given so many drinks and pounded heartily on the back so many times that she could hardly stand up. The cannon on the promontory was fired again and again, until the docks were choked with bitter smoke. Someone had made a mock Raider of wood and old clothes and hung it from a loading crane, where the crowd could hurl withered turnips and cabbages at it, and finally they doused it in pine-pitch and set it aflame to roars of approval.

People were full of ideas of what should be done in case those damned Syowyans ever dared to return. Some went so far as to advocate mounting an expedition to the other side of Terraus, to attack their stronghold. As people got deeper in their cups, the talk turned to increasingly lewd speculation about Outlander anatomy, but Aunt Matti dragged Rowan away before jhe could hear much of that.

Rowan made jhr way to Yrssu's place. Yrssu and Erkanni were sitting out on the porch, watching the celebrations at a slight remove. "They're saying we should go raid the Raiders," Rowan told them excitedly.

"That is madness," said Yrssu. "You Nuathans are knowing nothing of war."

"Well, we gave them a good pounding today, anyhow," said Rowan, gleefully adding the words jhe'd overheard, "the imago-babies, the fucking engendered Outlanders!"

At this, Erkanni turned to ask, "Were you at the defense too?"

"Just the last bit. Orry and I ran down from the Maypole as fast as we could. But were you one of those at the cannon? We didn't see you at the festivities."

"I was keeping watch with my spyglass," Erkanni was very proud of this telescope, a family heirloom. "And you know, the Raiders didn't look very fierce at all, to me. They were gaunt as scarecrows."

"Winter has harrowed them like a cruel-clawed beorn," added Yrssu.

Rowan looked in astonishment from one to the other, taking in their somber mood, so different from the jubilant giddiness of the townsfolk at the bonfires. "Don't tell me you feel *sorry* for the Raiders?"

"If you had seen what we saw, Rowan, you would too," insisted Erkanni. "They're just people, even if they weren't so lucky to be born into the great civilization of Nuatha."

"They're eftless abominations!"

"Well, for that matter so was Kassandra," retorted Erkanni.

Rowan stared at the Islander. "Kassandra?"

"The way she always calls herself 'she' — remember how we used to find that strange? And the way she keeps saying things about how she doesn't fit in with the children of the Colony?"

"That was only because she hadn't grown up there, Erkanni."

"Exactly — she joined New Athens as a teenaged orphan. The Colony children would have been the first generation of efts, wouldn't they?"

Yrssu added sharply, "Kassandra was explaining it, in that passage early in the winter. You Nuathans are remembering, are you not, how it was your own Founders who made you into efts?"

"Yes, of course," answered Rowan testily. "It's just not something we dwell on overmuch."

Yrssu snorted. "Nor do we, curse as it was."

"Curse. . .? Oh for Gaea's sake, Yrssu! would you rather have been born an imago?"

"That was not a question your Founders thought to ask us," Yrssu replied, as though having witnessed this ancient transformation in person. "Oh yes, my people are remembering very well the gifts of the *Siénttu*, both those of the left hand and those of the right: the locked gate and the shattered fence, that taught us to make no permanent abode; the mammút brought forth from old bones, whose path we yet follow; and the barren eft by which they would set themselves apart from the rest of humanity. Above all, we remember how they planted a lie at the heart of Nuatha."

At this, Rowan felt a flash of blinding rage. "Yrssu, what in Terraus are you talking about? I know your people have reasons for distrusting Nuathans, but for Gaea's sake, the Founders would hardly have gone around planting *lies*! Their whole purpose was to make sure as much knowledge as possible survived the Catastrophe."

Yrssu shook jhr head stubbornly. "They did. Kassandra was saying it, herself."

"Where?" demanded Rowan. They'd resumed working on the translation together, though of late Rowan had been much distracted by sailing excursions with Erkanni and the like.

"In the new passage I have been working on. She was talking about the writing of the Humanual, and how they decided to tell the children that the northern lands had all drowned."

"But they did drown, Yrssu! Terraus is the only land that was high enough to be left, when the ice melted and the sea level rose."

"That is what the Humanual is *saying*; but is it true?" asked Yrssu, maddeningly. Rowan glanced at Erkanni for support, but the Islander appeared lost in thought, gazing out over the silver-black harbor where the many celebratory bonfires were luridly reflected.

After such a disquieting day, the last thing Rowan wanted was to quarrel with Yrssu. Jhe took jhr leave, and walked home through smoke-filled streets that rang with the songs and laughter of determined revelers. On the hill above town, the tangled ribbons of the maypole still fluttered against the reddened midnight skies.

Chapter 24. Aftermath

I cast my thoughts into your far-off times.
— Kassandra Morgan-Ávvu

In the days following what everyone persisted in calling The Raid, there was much discussion of how best to improve Adare's defenses, and bold talk of forays to the East to teach the barbarians a lesson they would not soon forget. This, despite the fact that Nuathan vessels were not designed for the exposed seas on the far side of the continent. Only a few sober voices in the squares, Uncle Narv's among them, urged caution and circumspection. But those were little regarded.

Consultation with the folks at Yngencloven kept the skywave humming for hours. Mar thought it better that Orry not sail that summer, with all the unrest. So Orry threatened to join one of the forays to the far East if jhe couldn't go with Uncle Narv. Jhe went stomping around the house, refusing to discuss the matter any further with people who "hadn't been there" for the raid. As if Orry had been anywhere but helping the dancers at the Maypole, Rowan thought with disgust. Grandmother tried to talk some sense into jhm, having "been there all right," as she said, "with damp leaves on my backside from that hollow on the hill to prove it." Only when Uncle Narv said no captain worth his salt would ship a sailor who couldn't follow orders, did Orry pipe down, and return humbly to helping with preparations aboard the *Nioren*.

The Nuathan flag, which Rowan had rarely seen outside of a history book, had been appearing on many a house and storefront. Its green tree set within a sky-blue circle, bounded by a dark-blue ring on a white field, flapped wildly in the spring winds. Orry scrawled *RAID THE RAIDERS!* and *HEED THE ELEVENTH COMMANDMENT!* in chalk on walls thick with similar slogans, and decorated them with ships jauntily tilted in a strong wind. Orry tried to get Rowan to help, but jhe shook jhr head.

"You're no fun anymore!" Orry complained. "What's eating you, anyway?"

"Have you heard how the Raiders were all skinny and, well, kind of desperate-looking?"

"What, so we're supposed to throw up our hands and let them take whatever they want, just because those barbarians can't look after themselves properly?"

"I don't know what we're supposed to do." Rowan kept thinking of the sick and dying refugees Kassandra had written about. And then there was Kassandra herself, who had never been an eft, but was still a human being. Jhe didn't think Orry would get any of that, though.

Wanting to escape the stirred-up ants' nest that town had become, Rowan headed for a set of ramshackle wooden steps that went down to the shore. The tide was out, and jhe headed for the cool, dank shade under the docks. Jagged acorn barnacles climbed high up the blackened pilings, and lower down anemones and sea squirts drooped flaccidly as they awaited the return of the tide. The heady aroma of pitch and salt mud and lush seaweed felt strangely comforting.

Past the docks, summer's still-unfamiliar light was harsh and almost unbearably bright as it glinted off the water and haze of clouds. Rowan walked at the water's edge, and the stealthy wavelets erased the swooping line of footprints unevenly behind jhm. Miniature landscapes formed where streamlets cut curving banks of sand, spreading out in a fan of wavering diamonds as they reached the sea. A screeching flock of gulls rose up on silver wings as jhe walked by, but their clamorous benediction failed to lift Rowan's spirits.

Summer was upon them, yet for once Rowan did not welcome the ending of the school year. Everyone else was on to new adventures, but Rowan was headed back to the same old farm. There was a time jhe'd thought reading Kassandra was going to lead somewhere, prove something. Well, that had been a childish notion. All the same, Rowan did want to finish reading Kassandra's book before Yrssu left, and time was running out. With a sigh, jhe turned back towards town, and headed to Yrssu's place.

Yrssu was out on the porch, as if waiting for jhm to come by. "Do you want to hear how spring is going for Kassandra?"

The low light of the sun cast a bronze glow over the peeling shingles and worn railings. It looked unreal, like a scene out of a half-forgotten legend. Rowan lay back on the sun-warmed, velvety old planks, eyes closed, as Yrssu began to read aloud.

> The scientists have thrown themselves into completing a compendium of all knowledge, their so-called Humanual. Many choices must be made; painful omissions and oversimplifications. There has been some bitter wrangling over that, I am telling you. Biologists and physicists rarely see eye to eye, and within those groups the disagreements over what is most important to convey can be yet more fierce.
>
> No one listens to me, of course (it's an apt name my parents gave me), but I have serious doubts about some of their choices. For one, they have put nothing in there about how we ourselves broke the climate. They fear that sooner or later the convenience of coal and its ilk will prove too tempting, and people will wrongly tell themselves they can use it wisely. So, after much heated debate, a quasi-religious prohibition on using such fuels was adopted. I think they know the scientists of the future will eventually figure it out, but hope the less inquisitive will take to heart this new "fourth commandment". It shows

how little faith they place in their chances of founding a truly rational society.

This latest scheme, though, goes beyond mere omission. I think the guilt of having survived, when so many have perished, is affecting their judgment. The zoologists, especially, are much to blame, they who take such delight in the Earth's myriad creatures. The recent reports that even the giraffes, Afrikah's guileless and graceful giants, were dying of starvation, was more than they could bear. And of course they have all sorts of rational justifications for what they have done.

They have decided to teach the children that rising seas are going to cover the lands to the North, completely. This is ridiculous, of course: two hundred feet is all the seas can rise, if all of the ice melts. This will submerge the coastal cities, and change the shape of the continents; but no more than that. Yet to my amazement, the children believe this ridiculous claim. The North is no more real to them than Atlantis, or Hades. They will not listen to me, the outsider, when I try to tell them that our Earth does not hold enough water to drown such formidable lands, with hills and high plains and soaring mountains.

But the adults would erase those lands from all memory. The official line is that our best hope is to confine a low-carbon, high-tech society to this isolated continent. That way, the rest of the planet can return to a wilderness, and the worst of climate change may yet be averted. If we are very lucky, there may be some amount of recovery that humans are around long enough to see.

Yet would not that hoped-for recovery, that return to Earth's former equilibrium endanger the future inhabitants confined to this lonely continent? If it grows cooler again, this place will become an icy trap.

Karl has assured me that this is the least of our worries. He says it's far more important to ensure that humans can never again so endanger the entire biosphere. If that entails a small risk that we ourselves could go extinct, then so be it. Perhaps the planet would be better off without us.

The adults think they are making a wise decision, one that is courageous, and noble. I, who am younger and in no way to blame for this planetary apocalypse, see their desperate attempt at balancing the scales altogether differently. I see in the adults only guilt and despair, a useless grasping after atonement.

They think to cancel their debts by promising to remain sequestered here. They say they will accept Gaea's ultimate judgment on New Athens, whatever it may prove to be. *By what right do they seal the fate of the children of the future?*

Up north the judgment has already fallen, and it fell the hardest on those least to blame. I am not willing to accept judgment by the impersonal forces of Nature, and especially not to lay it on those who will come after us.

No. I refuse to be party to this deception. I do not submit to this verdict. Instead, in the name of future generations who may be given one more chance, I choose hope: the hope that, despite all evidence to the contrary, we humans are capable of wiser actions.

Yes, action: I am going to craft a message and launch it like an arrow through time. This book written in the timeless runes of my father's people will be one part of the message. I will seal it against flood and fire, and keep it safe until I can hide it in some place far from New Athens, that it may come to light when most needed.

The other part is of course the language it is written in, which must live in people's memories, generation after generation, or all will be lost. So they are tied together, the fate of this book and of the people who are able to read it, stretching in a long chain through time.

Do I dare to hope that living eyes will look upon these pages with understanding?

However much reverence the Kymrans have for their language, there are great changes ahead that will put this in jeopardy. They mean to leave the colony and learn to make a living in the bare wilderness. Not this year, but soon, when they follow the herds to summer pasture, they will not return with the coming of darkness. The caribou can already survive the winters out of doors, and it will not be much longer before the mammút will be able to join them.

Kymrans have their own notions of restraint, albeit different from those of the scientists. Their choice is to shun the technology that has led to so much discontent and degradation of both the world and the human spirit, and as much as possible go back to the ways of our ancestors.

I am thinking I will go with them. I must do what I can to ensure this message goes onward.

Rowan opened jhr eyes. “And so must we!”

There was one last passage still to translate. They went inside, and set to work.

Chapter 25. Decisions and Disembarkings

Can we ever find our way back across so wide a sea?
— Kassandra Morgan-Ávvu

The time of departures was at hand. People were streaming out of Adare on their way to sundry summer occupations, across the sea or inland, scattering in all directions. After the winter confines of communal town life, the lure of the open sky was irresistible. Never mind if physical labor was called for, fishing and sail-trade, hoeing and haymaking under the hot sun. Town clothes were put away in cedar cupboards, books left to gather dust on shelves, bags were packed and friends embraced and parted for the season.

Dialfi had arranged to work passage to the Akademy aboard the *Nioren*, to save the cost of the fare, so Rowan was going to lose everyone but Yrssu in one blow. The night before she was to set sail, they gathered at Bulkington's, a favorite haunt of students and sailors alike. From the entryway, snatches of out-of-tune sea shanties could be heard coming from a large room off to the right, punctuated by bellowed oaths and roars of laughter. But a bleary-eye man sitting at the bar looked askance at Yrssu, and muttered something about the place not serving that kind.

Erkanni said, "You mean stevedores?"

The bartender looked up from wiping glasses. "It's a rare pub as doesn't want their business, eh, Snurri? Go on, m'lads, there's plenty of room in the back."

They found a table in a smaller room off to the left. It was built right out on the pilings, and the reflection of golden nets of sunlight on green-black waters shimmered on the walls. The tables were scored with decades of adornment, courtesy of bored sailors handy with their pocketknives, that were interesting but hard to make out in the dim light. The floor was none too clean, and the whole place smelled of tar and of the rank coolness of whatever was exposed on the pilings at low tide.

When they all had their glasses filled, Rowan proposed a toast in Dialfi's honor. "What do the scholars say again, *Crisscross* something?"

Orry thumped jhr brimming mug on the table. "*Crescat scientia*!"

Crescat! they all answered, and drank deeply. It was considered bad form to do otherwise, after that particular toast. As the saying went, "A shallow draught intoxicates," and so on. The truth was, scholars liked their drink as much as anyone else. Not Rowan, though: to jhm, beer tasted like dirty dishwater. Jhe gagged it down for Dialfi's sake, hiding a grimace.

"Those words were not Anglic, surely?" asked Yrssu.

"No," answered Dialfi, "they're from one of the ancient tongues that scholars use. It means 'May knowledge increase.'"

"Are you certain it is not meaning, 'May the *Siénttu* increase'?" Yrssu said grouchily.

"Sometimes we toast with *Non satis*," Erkanni added, "but that's more of a joke for when you get to the bottom of your glass. Or when people forget to pass the pitcher down the table."

"Sorry!" said Rowan, passing it over. Jhe explained to Yrssu, "*Non satis* means 'not enough', or 'doesn't satisfy.' There's a saying, 'To know is not enough.'"

"*To know is not enough*, now that is one that I like," commented Yrssu. "Once in a while, you Nuathans are showing a bit of sense."

"Speaking of knowing enough," said Dialfi, "did you two ever got back to reading Kassandra?"

"Yes, and we finished it, too," Rowan told jhm. "We're going to read it to you tonight."

Dialfi sat back. "Well? what are you waiting for?" The others nodded eagerly.

Yrssu got out a thick sheaf of papers neatly rolled into a tube and tied with a leather thong: their entire translation, copied out by Rowan during those long months of winter. Carefully, jhe removed a few sheets from the bottom, and handed them to Rowan. "You should be reading it, this time, I am thinking."

So Rowan cleared jhr throat, and began. There was a bit of backlog to get through, and every so often they had to stop and order some food or another round of drinks, whenever the proprietor began hovering. At last they got to the passage about the Founders' lies.

". . . to my amazement, the children believe this ridiculous claim—" Rowan was reading, when Orry interrupted.

"Wait, are you saying the drowned lands have been there all along?"

"Kassandra is saying so," said Yrssu, and Rowan nodded.

"No *way*," breathed Orry — not so much in denial, as in dawning awareness of how wide the world might be.

"You know," put in Erkanni, "the old-timers on Faraday say that now and then over the centuries, castaways have appeared on our shores who came from lands not found on any map."

Dialfi had been looking over the rest of the passage. Now jhe said, visibly shaken, "Could they have deliberately deceived their own children like that? No, no; there must be some mistake. The way the Fourth Commandment taboo on burning coal was so vaguely worded, I'd more or less come to suspect — but this! The Founders taught us to seek to understand the world as it truly is, using the tools of reason and experiment!"

Rowan said, "Maybe we should go and see if those lands are really there."

Dialfi said slowly, "If the Akademy could be persuaded to mount an expedition . . . ."

Rowan's heart gave a lurch. "I don't know if that's such a good idea," jhe began, with misgivings jhe could not yet put a name to.

"No, it's not, because *we* should do it ourselves!" Orry banged jhr mug on the table, so the beer sloshed out.

"That would be a great adventure, to be sure," Erkanni, said, eyes alight with the idea.

"Those Gaeaists who objected to offshore fishing would hardly approve," pointed out Dialfi.

"Who cares? It's not like they'd dare to follow us!" laughed Orry.

"For that matter," said Erkanni. "We'd be lucky to find our own way back again. Once out of sight of land, it's nearly impossible to keep track of your position."

"Oh, that's easy," said Orry, "as long as you know how to use a sextant to find high-noon-north."

"You're mighty optimistic, sailor!" chuckled Erkanni. "Even when it's not overcast, the heaving seas will make a hash of your high noon-north." At Orry's crestfallen look, Erkanni added, "See, Orry, they make you learn all that in school, but no one uses the sextant unless they're in the middle of a calm sea with their dead-reckoning bungled up. Practical navigating is mostly a matter of landmarks and bottom-dredges."

"Then how does anyone sail where they've never been before?" objected Orry.

"No one's done that since ancient times. I think they must have lost a lot of ships before learning their way across the wide oceans."

Dialfi suggested, "With modern tools, though, we might manage a bit better."

"No matter what," said Erkanni, "crossing the open ocean will be very dangerous. None of you have seen the hill-high seas beyond Faraday, where only the albatross dares sport with the tearing whitecaps. No Nuathan ship is built to handle such waves."

"So we'll steal one from the Syowyans," suggested Orry, only half in jest.

Erkanni grinned, but went on, "And navigation would be a whole other problem. You could figure out how far north you were well enough, from the height of the sun and stars. But as to how far east or west — there'd be no telling, without landmarks. And the ocean might stretch thousands of kiloms in any direction you happened to try."

Orry was undaunted. "That's what makes it a voyage of discovery! We'll do it together, right?"

Rowan shook off jhr musings, and said, "Seriously, though, we have to decide how to tell the scholars about all this."

"I thought you wanted to keep it well away from the scholars!" laughed Erkanni.

"Yeah," chimed in Orry; "remember how you charged down the mountainside with it to keep it away from Dana, and later got the whole family to make a fool of poor Sa Torin?"

"That was before we'd found out what it was about," said Rowan, blushing a bit, as they all laughed at the memory. Rowan touched the bundle of papers on the table. "Dialfi, will you carry the translation with you, and Grandmother's copy of the runes? And find someone at the Akademy who will take them seriously?"

Dialfi furrowed jhr brow doubtfully. "They're going want to see the original, for purposes of authentification. Radiocarbon dating and so on. The name Kassandra is sure to generate some resistance, not to mention the depiction of the Founders' actions."

Rowan shook jhr head. "There's no time to get the book from Yngencloven now. Besides, I'm not at all sure it should go to the scholars."

Orry hooted. "Of course you're not!"

But Rowan said calmly, "The book is Kassandra's message to the future, not to the scholars alone. She warned of trusting the powerful too much, remember?"

Yrssu spoke up. "My people also need warning of the worse times that may be coming."

Dialfi looked at Yrssu, puzzled. "Can't you just tell them?"

"My word alone cannot bear such weighty tidings as *Emru*; they are needing to see it in Kassandra's own hand. But your scholars, they are practiced in reading truth from the world itself. Once set on the right path, they will have no trouble finding their way; is it not so?"

Dialfi was hardly going to argue with this depiction of scholars. "You're right. It's less a question of history, than whether the world is now cooling, and what to do about it. There are bound to be at least some scholars willing to look into that."

So it was decided. Dialfi was entrusted to carry with jhm to the Akademy both Grandmother's copy of the runes (the well-worn pages densely scribbled with Rowan's and Yrssu's notes and pocked with not a few coffee stains), plus the entire translation that Rowan had written out (perhaps not quite as neatly as a scholar would have done, but well above jhr usual standard). Kassandra's original, secure in its ornamented copper casket and buried at Yngencloven, Yrssu was charged to bring to jhr people.

Talk turned to the summer travels ahead. After a time, Erkanni noticed how downcast Rowan looked. "Why don't you sail with us this summer? I'm sure your uncle would be happy to have you."

Rowan shook jhr head regretfully.

Orry told Erkanni, "Jhe can't. Someone has to stay and help on the farm, and Rowan being neither sailor nor scholar is the one to do it."

Rowan turned away from Erkanni's concerned gaze, and said, "There's still one last bit to read from Kassandra."

> I cast my thoughts into your far-off times, oh future reader, when our loss and grief will be but the echo of an echo. Is the world we left you once again a kind and gentle place? Is your air full of birdsong and the drone of insects, of the perfume of blossoms and apples and balsam fir, and every shade of green my heart aches to see again? I hope the rain falls softly on your faces in spring, and the sun beats down with brazen might, though from no higher than the outspread span of your hand.

Can you possibly understand how it was for us, who knew so much but did so little? Our air was as full of facts as the great cities were of smoke and coal-dust. We knew things both wondrous and strange, both trivial and devastating. We knew within minutes when a missile was launched, or terrorists attacked, or an earthquake happened on the other side of the globe; we knew how quickly the forests were being logged and burned and the coral reefs dying; we knew just how few tigers and blue whales remained. We knew how many humans walked the overburdened planet. We knew that thanks to our inability to stop burning fossil fuels, the glaciers and ice sheets were dissolving, the seas were rising, and the storms and the droughts worsening.

Oh, we knew.

We watched, paralyzed, as the disaster unfolded, and grieved; grieved in anticipation, like someone with a slow illness gradually wasting away, losing more day by day and year by year. And all the time, we knew it was eminently fixable, by none of us alone but by all of us together, if only we could have summoned the energy, the spirit, the collective will. Far too little was done, and we frittered the time away until no choice was left that could have staved off catastrophe.

And there was no heroic action, even at that moment of greatest clarity when the choice could not have been more clear. People chose to continue the destruction instead, chose to struggle individually, to build higher walls and grab and keep what they could for as long as they could, which was not long. Cynics who'd heard of game theory said it had been inevitable all along.

We could have risen beyond this mindless competition. We had shown flashes of potential before, however riddled with flaws and selfishness – in the rebuilding after great wars, in acts of forgiveness for the staggering wrongs of genocide and segregation and slavery, in ceasing to damage the ozone layer, in the marshaling of resources for the race into space, in the restraint we were slowly and fitfully learning over nuclear weapons.

We of New Athens may be all that now remains of that great flowering of civilization. It was what they'd planned for decades, and yet, now that it has come to pass, the adults seem unhinged by shock and grief. At least, that's the only way I can understand why scientists, whose deepest motivation is to understand and face reality, think they can protect the world by glossing over what caused this Catastrophe, and keep humankind fenced behind a violent, gale-prone sea with the lie that this is the only land left on Earth.

Yet if the planet ever does heal, this place of refuge will become a deathly trap. Snow will begin lingering further and further down the mountainsides, and rivers of ice will once again creep down their flanks. If people do not realize how great and lasting the change – that it is no mere spell of harsh winters and cold summers, but a return to another regime entirely – they will not know until too late how they must act to save themselves.

You born into such times will know heart-rending loss even as we have, and all but unbearable change. The Great Riddle will again be set before you, as it must be set before every intelligent, tool-wielding species. Perhaps no race in the history of the cosmos has ever solved it. Nonetheless you must set out on the hopeless quest, your eyes on the guiding stars; for it is our fate to strive against darkness, and make answers out of impossibilities.

So I consign this testament to the Earth.

Early the next morning, Rowan and Yrssu braved pounding headaches to see the others off. After a quick goodbye, Orry made jhmself scarce, afraid that Uncle Narv would change his mind and send jhm home at the last minute.

Yrssu and Erkanni had a few quiet words, then Erkanni turned to Rowan. "It's a good thing you're doing, to help your folks on the farm, you know."

Rowan shrugged. "Orry's right; I never tried to do anything else."

"Rowan, you just spent the winter helping a gnomad translate a book written thousands of years ago, that upends our whole notion of the world. Kassandra found who she was looking for. You know that, don't you, Rowan? How did she put it, someone pure of heart, strong of spirit, and open of mind."

"Maybe the world was better as it was, though."

Erkanni was puzzled. "You didn't make the world start this drastic cooling, Rowan. But thanks to your discovery, we won't be helplessly caught in a snare of our ancestors' making."

No, but we might be caught in a yet older and more subtle one, thought Rowan. Jhe reached out and touched the pendant hanging around Erkanni's neck. "I still can't believe how it's just like the one Kassandra put in the casket with the book. Erkanni, what if your fohn had come all the way from Josiah, handed down from father to son all this time?"

Erkanni looked hard at Rowan. "Selkie to son, you mean?"

"If you like." Rowan met his gaze. Jhe'd thought a lot about what Erkanni had said, the night of the Raid, about what it had been like for Kassandra to live among those Colony efts, and various other odd comments over the course of the winter. Jhe had come to jhr own conclusions as to the nature of the Islander, and had more or less made peace with the strangeness of that.

Erkanni broke into a smile, and the light in his eyes was brighter than Rowan had yet seen.

There came a piping call from the foredeck. "I'd best be off. I'll be seeing you, Rowan." He reached out his hand and touched jhr cheek, then crossed the gangplank and disappeared forward.

The ship slowly nosed away from the dock and headed out on a broad reach. With no crew duties as yet, Dialfi leaned over the rail waving both hands, calling something that the wind snatched away.

Rowan waved back, not trusting jhr voice.

As the ship swiftly tilted off towards the broad Ross Sea and distant Getz, Yrssu beside jhm said softly, "*Ang tarn arra kern.*"

But Rowan shook jhr head, eyes blinded by tears.

Chapter 26. Rowan's Road

I do not seek one schooled in the ways of power.
— Kassandra Morgan-Ávvu

Rowan straightened jhr aching back and rubbed with a grimy hand at a strand of hair tickling jhr forehead. Hoeing in June was not unlike trying to slay the many-headed Hydra. New weeds sprang up undaunted behind jhm even as the limp bodies of their predecessors littered the path, wilting in the hot sun. Rowan leaned on the hoe like a walking stick, peering across bright pastures to the cool and shadowy forest beyond.

Rowan's hands had already hardened again, and jhr bronzed skin tingled and tightened with pleasant awareness of long days spent in the wind and sun. Freckles littered jhr face and chest, as if the vanished stars of winter had found refuge there.

Yrssu had no such tan, having covered up against the sun in the Kymran fashion. Jhe had taken Far up on his offer to help on the farm through the summer, in return for enough wages to cover train fare to the southern end of the line. "I would be walking all that time in any case, so I can better be putting my muscles to helping you Ynglings, in the stead."

Rowan wondered at this; surely, Yrssu could hop the train as jhe'd done in the autumn for no fare at all. Unless jhe were concerned about reports of increasingly violent altercations with gnomads in the hinterlands? But Rowan didn't ask questions, being grateful for Yrssu's company for a bit longer. After seeing jhr school marks for the past year, which had been even worse than usual, Far had said it might make more sense for Rowan to stay on the farm through the coming winter. Rowan didn't have the heart to argue. Erkanni might not be coming back to town in any case, and Orry had jhr own circle of friends that Rowan did not feel particularly close to. Jhe might as well be of use to the folks at home, making jhmself useful.

That summer, Rowan did a lot of thinking while saying little. Jhr parents wondered at jhr unwonted quietness. Far thought jhe was just growing up, but Mar shook her head at this, and watched her middle child with quiet concern.

The time came to bring the sheep back from the high pasture. A pack of youngsters from neighboring farms had been looking after them all month, along with their own larger herds. Rowan and Yrssu set off with the dog Kei and packs full of food and a couple of blankets. Even though they'd only be away a few days, it felt like a holiday, climbing up and up on a steep trail into the wilds and leaving the farm with its endless drudgery far below. When they found the shrill and overly active youngsters around dinnertime, Rowan felt strangely old and sober among them. Jhe and Yrssu sat by the embers of a dying campfire and talked late into the night, as Dana and Dialfi had done in past years.

They spoke of many things, but especially of Kassandra's message. Rowan at last voiced jhr worries about what would come of people learning the truth about the so-called Drowned Lands, and the rest of it. "It's not just a matter of finding the lost lands of the North, the way Orry and Erkanni seem to think! It's not enough to trust the scholars to fix everything, the way Dialfi thinks. Are we really so different from the Ancients? I don't think so. They weren't terrible people; they were just caught in a situation too complex for anyone to find a way out. Kassandra's message was not just that the Founders lied about the Drowned Lands — as you told me, the Kymran pretty much already knew that — or that they suppressed the details of what caused the Catastrophe and substituted a taboo against using fossil carbon."

Quietly, Yrssu said, "What, then?"

"It's that we have to find an answer to the Cosmic Riddle. What if there is no answer? What if people spread back north, only to unleash another Catastrophe?"

Yrssu nodded, as if satisfied in some way. "Rowan, you bear the mark Emru."

"*Danger foretold.* Is it the danger of the cooling, or the danger of overrunning the Earth again?"

Yrssu only said, "That is for you to discover."

"It's too big of a question for me!" cried Rowan.

"Maybe," said Yrssu slowly, "you should come with me to the Waste, and talk with our elders about these matters."

Rowan stared at the Kymran. "You would bring me with you, truly?"

"It is not good to walk the Waste alone, nor will it be easy for me to cross through the borderlands, the way things are nowadays. And perhaps it would be helping you know what to do with Kassandra's warning."

A couple days later, when they'd brought the sheep home, Rowan climbed the stairs to Mar's workroom. It would have been easier to talk to Far, but somehow jhe felt it had to be Mar, this once. Jhe pushed aside the tapestry that served as a door to Mar's workroom. There were the well-stocked shelves holding all the world's colors, waiting their time to be woven into patterns yet undreamed.

Mar's head, bent over the loom, blazed silver at the edges in the low-angled evening sunshine pouring through the window. The shuttle clattered busily back and forth. Then Mar paused the loom and looked up. "Oh, Rowan! I didn't see you come in." Mar tightened one of the threads of the warp, while studying the emerging pattern with cocked head. "It's so quiet around here these days; I still haven't gotten used to your sibs being away. Thank Gaea we still have you with us."

Rowan smiled awkwardly. "And Yrssu. Though jhe will be leaving soon."

Mar was studying the emerging pattern, and made a slight alteration in the tension. "I don't suppose you could persuade jhm to stay on and help with the harvest?"

"No chance. Jhe's got to join a camp before winter sets in."

"But jhe could just as well stay here until the spring," pointed out Mar.

Rowan was happy to see how Mar had accepted Yrssu, but explained, "Yrssu's been pretty homesick lately. Besides, jhe wants to bring word to jhr people about what we read in the book."

"The book. You know, you never did tell me how that turned out," Mar said, with gratifying curiosity.

So Rowan told Mar what they'd read about the Catastrophe being largely caused by a sudden warming of the Earth, brought on by people adding too much fossil carbon to the air with their burning industry. "Dialfi understands the physics of it, and says it explains a great deal that the Humanual had left opaque."

"That sounds like our Dialfi, all right," smiled Mar sadly. Clearly she missed her eldest a good deal.

Rowan went on to explain what it had been like for Kassandra, who'd lived through the cataclysmic Founding, struggling to find a place to belong in a secret colony she'd never been meant to join. Her sense of betrayal when she'd learned of the plan to deceive later generations into thinking theirs the last land on Earth, and her fears that one day, when the Earth began to heal and cool, Nuatha could find itself in great and unguessed danger, and had crafted a message to the distant future in the form of the book of runes.

Mar silently took in this astonishing series of revelations. Rowan's face was lit by the lowering sun, as jhe poured out jhr heart to Mar as jhe had not done since early childhood. ". . . and you know, after the Raid, Mar, people starting acting so strange. All this talk of going to war with Syowya. And they've been blaming the Kymrans for the failing southern farms. I guess it's because Kymrans can be driven off, unlike late snowstorms and early freezes. Don't people understand that everyone is having a harder time these days? Fighting each other won't do any good, if our world is changing back to the way it was before the Catastrophe."

Mar's hands were resting quite still beside the loom, a strange sight to Rowan. "So that is what you read in your book, Rowan, you and Yrssu. Dialfi told me how seriously you worked on the translating, but jhe didn't explain what was in it."

"It wasn't until the very end that we realized what the message really was," Rowan said. "Now Dialfi's showing it to the scholars, and hopefully we can figure out a way to deal with this cooling that seems to be happening. We may even have to seek out the lost lands of the North. That's what Orry's hoping for, anyhow. And Yrssu will bring word to jhr people, of course."

Mar, more comfortable in the realm of the practical than the sublime, replied, "Well, we've certainly seen a rough spell here, lately. Are you sure you can't persuade Yrssu to stay on a bit longer? It would be a great help, and give you some company, too; it must be lonesome around here for you, these days."

"Sure, I can ask. Anyhow, before jhe goes, we'll bring in the rest of the hay, and tackle that broken fence in the north pasture."

"Don't overwork yourself, Rowan," Mar said, as she turned back to her weaving; "no one expects you to do the work of three—"

"I don't," interrupted Rowan; "The truth is, Anno does an awful lot of it, now that she's feeling better."

Rowan still made no move to leave, and Mar looked hard at jhm. "What are you getting at?"

Rowan cleared jhr throat. "I sort of thought it might be better if I went with Yrssu. To help jhm over the border, and to see what I can learn from the Kymrans. For one thing, Yrssu thinks they might have a map of the whole world, preserved from pre-Catastrophe days . . . ." Rowan's voice faded, and jhe watched Mar anxiously.

Mar's expression was unreadable. She gazed a long while at the wooden figure carved into the rafter overhead, at the kind, assured smile, the powerful shoulders and graceful curve of backbone.

At last she turned to Rowan. "Yes, I see that you must go."

"But will the farm be all right?" Rowan was able to ask, now.

"We'll manage. We have Anno, as you said; and Matti will come, if we need her."

Rowan now turned to go, but Mar gestured for jhm to sit down. "I would speak with you a little more. Wherever your path leads you, it will be a long time before we see each other again."

Tears sprang to Rowan's eyes, all unexpected. Mar continued, in a steady voice, "It's going to be different around here, but that's the way of the world: the same for a great long while, then all at once everything changes. Anno has become an imago and you three have found your callings, all in the same year."

"I never thought you'd understand."

"Rowan, we are not so different, you and I. No, don't shake your head; that doesn't always make it easy to get along; quite the opposite, in fact. I want to explain something to you. When I was young, I was very restless, couldn't put my hand to anything for long, and to tell the truth, I got into a lot of trouble. Well, you don't need to hear about all that. I was searching for something, perhaps, without knowing what it was; some purpose; some worthwhile task to consume me. My parents were almost in despair over me — and no, before you ask, your father and I have not felt that kind of anxiety about you."

Mar had never spoken like this to Rowan before.

"Then I saw the work of a master weaver and something clicked in my mind. I discovered color, you could say. I wanted to make colors move and dance like that more than anything. I was on fire with it, nothing else mattered; I would learn anything, do anything to master it. Weaving is how I make sense of the world."

"And that's how it's been ever since," concluded Rowan. This was the Mar jhe knew.

"Not quite," Mar smiled. "Later, I met Sol, and had you three. Listen, I may not know much about this book — though now I wish there was time for you to tell me more — but I can see it is for you what weaving is for me — it is the thread that you must follow wherever it leads. And so this is the blessing that I give you as I send you out into the world, my middle and nearest child, who with your sibs make the best and most important weaving I have ever done. I wove your bones and sinews within the loom of my body, knowing even less how I did so than I know how I do my craft, but with great love. I have watched you grow and become yourself all these long years, and now at last I cut the tense lines of the warp and release you out into the wide world.

"I have no doubt that much will be asked of you in the end, if you take this path. But follow your thread always, Rowan, and nothing will be so ill that it cannot be borne."

Chapter 27. Southwards

And so I shook the dust of the settled places from my feet, and entered the wilderness at last.

— Kassandra Morgan-Ávvu

Rowan paused to tighten jhr laces and to dig out some gloves. Pulling them over stiff fingers, jhe tilted jhr head to gaze up at the craggy peaks whose flanks they'd begun to scale. This was the great shield of mountains that formed the border between Nuatha and the Waste. They hid the sun for hours even in full summer. They still held the chill of winter; it came pouring down their dark rocks and out of dank gullies that never saw the daylight.

They'd reached it by train, and without paying a cent or hiding on the roof, either. It had been Anno's idea, to have one of them wear the veil so that they could ride to the southern monastery free of charge.

Far had burst out laughing. "Brilliant!"

"It's a bit irreverent, to use the veil to avoid train-fare," objected Mar. But Far pointed out that Dialfi would be following the traditions of the scholars when jhr time came, so really they would only be putting their due to a slightly different use. "Besides, the veil will hide Yrssu from any unfriendly eyes."

After a very early breakfast and goodbyes that had felt strangely unreal — a tight, wordless hug from Mar, the packet of traveling cakes from Anno, Grandmother's irrepressible twinkle as she whispered, "So you do get to go live with the gnomads after all, lucky one"; after Far had brought out the heavy veil used for one going to the monks, while telling many a joke that couldn't quite ward off the tear in his eye; and had driven them to the station, where he gave them two sacks of finely ground salt, and pressed into Rowan's hand his treasured sun compass on its silver chain, that he'd had from his father the wandering bard — after all that, there was nothing to do but wait.

The train was running late.

A cart clopped around the bend and pulled up beside Far: Silas, the farmhand at the Ettencotts'. "Fine morning, eh?" he said. "Here to pick up some equipment?"

Far muttered something about bringing a kinseft to the monks.

"What, at this time of year? Bad luck." Silas wiped his nose delicately on his sleeve. "And with your eldest off to the Akademy, like our Dana. Not that Dana ever had much to do with the hayin'!"

Rowan looked straight ahead, taking refuge in dignified silence. Jhe wished it had been anyone but a farmhand from the Ettencotts'. Not that it really mattered; only somehow, it gave jhm a nervous feeling.

Thankfully, the train pulled up not long after. They settled into the nearly empty carriage. The train skimmed past ever more hardscrabble farmland, skirting the massive coastal peaks rising up slowly higher on both sides, to heights where the snow lay deep and white even in late summer. Rowan was fascinated, never having taken the train in this direction. Yrssu, somewhat hampered by the veil, gazed out at the view with pleasure.

This peaceful reverie was interrupted when a dozen people noisily entered the car, a veiled person protected in their midst. They seemed to think a party of just two was a sad thing, and immediately set about trying to amend it as best they could, settling themselves with cheerful bustle in the nearby seats.

"You too, my dear?" they asked Yrssu, who nodded warily.

"A bit small, isn't jhe?" whispered someone noisily.

"There's some as get their growth after the Change, you know, Lanara."

Yrssu straightened jhr hunched shoulders and sat as tall as possible. Rowan thought of changing cars, then decided it would only attract more attention.

They were a friendly bunch, full of jokes and stories, passing around bowls of crackers and cookies and scattering the crumbs with abandon. Rowan had always imagined that going to the monastery would be a decorous and serious business, but apparently not for these folks.

"Do you remember Jotte's first trip?" asked a large woman in a tenor voice.

A seat-mate giggled, "Her *first* trip? Wasn't one enough?"

"Oh no, not for Jotte." The large woman leaned forward and launched into the tale. "Jhe'd made a bet with Anka that jhr time would come before autumn, and managed to work jhmself up into some sort of delusional state. Prickly skin, moodiness, aches, the lot. Only it was all in jhr head! Somehow it wasn't discovered until after the—" here, her friend elbowed her and she lowered her voice to a hoarse whisper. The only thing Rowan managed to catch was, " . . . in the canopied rooms, you can imagine what a scandal *that* was? They put jhm on the next train home with a severe reprimand. Oh, jhe didn't hear the end of that for a month of Fridays!" The woman guffawed through her wide, rubbery lips, spraying out spittle.

Then she reached over to poke Yrssu in the ribs. "You're a skinny one, aren't you? Some say that means you'll turn out a man." Yrssu just shrugged. If jhe spoke, they would catch the Kymran accent, which though fainter than it had been in the fall, was still quite evident.

"Oh, I understand," the irrepressible creature went on; "you aren't at all sure you like coming to the end of efthood. But believe me," she nudged her friend, "there are compensations, as you'll see for yourself soon enough. Right, Yanneh?" She and the woman beside her broke into cascades of laughter.

All this was merely annoying. Worse was when they began discussing recent problems with the gnomads. *I hear it's gotten so's you can't leave a door unlocked, near the borderlands. They send their children over to steal things from the storehouses, coffee and flour and eggs and anything they can get their grubby hands on, thinking we're too soft to do anything about it.*

Now that the patrol's gotten some of them Adelian wolfhounds, they'll put an end to that sort of nonsense.

They were saying on the radio how one family woke up not long ago to find them camped right in the middle of their half-grown barley, those horrid beasts rampaging about.

How dare they trample all over decent, hardworking folks' fields?

They've got no respect for borders. You don't see us marauding about in their country!

Well, maybe that needs to change.

Rowan stole a glance at Yrssu, but could see nothing through the thick veil. Jhe seemed to be breathing rather rapidly. Rowan squeezed jhr hand, and turned back to the window. They'd planned to slip off the train one stop before the Monastery. But how in Gaea's name would they manage it, with this noisy group all around them? Rowan had no doubt they'd make a fuss about anything, even if were only a trip to the toilets.

As the long train ride wore on, however, full of food and emptied of chatter and gossip, they all dozed off to the soothing rocking of the wheels.

Rowan nudged Yrssu as jhe heard the muted call for their station. The train began to slow, and they hurriedly gathered their bags and stepped gingerly past the sprawled legs in the aisle. Rowan held jhr breath as jhe bumped into one particularly inconvenient ankle, but the sleeper only made a face without opening her eyes. They'd made it to the steps at the far end of the car, when someone sat up rubbing her eyes and caught sight of the pair of them. She sat up abruptly, calling out, "Are we there already? Hey, we nearly slept through our stop!" She began nudging her companions awake.

Rowan and Yrssu leaped down the stairs and made for the cover of the forest as fast as they could, Yrssu tearing off the veil as they went. Behind them they heard confused calling, then, after a while, the sound of the train starting up again. They plopped down on fir needles, panting, and began to laugh and laugh, until their sides ached with it.

"Did you see that sleeper with the spit dribbling down her ear, who looked so confused?" gasped out Rowan.

"They will be telling stories about us for years!" chortled Yrssu, when jhe managed to catch jhr breath.

A few other people had gotten off too, backwoods trappers and hikers. Rowan and Yrssu sat on a large boulder, looking around and adjusting their gear, as these others set off down a well-worn trail that followed the river. "That is one way we will not go," Yrssu said quietly.

"We might blend in better on a proper trail," Rowan suggested. "We'd just look like ordinary hikers."

"We will not blend in — my hair, and yours too for that matter, the shape of my tent, it will all stand out. Neh, better that we stay away from people now."

They entered the forest of towering firs and hemlock at a gap between two huge trunks. As they ducked under brambly vines and climbed around fallen root masses, Yrssu looked uncomfortably around the thickly grown, labyrinthine twilight.

"Not safe like open country; too much is hidden," jhe muttered. Once they were well inside, the underbrush thinned somewhat, and at least they could choose their way better. The plan was to walk due south seeking a way through the mountains, keeping to stream-beds and following any small paths they might find.

When they reached a bit of open country, Rowan pulled out the journey-watch Far had given jhm. It was a very fine one; it kept precise time, and never needed winding, having an exquisite ratchet mechanism to wind itself from the motions of your walking. It had two folding arms opposite one another that could stand up to cast a precise shadow, and a swivel mechanism with a sealed bubble to level it. In the back was a compartment with a sliding cover that held a piece of sunglass, to look through on cloudy days; looking through it revealed hundreds of tiny lines that pointed to the invisible sun.

At first, Yrssu could not see the point of it. "Why do you need to know what time it is, now that we are in the wild lands?"

"It's not so much to keep time," Rowan explained; "as to know where you're headed." Far had taught Rowan how to use it as a sun compass way back in jhr childhood when they had wandered the hills near Yngencloven together. He'd explained how the face of the watch was like the land from above, as a crow would see it, or a hovering skua. Midnight on the clock-face corresponded to due south, and twelve noon to north. To the right lay the hour of six in the morning, pointing widdershins. Opposite it, eighteen o'clock, pointed sunwise. The twenty-four hours of the day made a fine division of compass points, so that you only had to line it up with the hour hand pointing towards the sun to know your orientation.

"A little sundial that runs on its own," said Yrssu. "Is that what a clock is?"

"I guess so," answered Rowan. "Have you ever seen the orrery, at the museum?"

"No, what is that?"

"It's a machine that copies the movements of the sun, moon, planets and stars, so they go spinning round each other. It helps you understand why summer is so light and winter so dark, and why we only see the full moon in winter. But do you know, Yrssu, I've been thinking how it would be quite different, in the north."

Yrssu looked curious, so Rowan went on with a sideways grin, "And so it is, and so I shall tell you: our planet is spinning like a tilted top." Rowan rotated jhr fist, jhr thumb at the top standing for the land of Terraus. "That's what makes everything seem to circle us; really it's the planet that's going around and around. But it's also orbiting slowly round the sun — that's my head—" Jhe moved jhr arm to demonstrate, as Yrssu laughed, "which makes the year. We face towards the sun in summer, but in winter we face the other way, and look upon the stars."

"But how would it be any different to the north?" asked Yrssu.

"Erkanni told me how in Faraday, the sun rides higher in the northern sky than it ever does in Adare, and lower in the south. Far in the north, the sun must go right over your head."

Rowan pointed straight up, to a place the sun should never be. Yrssu looked incredulous.

"Look," insisted Rowan, "if you lived right here," pointing to the middle of the fist-Earth, "you'd never point away from the sun at all. So there wouldn't be any suncircles or winternights, but only the little day-nights of fall and spring, all the year round. How must people living in the northern lands manage? How would they know when to plant their crops, and when to go to school? I wonder what sort of holidays they have. Maybe they pay no mind to the year's passage at all!"

Yrssu clapped at this performance. "Surely, you are becoming a storyteller of sorts. Perhaps you already feel the air of the Waste blowing over you. —But it is time I began to teach you Kymran speech, for you will not find many speakers of Anglic on the other side of these mountains."

Rowan said smugly, "I've already picked up a lot, from Kassandra's book."

"Oh, that won't help you much. It has very little everyday language in it. Here, listen." And Yrssu began a lesson in the basic vocabulary useful around a Kymran camp.

A dekilom on, Yrssu was still at it. "Now, are you remembering the word for a caribou whose fur has fallen from its horns?"

"Was that *khaloavy*?"

"Good. And for a yellow one who usually births twins?"

"*Kualtu.*"

"Yes, if you are about to harness her. But if she is to run free, it is *kualdu*. Now, try saying *juonna härker nethallen.*"

"*Juona herker nezhahllenn*?"

Yrssu burst out laughing. "What?" said Rowan, annoyed.

Through guffaws, Yrssu choked out, "You just said, 'the potato has a gnat-bite on his elbow.' At least, I think you did. You may have said, 'the potato bit the gnat with its elbow.'"

"I did not, neither one!"

"No, see, you are needing to use the short 'o', with the high tone, and the proper 'th', not your awful Nuathan 'zh.' And also — oh, just listen." Yrssu repeated the sentence slowly.

"It sounds exactly the same to me."

"Then you will need a great deal more practice before anyone will understand a word you say."

Rowan tried to keep jhr patience. "Honestly, Yrssu, can't we start with more ordinary words?"

"It is nothing but ordinary words I have been teaching you."

"What about hello, goodbye, please, and thank you?"

"You can wave for hello and goodbye, hold out two hands for please — not just one, that is very rude — and put your palms together for thank you."

"You Kymrans must be a quiet bunch, when you're not talking about your animals. But how do you say, 'where is the bathroom?'"

"What in Gaea's name are you talking about, Rowan? Where isn't the bathroom? Just go a ways from the camp if it is a long-term one. That reminds me, a settled camp in midsummer is called *muanttu*, and a camp where several clans meet is . . . "

They walked on and on, upwards past a series of valleys slashed through by leaping, foaming streams, ice-cold with snowmelt, breathing deeply of the fresh forest scents.

It was tricky going along the rushing streams, along rocks dark and wet with spray hemmed in by the thick, steep forest, but they got surer and bolder as the day wore on, until they were leaping from one rock to another like goats on a mountainside. They walked on and on; even so late in the summer, the darkest it ever got was the shadowy gloaming, when the sun dipped behind the highest peaks. They stopped at last in a sheltered hollow near the top of a rise. Yrssu fixed a warm meal over a fire he built with unthinking expertise.

As they settled down inside the tent, Rowan asked, "Where are the runes?"

"What runes?"

"You said Kymrans wrote runes all over the walls of your tents."

"Oh, not on a little one like this – that is for real homes, when you marry and set up a family. There is only just a token line from the Humanual, right up there, see? It says, 'All life requires a separation of the inside from the outside.' That is the sort of thing we write on small tents."

Chapter 28. The Chase

There was a poem that my mother used to recite, that I wish I could find again. But I can only recall a bit of the ending: "I hear a dead man's cry from Autumn long since past. I cry to you, beyond this bitter air."

— Kassandra Morgan-Ávvu

All through the next day, Rowan and Yrssu climbed switchbacks through forest interspersed with steep, boulder-strewn scree. The faint paths came and went, the work of deer or humans or of their imaginations acting on the landscape. Here the trees grew at such a steep angle to the mountainside that their trunks curved out in graceful J-shapes, as though prepared for the ground to slide out from under them.

In midmorning, they stopped for lunch on a high overlook, where they could look back down the wide green and golden valley they'd started from. The land lay spread out like a living map, silvery train tracks curving off towards the east to cross a broad river, fed by mountain streams and waterfalls pouring off the peaks all around them.

Rowan made out the little station where they'd left the train the day before. Well, distances were deceptive in the mountains, and hiking off trail was bound to be slow work. As they watched, a train pulled in, and tiny figures got off. Several of them walked over and sat down on the very boulder where Rowan and Yrssu had crouched, waiting for the train to go. For some reason this made Rowan shudder. But it meant nothing; it just happened to be a good rock for sitting on. They shouldered their packs and went back to picking their way over the rough and broken ground.

Soon after, a cold wind came up, and the sky became dark with clouds. They decided to make camp early. There was not a bit of flat ground to be found; but finally they chose a small, not too uncomfortable spot, tucked back among a trio of tenacious firs. They went to sleep amid the roaring of winds, Yrssu having assured Rowan that the narrow, pyramid-shaped tent could not be blown off the mountainside.

They awoke to a vast stillness. A dim, filtered light was coming through the walls of the tent. Yrssu opened the flap and gave a surprised laugh.

"What is it?" asked Rowan sleepily. Jhe was stiff from the long hike and unready to climb out of the warm blankets just yet.

"Come and see."

Rowan crawled over and looked out at a world become white and smooth, the hollows were tinged with shadows of blue and rose and yellow by the morning sun. "It's beautiful," Rowan breathed.

“These mountains are indeed mighty. Who could have guessed we would be wanting skis in summertime?”

“How will we manage to get through it?” Rowan wondered. It was at least knee-deep, more in many places.

“Better to wait a while, I am thinking. Soon enough it will melt down, or at least make a crust we can walk on.”

They gazed out at the silent, white landscape. “Look!” Rowan pointed down along the route they’d hiked the day before. A trio of ant-sized figures was emerging from the forest. Beside them a dog plunged through drifts, hampered by a long leash, the faint trace of its barking carrying up the slope.

Yrssu said, “We are far from the train, and from the main trail also.”

“That’s where hunters go, too,” Rowan answered reassuringly.

“Maybe it is gnomads they are hunting,” Yrssu suggested quietly.

“Nah, they’ve got nothing to do with us.” Rowan tried to believe this was true.

They passed the time as best they could while waiting for the snow to harden up enough to walk on. After breakfast Yrssu tried to give Rowan another language lesson, but Rowan found it hard to concentrate. Jhe looked out of the flap, and caught sight of the hunters again, a ways up the slope but further to the left. While Rowan and Yrssu watched, unreasonably holding their breath, they crossed a drift, marring the smooth curve with the broad track of their snowshoes. They disappeared in the cover of forest, one lagging slightly behind the other two.

Yrssu got a roll of cloth out of jhr pack and spread it out on the floor of the tent, pushing their clothes and bedrolls to the walls to make room. The cloth had a grid of long, straight lines some of whose intersections were marked with stars and other shapes. Yrssu got out two small sacks and folded open their tops, revealing light and dark bits of polished wood, about the size and shape of fava beans.

Yrssu explained, "This game is called *Vittà*. Here. You are day, I am night. Night is the elder, you see. We are each striving to persist; and also to overwhelm the other, or perhaps to come into balance — there are many different styles of play." Jhe showed Rowan the basic rules of capturing chips, and of securing territory, and they began to place the chips on the grid. As Rowan gained confidence with the simple rules, jhe eagerly mounted attacks on the dark chips. Time and again, jhe would be a move away from a large victory, and then a dark piece would slip in and capture one or two of jhrs, and the attack would collapse into disarray, the hunter turned hunted, the carefully constructed wall itself surrounded by enemy lines.

"You are too reckless, too impulsive." Yrssu shook jhr head when Rowan made the same mistake yet again.

"Who cares; it's only a game," Rowan groused. "Can't we be on our way? We're going to freeze if we sit here much longer."

They looked out of the tent flap. The landscape was pale and very still. The sun was sinking behind the coastal range, putting them in deep shadow. A lone bird soared far overheard, calling eerily in the silence.

Yrssu tested the snow and said it would do. They packed up quickly, bundling the tent into the top of Rowan's pack. Yrssu kicked the snow around to cover the bare ground where the tent had been. This inspired Rowan to climb one of the snow-laden firs and shake snow down from the branches, in imitation of what happened as snow melted and plopped down onto the ground. The result was quite impressively naturalistic, and jhe grinned at Yrssu triumphantly.

A shout rang out, and, from jhr place on the springy branch, Rowan saw two figures on a slope to their left, pointing at the still-quivering boughs.

Yrssu didn't waste time in recriminations. "Let's go!"

Rowan paused, shading jhr eyes with one hand. If these hunters really were after gnomads, all jhe had to do was show them they had the wrong quarry. Waving, jhe called, "Good e'en! What are you hunting with such a fine dog, mountain lion or beorn?"

The hunters' silent and sinister response was to head down the slope straight towards them. With the shuffling gait peculiar to snowshoes, they loped expertly over the snow. The dog strained at the leash, barking madly.

Rowan gripped the branch and swung down. Jhe shouldered jhr pack and they headed downhill.

It was impossible to move quickly. The crust would hold for a few steps and then treacherously give way so that they would plunge in up to their knees. The sharp edges cut into their trousers and scraped and numbed their legs.

At first their pursuers shouted words that could not be made out, but soon gave up and saved their breath for the chase. Yrssu and Rowan kept to cover among the tumbled boulders and crooked flanks of the mountain.

Bare ground or snow made no difference; the dog would be able to track them either way, so they took the fastest route they could find. Coming to a steep-edged ravine, they slid down with breakneck haste for the stream that must run along its lowest point. They found it among low-growing brush that splintered with loud cracks as they hurtled through it.

They tried to confuse the trail by running downstream in the icy water, luckily only ankle-deep. But the stones were slippery, and their numbed feet got more and more clumsy at keeping their footing; and anyhow following a stream was not a very clever trick, given the unmistakable trail of broken brush leading to it. But hearing the hound barking in the distance, they stumbled along faster, willing their frozen feet to action.

In their panicked run downhill they'd already lost much of the height they'd so laboriously gained the day before. A memory of the living map they'd seen from the overlook flashed through Rowan's mind, and jhe feared they were letting themselves be driven to the open country of the wide valley and the train tracks, where there would be no hope of escaping these pursuers, whoever they were.

Just ahead, the stream joined a river which ran fast and foamy. They paused, then rushed on along the river, heading downstream. On the other side, they could see a tumbled field of boulders, the remains of a landslide that had torn through the forest, stretching up and up to steep cliffs. Rowan pointed, and Yrssu nodded agreement. If they could cross the river, it would be a good refuge. That rough terrain of crannies, steep cliffs, and loose rock would be more difficult for their pursuers to navigate, while holding the leash of a lunging wolfhound, than for Rowan and Yrssu with their youthful strength and free hands. Plus, as Rowan was quick to notice, there would no shortage of rocks to rain down on their assailants should it prove necessary.

They came to a great, long log that had fallen across the river. Yrssu panted, "the spray may clean off our scent." So they crept along its slick, barkless trunk. Partway across, Rowan slipped and barely caught jhmself, staring into the rushing dark waters just below.

The hound barked in the distance. "Hurry up!" said Yrssu. "That wolf-dog runs fast!"

"It's okay, he's on a leash. And he'd better not get loose, because if he comes running up without his masters, I'll kill him. I'lll bash his head in." Yrssu had never seen Rowan like this before, on fire with a sort of furious joy. There was nothing remotely Nuathan in it. Yrssu no longer doubted that story of the great-great grandmother.

A little beyond the crossing, they came to an immense disc of roots from a fallen fir, whose trunk pointed upriver towards the steep boulder field. At Rowan's gesture, Yrssu made a great leap up into the tangled root mass, catching it high above the snuffling nose of any dog. Hanging by jhr arms jhe swung back and forth until jhr momentum was sufficient to leap out onto the long elevated trunk. Jhe reached down to offer Rowan a hand. But Rowan handed the casket up to Yrssu, saying gravely, "Keep it safe, whatever happens."

"What are you doing, Rowan? Come on!"

Rowan was sniffing a feathery-leaved, yellow-flowered plant jhe'd noticed growing along the river. "I'm going to use this fennel to try to throw them off our trail."

Yrssu looked unhappy. "We should not split up, Rowan."

"It'll just take a few minutes, then I'll circle back and meet you at that boulder field." They met one another's eyes for just a moment; then Yrssu nodded assent.

Rowan hurried back to the river crossing and listened: no sound of their pursuers yet. It would be much better to lay the trail on that side. Jhe retraced jhr path over the wet and slippery log as quickly as jhe dared. At a nearby clump of fennel jhe yanked out a large handful. Then jhe trampled in it, releasing a pungent scent and thoroughly smearing the bottoms of jhr boots. Jhe wiped jhr hands on the ground to ensure jhr own scent was well-mingled with that of the fennel. It was a trick jhe and Orry had used when playing hide and seek with their dog Kei in the woods. Even now, Rowan smiled to remember being perched in a tree watching Kei snuffling earnestly along, like a pig after acorns.

As jhe set off, Rowan let fall one of jhr precious gloves. It was vital to convince the dog to choose this false trail over the river crossing. Jhe went in a long curve downriver, pausing every so often to wipe jhr palms on the ground and renew the scent of fennel on jhr boots. Jhe dropped the other glove for good measure. Jhr breath came steady and deep, and jhe felt like jhe could run forever if need be. Jhe followed a ridge that fell away steeply on jhr left through scree and stunted pines, to the broad valley where the train ran on towards the mountain monastery. The river was off to the right; jhe meant to lay the trail well away from it before looking for another crossing.

Faintly on the breeze came barking from somewhere behind jhm. Suddenly it rose in pitch and intensity, which probably meant they'd come to the fennel and the first glove. Time to finish this, for the tracking would be fast now. Rowan spotted another fallen giant of the forest, and skidded to a halt beside it. Jhe pulled off jhr fennel-scented boots and hung them around jhr neck, jammed the remaining fennel into the gaps between the scales of a large fir-cone, and stuffed it inside jhr sock. Jhe sent this fennel-and-Rowan-scented bait hurtling down the scree field towards the train tracks, into a wooded area below. Then, copying Yrssu's trail-breaking move, jhe made a great leap up into the tangled root-mass and thence to the high trunk.

At the end of the log highway, Rowan pulled on jhr boots, and began to work jhr way down from the long ridge towards where the river should be, and the boulder field beyond that. The densely wooded terrain gave a sense of safety, but made it difficult to keep track of jhr direction. The sun compass was useless in the dim light, and it was impossible to keep going in a straight line for any distance, frequently barred by thick brambles or many layers of logs fallen every which way. All jhe had to do was find the river. Jhe kept thinking jhe heard running water, but it was only the wind, or one of the innumerable little streams running off the steep slopes.

The hound's cry rang out again, muffled by the tree cover so that it was hard to tell where it was coming from. It sounded like it might be somewhere ahead, where jhe thought the river must be. Had jhe so completely lost jhr bearings in the dark of the forest? Or had it found where jhe and Yrssu had crossed on the slippery log? What if the dog had not been deceived by the fennel, but had crossed the river and followed Yrssu's trail into the boulder field? It might already have cornered the Kymran, whom jhe'd left all alone, who was terrified of big dogs, who was carrying the casket with Kassandra's vital message.

After what seemed like hours, jhe caught sight of water glinting through the trees. That lonely fording of the snowmelt-fed mountain river was the hardest thing Rowan had ever had to do. The waters were black and chill, flowing with silky power. So cold, so very cold. Every step into deeper water took more effort, more will. As the waters rose hip-deep, the pull of the current kept throwing jhm off balance. The only thing that saved jhm was a thin branch caught up across the river, too thin and willowy to hold real weight, but just firm enough to steady a trembling hand. Jhe had to navigate a series of underwater boulders that could be felt but not seen, slippery and of uncertain shape, curving down into unknown depths, their gaps catching at the numbed blocks that were Rowan's feet. And still the water rose. Jhe struggled to hold the heavy pack above the water. Cheeks wet with tears, Rowan went on, as strength and hope were carried away by the pitiless current. The water had reached jhr chest; jhe was light as a feather; the slightest push would send jhm tumbling down river. Only a tiny part of Rowan even cared, if only it meant this ordeal would end. Then the waters began to drop, down thigh and knee, and jhe was skidding over jagged pebbles and then staggering out onto the far bank, legs trembling uncontrollably. Jhe somehow managed to keep to the bare rock as jhe stumbled uphill through the unstable scree.

The boulder field lay in the shadow of a high peak, far above and white with snow. Here, though, strong winds that were still blowing had cleared most of the snow away. Shaking with cold, Rowan worked jhr way upstream along the river, creeping between the taller boulders and ducking under massive logs that lay like scattered toothpicks, all pointing downhill, the strewn remnants of many a landslide. How on earth was jhe going to find Yrssu in such a place? Laboriously, jhe worked jhr way up the slope, skirting a scree of flat rocks that would go skittering downhill, for all to hear and see, at the slightest misstep.

As jhe crawled over a gap between two large stones, a hand from below grasped jhr ankle, and jhe bit back a yelp of fear.

It was Yrssu. Jhe had found a hiding place in a crack formed by several massive boulders, out of the wind. Yrssu helped get out dry clothes and they piled everything that wasn't completely sodden around and under them, trying to get Rowan warm, but the rocks were as relentlessly cold as are all things never touched by sun.

"Why are they after us?" Rowan asked at last.

"Could we be in trouble for having ridden the train like that?" wondered Yrssu.

"Not so much that they'd send hunters with a wolfhound!"

Just then, Yrssu put a hand to jhr mouth, and cocked jhr head upwards. Then Rowan too heard the harsh, clatter of people walking on scree. They were talking, but the bitter wind pouring down from the mountain-tops snatched their voices away. As they got nearer, though, Rowan could make out their words.

—Little rats! They could be hiding anywhere, Gaea-damned sneaks! one of them snarled.

—Perhaps we should try further upriver? a more refined voice asked.

—Jock'll pick up their trail again soon enough, yer Luminance, never fear.

Had jhe really heard that, or had jhe only imagined it?

The footsteps stuttered away and blended into the softer sounds of wind and river, and Rowan could breathe again. "Yrssu, one of them is a scholar. Only a high scholar is addressed as 'your Luminance.'"

"Maybe scholars like to hunt gnomads, too."

Rowan shook jhr head, with sinking heart. "It's got to be about the book, Yrssu."

There came the baying of the hound farther off, then silence. They argued in whispers about what to do. Yrssu wanted to hole up until the hunters moved on, however long that might take. "For all we know, they are right here, just waiting for us to come out."

Rowan said, shivering, "But no one is as patient as a hunter in ambush."

Yrssu replied, “I am; though I’m sure you are not.”

“How are we to know when they’ve left? We’ll just get weaker and colder, and have to make a break for it in the end all the same.”

Yrssu considered awhile. At last, jhe proposed they abandon their packs, that they might creep unseen through the boulder field, and run swiftly if spotted. “It is a desperate choice. And yet — what freedom, also, to enter a new country with empty hands.”

“*Freedom*?” said Rowan skeptically, jhr chattering jaw making it hard to talk.

“What is freedom but such lightness?” Yrssu sat lost in thought for some time, then stirred jhmself. “We will soon find people to give us aid. The hunters will get none, even if they are so foolish as to follow us across the border.”

They did not leave quite everything. After eating all the food that wasn’t worth carrying, they secured their water bottles, and filled their pockets with dried meat, their knives, the watch. Rowan put some odds and ends including the sacks of salt, a valuable trade item this far inland, into a bag jhe could carry over one shoulder, and started to tuck the precious casket in among them. Then jhe froze, mind racing over various possibilities.

Yrssu watched jhm. “Leave the salt. That bag, it will only be slowing you down.”

Rowan nodded, setting it aside. Jhe carefully folded the casket into a long-sleeved shirt, and tied it firmly around Yrssu’s waist.

“Why are you giving it to me?” Yrssu asked in surprise.

Rowan put a hand on Yrssu's knee. "Whatever happens, Yrssu, get the book safely to your people." Jhe slung the bag back over jhr shoulder and reached up for a handhold near the narrow gap between the sheltering boulders. The heavy salt bumped into the small of jhr back like another pounding heart, as jhe squinted at the overly bright sky.

"Rowan—"

"I don't know what they would do to you, if they captured you, Yrssu."

As Rowan and Yrssu crept cautiously out of the crack, to shouts rang out. They heard only the wind, and the wind-like sigh of the river below. They headed uphill, keeping always under cover, for the tumbled boulders were so large that they could creep through their gaps like mice.

From far down the river came the baying of the wolfhound. Reaching the cliff-face, they crawled along it towards the right, looking for a way beyond. It was sheer for a long ways and would expose them to any watcher. Finally they made it to the forest's edge, with its towering firs. Yrssu entered the welcome dimness. Before they lost sight of the sun, Rowan paused to take a heading from the watch.

Someone seized jhr arm, and Rowan's heart almost stopped. "Run, Yrssu!" Way down below, the dog began barking furiously.

Holding the bag tightly with both hands, Rowan glared defiantly at the scholar. Though far from old, she had begun to acquire the careworn lines around her mouth and on her forehead that marked imagoes off from efts. Her gaze was direct, unthreatening and unthreatened.

"I am glad I guessed correctly, and waited for you here. As your friend, I think, is waiting for you just beyond those trees."

Rowan's heart sank.

"I was not raised in the city, and know something of hunting." She shaded her eyes and looked down over the boulder-strewn slopes, to the hunters picking their way upwards.

"Yrssu, go! The hunters are coming now!" Rowan listened intently, but could not hear whether jhr words took effect.

Gesturing to a moss-covered log, the scholar suggested, "Shall we sit? This has turned out a far longer journey that I had anticipated."

Rowan sat down warily. "Why did you come after me, then? Was it for the book?"

The scholar nodded.

"But I sent my sib with a perfectly good copy, along with our translation."

"And for that, Rowan Yngling, we thank you. Your translation looks to be an interesting addition to the other versions we had in our possession."

"So you already knew all about Kassandra's book?" Rowan asked, disappointed but also curious, and determined to delay as long as possible the moment the scholar found out jhe was not the one carrying the book. There'd been no sound of movement from the forest, but jhe fervently hoped Yrssu had crept off at last.

"It is known to a small number of us, yes," the scholar answered.

"Why to only a few?" Rowan was aware jhe spoke rudely, but as there had been no introductions, how was jhe to know this was a Luminary?

"You, who have labored over a translation, must surely be aware that there are parts of the account that could cause people to question our Covenant with Gaea."

"Do scholars prefer that people believe lies?"

"Of what lies do you speak?" the scholar asked mildly, adding, "I have not yet read the whole of your translation."

"That the lands to the north were all drowned!"

The scholar sighed. "You have stumbled onto that which must remain hidden, if Nuatha is to continue to prosper, and the wide world as well. My foremost charge, and that of my order, is to defend the Earth against the ravenings of humanity."

"Yes, I get why the Founders wanted us to stay here. But what about the cooling?"

"The what?"

"This past winter was just the worst in a series of bad ones, or haven't you noticed down there on Getz?"

The scholar tilted her head. "The city-bred folks didn't think it amounted to much, but my family's on the mainland, so I'm not unaware of this concern. But I fail to see the connection to Kassandra's account of the Founding."

"Kassandra was a sort of a scholar too, young as she was," Rowan was inspired to say. "She worked on forecasting the course of the climate Catastrophe, back when the Colony scientists still had time for that sort of thing. Then, when things fell apart in the north so suddenly, it made her wonder if the world might cool off sooner than anyone had thought possible. And if it does, Nuatha will go back to being an icy wasteland."

The scholar sat in silent thought. Rowan wondered if the scholar had truly known nothing of this.

The hunters burst into view, and the scholar held up a hand to halt them. "Don't you dare loose that dog!" cried Rowan.

The scholar said quietly to Rowan, "I would like to have the gnomad came to the Akademy with us, to help substantiate this new translation."

"Yrssu will never agree to come," Rowan said flatly. "Look, either you believe our translation or you don't."

"And what precisely did you two mean to do, traveling to the Waste?" wondered the scholar.

"What else? We were going there to warn jhr people!"

"You do not need the book for that, however." The scholar glanced at Rowan's bag and Rowan held it more tightly.

"Yes, we do. The Kymrans have a great reverence for the written word, and will believe what they would not readily believe from our tongues alone."

"Yet that is nothing, beside the wishes of the Akademy."

"Are you forgetting that Kassandra was half-Kymran? We'd never have been able to read her account without their runes! Your Akademy can go — can go study nature if they want to *substantiate* Kassandra's prophecy."

The hunters looked shocked at the way Rowan spoke to the high scholar, and the hound growled deep in its throat. The scholar again gestured for them to back off. "An interesting proposal, to be sure. Meanwhile, how about going to fetch your friend, if you would rather we did not send the dog to do it?" Smoothly, she took possession of Rowan's bag.

"Hey!" Rowan wasn't sure how much of a fuss to make. As long as she didn't start to open it...

The scholar spoke quietly. "You now have a choice before you, Rowan Yngling. If you bring your friend back, I can offer you both a place at the Akademy."

Rowan was about to make an angry retort, when something in the scholar's gaze stopped jhm. She walked Rowan a few steps closer to the trees, and continued in an undertone, "If you run, on the other hand, the consequences may be severe. Dialfi I can protect, but you would likely be a fugitive in Nuatha henceforward." She paused, and the leashed dog growled again. "If you do choose to run, I will delay the pursuit as long as I credibly can."

Rowan stared at the scholar in astonishment.

"Go!"

Rowan dove into the forest, and there was Yrssu, wide-eyed. Rowan hissed, "Hurry, while they still think they've got the book!" They scrambled deeper into the trees. A few minutes later, an angry shout suggested that deception had been uncovered.

"*Ahiru ikká, em haakhannu ertái,*" murmured Yrssu.

"What?"

"It is said, 'Pray not for rest, but always and only for strength.'"

And so the weary race began again.

On and on they went, as the sun circled them, Rowan mechanically checking the watch and keeping them as near southerly as the terrain permitted, trying for the shortest route across this young and fierce spur of mountains that guarded the inner plateau. Had the sun gone all the way around the sky since they'd crossed the river? Rowan had no idea. Though jhe checked the watch at intervals to make sure their heading was still good, in jhr exhausted state jhe could only use it to guide their movements in space, but was unable to make sense of their effortless movement through time.

Eventually, they came to see that it was a race not just against the hunters and their dog, but against hunger and the deadly fatigue it brought. Hunger gained on them, even as the hunters appeared to be left far behind. Rowan's hand kept straying to jhr pocket as if it had a mind of its own, even when the meat had all been eked out, and jhe'd long since licked the remaining dust of it from jhr fingers. Drinking water from the plentiful rivulets that crossed their path became merely nauseating, but jhe forced jhmself to swallow and fill the bottle each time, knowing that to do otherwise was to open a crack towards giving up. Rowan felt lighter and lighter, as though at any moment jhe would begin to float over the ground, the way a falling leaf dipped back and forth, only going upwards, endlessly upwards.

Round and round Rowan's thoughts ran Grandmother's words, a chant keeping pace with jhr weary steps like another heartbeat. *To think you've found the treasure, at long last . . . a treasure not of gold, nor yet of jewels . . . Kassandra will take you into the distant past and shape for all of us the future.*

Passing through a gap in the trees they came out into open country, the ground falling away before them in a misty slope of pale green, and on into the endless blue and indigo distances, watered by sparkling streams that ran down the mountainsides. Rowan had never seen an entire horizon so smooth, so gently rounded. The awareness came to jhm, in a slow dawning, that they had reached the Inland Plateau, realm of the gnomads, where mammút roamed and caribou, and oceans of waving grass, and mazes of tussocky swampland went on and on, a land of eternal light in summer and unmitigated darkness and howling winds in winter. Yrssu beside jhm gazed as dumbstruck as Rowan, drinking in a landscape unseen for many long years.

Epilogue (by skywave, 5985 kHz)

There at the mountains' edge I stood swaying, faint with hunger and exhaustion. My spirit rose out of me like a bird and soared over the vast plains of that windswept wilderness, circling and circling upwards in a sweep as wide as the sky. That land we called the Waste! It was the unknown heart of our world, despised and ignored. I first saw it in summer's clear and newborn light, but in the darkness of the saga-night I would come to know it truly.

The journey outward begins with the journey inward, as all true work begins with sleep and with dreaming. The north of our future would abide. Now we were headed to the world's spindle, the uttermost South.

This is Rowan Askve Yngling, signing

Over—

—And—

—Out.

Supplemental Materials

Antarctica. Nuatha is a country at the fringes of what used to be called Western Antarctica, a continent that was for a time known as *Terra Australis Incognita*, the Unknown Southern Land. Its existence was first intuited by the ancient-Greeks, millennia before any human had set eyes on it, and so from that faith and tradition alone, its place on ancient maps was secured.

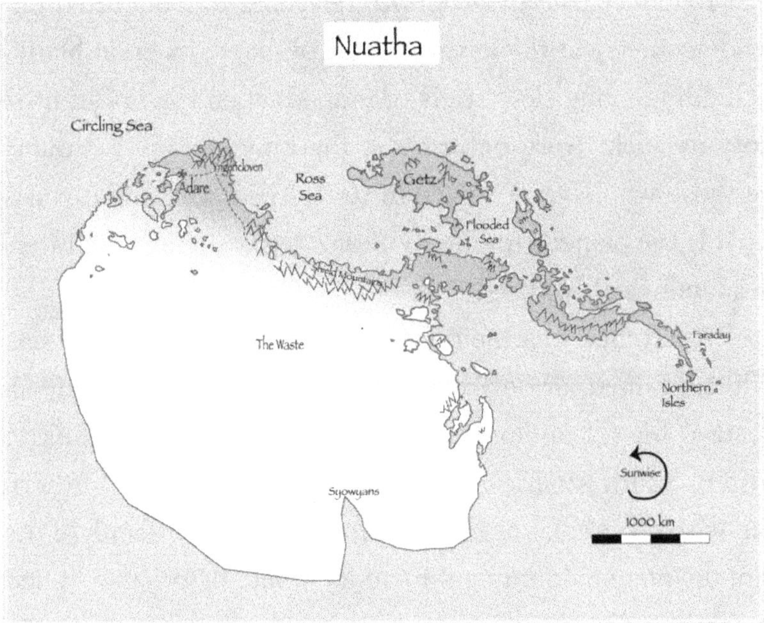

In the Age of Exploration, the latter half of the second millennium of the Common Era (C.E.), ships pushed further and further southward seeking that fabled last continent. For it was rumored to be a land of warmth and ease, an earthly paradise; but as far southwards as they pushed, they found only hill-high waves, fog, and contrary winds. At last, it was regretfully removed from the maps, not without a sense of *Fernweh*, a longing for a place that had never existed in the first place.

Late in the second millennium, Antarctica was discovered after all. And so has it always hovered between existence and unreality.

It is the coldest of continents, and the windiest, and above all the most cut off from the world, separated by a raging ocean that rings it like a great moat. Even in the 21st century C.E. it remained *Terra Incognita*, relegated to a distorted unwound geometry at the lower margin of maps, its great blankness holding many clear trails of individual endeavor but little history as such. Here nature was the only enemy, yet many were those who sought solace in its merciless, inhuman vastness. It is the planet's forgotten nether region, almost extraterrestrial, our earthly Mars.

Antarctica was the only continent that had never been inhabited, tamed, or destroyed by humans. It lost virtually all terrestrial life 35 million years ago, when its tenuous link to the tip of South America was severed, and the great Southern ocean with its circular current cut it off from the warmth of the rest of the planet, dooming it to an icy coma. Before this, it had held forests of birch and beech and evergreens, a profusion of birds and mammals, all in a strange land where the sun never set for half the year, and never rose for the other half. What must it have been like for them when the cold set in, inexorably freezing its lifeblood, the snows lying ever deeper until the mighty mountains were drowned to their necks in it, the last stunted remnants of forests huddled on the slopes of sheltered valleys, shivering in the blasting winds.

The twenty-first-century citizens of Antarctica are scientists from all over the world, a model of international cooperation and ongoing inquiry into the mysteries of our world and cosmos. Its minerals have never been exploited. Not a single murder has ever occurred there, let alone a war. Money is barely any use; compasses spin wildly, so that all cardinal directions but north shrink to meaninglessness. Time itself behaves strangely: that granted by the heavens above, where day and night can stretch to weeks or months, and that invented by humans on earth below. For the twenty-four wedges of clock-face time zones that we project on the globe become ludicrously narrower as they approach the pole, until a person can stride through all of them in the course of a short walk. They converge to a point where a post stands at eye level, marking the axis of the Earth. This post is whimsically topped with a reflective sphere that mirrors all it sees. Most would call this place the remotest spot of land anywhere on this Earth, yet is it not rather the center around which all else revolves?

History of Nuatha. The global warming of the early third millennium C.E. caused the breakup of Antarctica's western ice sheets mere decades after glaciologists first realized their extreme vulnerability. The former Antarctic Peninsula became an archipelago across the now ice-free Ross and Weddell seas. The far greater inland ice sheet of Eastern Antarctica held out longer, but in the end it too melted much faster than anyone had imagined possible, as its great glaciers sped up and its great weight slid over the underlying dirt and meltwater like so many greased ball bearings. This melting caused the seas to rise a devastating 60 meters in just over a century, Greenland's ice sheets having given out too. All the great coastal cities were underwater ruins, but they had by then already been abandoned by the desperate and hungry people of a dying civilization.

The coastline of mainland Antarctica, consisting mainly of high mountains and an immense plateau, has changed little from the time of the ice. But the monochrome landscape has been utterly changed to boreal forest (primarily birch, aspen, willow, fir, spruce, hemlock and cypress) and grassy tundra interspersed with lakes and swamps. Areas near the coast are now suitable for dairy and sheep farming, supplemented with fishing, not unlike medieval Scandinavia, Iceland, and Greenland.

The first Nuathan settlers lived at the northern tip of the Peninsula, where there had always been a few hardy grasses, and where warming proceeded most quickly. Initially, the seas supported them far more than did the rocky barren earth, even providing them with seal skins for making boats in that treeless land.

After the great melting, and the cataclysms of volcanism and crustal upheaval in the wake of receding ice that had so weighed down on the land; after fertile falls of volcanic ash had enriched the bare rock and the soil began to support plant growth (with the spread of vegetation greatly accelerated by human terraforming), people spread southwards and westwards (or, as Nuathans would usually say, sunwise), eventually settling the great island of Getz, and finally the riverine lowland valleys of Victorialand, and around the mainland to Adelie.

In present-day Nuatha, a mixture of wind, hydroelectric, solar, and geothermal is used to generate electricity and heat buildings in a highly-localized energy distribution system. With windmills to pump well-water, the greatest need for electricity is to light dwellings and workplaces during the long, dark winter. Because the winters are not very cold, sufficient heating is obtained from a combination of geothermal, passive, and wood or charcoal stoves. There is an absolute prohibition, which has come to have the force of a strong taboo, against the use of any fossil fuels, though the mountains are known to be rich in coal.

Some seven and seventy generations have elapsed between the time Kassandra walked the land with the first of the mehemoth herds, and Rowan's finding her account of those days. Remember, however, that Nuathans with their intervening eft stage have much longer generations than do we untransformed Outlanders.

Nuathans tend to think of Nuatha as being synonymous with the continent of Terra, though they live only on the archipelago and a small part of the westerly mainland. They largely ignore the vast inland plateau, which they call the

I was funded for one year by the Seaver Foundation in 2016-2017 to work on this project, for which I am most grateful. In conjunction with this I also thank professor Sally Horne-Badovinac for cheerfully allowing me to work in her lab as researcher-cum-writer under these auspices, and then-Chair of Molecular Genetics and Cell Biology Rick Fehon for smoothing the administrative way. Stephen Santell, Catherine Will, Adrianne Coates, Farrah Q. Jensen, Blenda Robertson, and Pilar Frankowitz kindly sorted out the logistics of the oddball scenario of a biologist being supported by a grant to publish a novel, for which I thank them.

Others I must thank include Ed Munro, staunch ally with an unflagging belief in my abilities, and Alice, who pointed me towards the Kymrans. My brother Paul tirelessly edited the details and offered insightful counsel on the big picture: I could not imagine a better editor for me or for this book. My brother Daniel, a poet and novelist in his own right, saw and loved what I was trying to do, and inspired me to keep reaching for it. I am most fortunate to have a large circle of extended family and in-laws who have read various stages of this work and offered much-needed interest and critiques. Finally, I heartily thank Yvonne Beckham, Ed Munro, and Vic Foe for the chapter-a-night read-aloud sessions in which we made a nearly penultimate pass through the novel and mercilessly stress-tested it. Their patience and discernment and attention to detail are much appreciated.

About the Author

Kristin Sherrard is an erstwhile marine biologist from the Pacific Northwest, who currently lives in Chicago and studies fruit flies. Hey, all cells are beautiful under a microscope. From an early age she knew she wanted to be either a biologist or a writer. There's time for a lot of interesting work when you live within walking distance of everywhere you need to go on a daily basis, and when you avoid social media. However, you can find her online at www.beyondthisbitterair.com and blogging about fruit flies at kmsherrard.tumblr.com.

More books in the series are forthcoming.

CPSIA information can be obtained
at www.ICGtesting.com
Printed in the USA
JSHW040817100621
15606JS00002B/26

9 781663 554062